Praise for Jayne Rylon's Dream Machine

"If you are in the mood for hot sex, really smart men, and even smarter women then Dream Machine is just what the doctor ordered."

~ *Stefani Clayton, JERR Review*

"Ms. Rylon is a true talent and her love scenes are scorchers!"

~ *Coffee Time Romance*

"Jayne Rylon's story is absolute perfection. The intense emotions and evocative imagery captivate the reader. There is so much to appreciate in this novel and it is not over done. this is the way a hot and steamy romance should be written. I definitely can not wait for more from this absolutely phenomenal author."

~ *Ecataromance*

"Wow – Nice and Naughty by Jayne Rylon is erotic romance at its best! It makes me want to call all my girlfriends and say, 'You have to read this!'"

~ *Erotic Romance Writers*

"This book is super hot with extremely naughty bits that will make you squirm. Guaranteed. If you like molten hot contemporaries, then check out Dream Machine by Jayne Rylon!"

~ *Bianca D'Arc, Author*

"Dream Machine kept me reading late into the night and Ms. Rylon is now an autobuy for me."

~ *Whipped Cream Long and Short Erotic Romance*

Look for these titles by
Jayne Rylon

Now Available:

Nice and Naughty
Night is Darkest

Print Anthology
Three's Company

Dream Machine

Jayne Rylon

A Samhain Publishing, Ltd. publication.

Samhain Publishing, Ltd.
577 Mulberry Street, Suite 1520
Macon, GA 31201
www.samhainpublishing.com

Dream Machine
Copyright © 2010 by Jayne Rylon
Print ISBN: 978-1-60504-556-6
Digital ISBN: 978-1-60504-531-3

Editing by Angela James
Cover by Natalie Winters

First Samhain Publishing, Ltd. electronic publication: May 2009
First Samhain Publishing, Ltd. print publication: March 2010

Dedication

To the people who don't know that I'm an author but would be proud if they did.

Chapter One

"This is a bad idea."

Dr. Kurt Foster revolted against the ultimatum his colleague, Dr. Luke Malone, had just delivered on behalf of the Elembreth University Psychology Board. Kurt shook his head then continued, "I won't fucking do it."

"Don't make this harder than it already is, Kurt. You no longer have a choice."

He registered the genuine regret in Luke's expression when the other man slid the rejected paperwork across the glossy surface of Kurt's desk.

"They denied your plea. There are consequences to decking James, even if the bastard deserved it."

Kurt yanked open a drawer, dumped the folder inside then slammed it shut, wincing as he flexed his scabbed knuckles. "She's been violated once. I won't let her be subjected to it again without her permission."

"Calm down. I admit it's not typical procedure but I'm here to do the only thing in my control to prevent the board from kicking your ass out and firing you from the job you love." Luke inhaled, his gaze darting away for a moment. "The board has ruled. You're to conduct the Dream Machine experiment with Rebecca."

"Yes, sir, Mr. Board President." Kurt sneered. Luke didn't deserve his foul mood but he couldn't suppress the urge to swipe at someone while everything he'd built crumbled around him. He shoved back then began to pace, scrubbing his hands through his hair. "Fuck! I don't mean that, Luke. I just..."

"I know." Of course the renowned psychologist understood. "You feel guilty because her dreams were invaded, because watching them made you want her more and because you're afraid she's not ready. But you have an impeccable record. You know I think of you as a brother, but I'm speaking for the board when I say you're the right man for this job. This is the only opportunity you have for a true control. You'd never be allowed a blind trial if Dr. Dipshit hadn't broken into your lab. He proved it's safe. And that Rebecca wants this. You starred in every single wild dream of hers. She needs you."

The fury Kurt hadn't succeeded in pounding out on James prohibited him from answering. He'd never intended his invention to be used like this. As a leader in the field of sexual therapy and repression research, he strived to help people, not hurt them.

Two nights ago, he'd forgotten to lock the damn door to his private laboratory, which adjoined the university practice. His assistant, Rebecca Williams, had paid the price for his moment of carelessness. And she didn't even know it yet.

Now, he had to fix it.

If he didn't agree to the board's demands, they would find someone else to take his place. Probably Luke. Jealousy sealed his fate.

Defeated, he sank into the plush leather desk chair.

"How's this going to work?"

"The board is giving you seven days to prove the Dream Machine is a viable treatment for sexual repression. They agreed to allow you to operate without a witness in person, but you have to record the proceedings for me to review each day. If you tell her about the break-in, the board will terminate the study. I won't be able to intervene to protect you again. You'll bring her to a board meeting midway through to present your progress. If they see merit in the work, they'll allow you to continue to completion."

Kurt knew Luke well enough to identify the heat layered beneath concern in the other man's eyes. He growled low in his throat. "Don't be thinking about her like that."

A rich laugh rumbled from Luke as a wicked grin spread

across his face. "I admit it. I'm envious. Just think, this is your golden chance to have her without ruining your working relationship. She's not the innocent young woman you first met as your student. She's about to graduate at the top of her class and, no one knows better than you, her stellar performance in the university psychology intern program makes her a clear candidate for a permanent position."

The knot of worry, frustration, anger and betrayal lodged in Kurt's gut loosened for a moment. "Does that mean my nomination was voted on?"

Luke confirmed the only good news he'd had today. "The board agreed this experience will complete her training. If she can learn to cope with her emotions instead of repressing them, their last reservations on her character will be invalidated. If the experiment is successful, and if she accepts the position, the board will appoint her as your partner. The decision was unanimous."

"Then it's a deal." Kurt would do whatever necessary to ensure Becca's dream came true. It was the least he could do. "But how the hell am I going to get her to agree to be my subject without filling her in on the details? I won't do this without her consent."

The wattage of Luke's smile doubled. That look had lured in many willing women over the years they'd been friends. It appeared charming but the devilish smirk meant he'd been up to no good.

"Shit, you already started didn't you?" Kurt groaned.

"Let's say the wheels are in motion. She'll come to you. Soon."

"Don't tell me. I don't want to know." Kurt rose, shaking his head.

Luke met him halfway around the desk then clapped his hand on Kurt's bruised shoulder. They walked side by side toward the office door. "Call me when you have the first stage finished then I'll gather the board. And please, be careful."

"Got it. Luke..." Kurt pivoted, tempted to hug the man who'd been his closest friend for years. After a brief but awkward silence, he settled for silent communication. "Thanks."

Luke responded with a tiny nod before slipping into the lobby.

CB

By four o'clock in the afternoon, it'd already been a long day for Rebecca Williams.

Well, two days. She'd pulled an all-nighter studying, then taken her early morning final exam before going straight to work at the clinic. Dr. Foster was booked solid, which meant a lot of prep work for her. There hadn't even been a second to talk to him about the memo on her desk. As soon as he finished his meeting with Dr. Malone, she'd do it.

She promised herself she wouldn't back down.

Her pencil paused in mid cross-through on the last item of her to-do list when the front door burst open. A woman barged into the lobby, her eyes puffy and red from crying. Mussed hair stood out from her scalp as though she'd run her hands through it a million times.

"Mrs. Henderson?" Rebecca hardly recognized the disheveled woman. She jumped to her feet, meeting the woman halfway. "What's wrong?"

The woman rushed straight to her and flung her arms around Rebecca. "I caught Jim with some piece of trash. In our room. Right on my own bed." The words were muffled against Rebecca's shoulder. Sobs wracked her body. Steering her down the hall, Rebecca led Mrs. Henderson to privacy in a vacant patient room.

"Everything's going to be all right. Have a seat and I'll get Dr. Foster. It'll be just a moment." Rebecca helped the woman to the chair while she tried to soothe her with a calm voice.

"No! Don't go. I'd rather talk to you." Mrs. Henderson grabbed her hand, preventing her from turning away. "Please."

How could she deny the woman?

"Of course." She settled on the adjoining chair, Mrs. Henderson still grasping her hand like a lifeline. "Where would you like to start?"

ॐ

Rebecca updated Mrs. Henderson's case file with the details of their session when her cell blasted the shrill emergency ring associated with her sister. She dove for her purse then dug out her phone. *Can this day get any worse?*

"Calm down, Elsa." Rebecca quieted her hysterical younger sister over the phone. "I think everything's going to work out. I didn't tell you yet because I don't want to get your hopes up again but I have a plan. I can't really talk right now, I'm at work. I'll know for sure by tonight. I promise I'll call you then."

"Becca, that's awesome!" Her sister's elated voice proved she had skipped over the maybes going straight to assuming everything was taken care of. *Great.* "I'm going to tell Mom. Talk to you tonight! Love you!"

"I love you too, Elsa." Rebecca wasn't sure her sister heard her response as she went off in the background, screeching for their mother. She hoped the woman was having a good day but she could only worry about so many things at once. Sighing, she slipped her cell phone back into her plain purse.

As she tucked the black bag under her desk in the reception area of Dr. Foster's university practice, the door to his office opened and Dr. Malone emerged.

"Thanks for covering, Rebecca. See you soon." The tall, handsome doctor always found time to chat with her, no matter the difference in their ranks. She enjoyed seeing him but, today, she was swamped and finding it difficult to focus on anything but the decision she'd made earlier.

"You're welcome, Dr. Malone. Have a good day." She responded automatically, without questioning the curious look he shot her before making his way out the front door.

Slotting Mrs. Henderson's file back into the cabinet, she decided it was now or never.

Rebecca snuck one final glance at the paper fluttering in her hand, willing herself to stop shaking. She paused then drew a deep breath to fortify her nerve before knocking on the heavy wood-paneled door to Dr. Foster's office.

"Come in."

She nudged open the door to his workspace then turned to guide it closed, eliminating the risk of anyone overhearing her outlandish request. Resisting the urge to make up a lame excuse and duck back out, she scanned his inner office then took a wary step forward.

The area was spacious but comfortable. Soft incandescent light emanated from lamps positioned around the room. The warm illumination made the space seem intimate for its size. Plush carpet covered the floor and substantial masculine furniture in rich jewel tones clustered to facilitate group conversation.

Dr. Foster had designed the soothing atmosphere to encourage his patients to relax during their sometimes intense sessions. The innovative psychologist specialized in relationship therapy and sexual repression issues while holding a distinguished position here at Elembreth University, where he both taught and maintained a small clinic.

"Rebecca, is there something I can do for you?" Kurt—no, Dr. Foster—asked. She kept slipping lately.

"Yes, Doctor. First, while you met with Dr. Malone, Mrs. Henderson came in."

"Damn. Is Jim screwing around on her again?" Dr. Foster cared for each of his patients on a personal level. She admired the fact that he didn't need case notes to remember the details of their situations.

"Unfortunately, yes."

"Tell her to come in. Luke was my last appointment for the day, I can see her right now."

Rebecca hesitated. Would he be angry she'd overstepped her place by talking with Mrs. Henderson? His displeasure would make her offer even harder to make.

"Actually, she's gone now. She requested a session with me instead."

"About time." He didn't seem the least bit concerned.

"You don't care that I met alone with one of your patients?"

"Of course not. You're ready for this, Rebecca. You've put six years into your residency here at the clinic. You did have

14

your last exam today didn't you?"

She nodded.

"Since you're my best student, I know you aced it. Therefore, waiting for your degree on graduation day is a formality. You're a well-qualified therapist. Mrs. Henderson is one of my more dramatic patients. How did you feel dealing with her radical emotions alone?"

"I did as you've taught me. I listened actively with compassion, then worked the case by giving feedback on what I heard, provided the statistics of cheating husbands, supplied her with resources for local support groups and talked her through how to find help if she chooses to divorce him."

"Sometimes it takes more than facts and methodology to heal someone's heart. But for your first time flying solo, it sounds like you did very well."

Pride swept over her. She'd worked her ass off for this. His approval meant more than the piece of paper that would bestow her official title.

And his sexy smile made an excellent reward.

Dr. Foster could make a blind woman do a double take. In his mid thirties, he had slight laugh lines crinkled around his dark grey eyes. Their stormy depths contradicted his inviting personality, which enhanced his charm and made her curious about what lay beneath his enigmatic surface.

Standing over six feet tall, he towered above her. His height and lean but powerful build combined with his wavy black hair, which he kept long enough to graze his shirt collar, to give him a dangerous edge. It caught her off balance at odd moments during the day when her overactive imagination insisted she'd caught him staring at her.

To Rebecca, his psychical perfection was only a fraction of what made him attractive. Touted as the genius of his field, he had risen to his prestige early, though with some controversy. His opponents argued against his sometimes-extreme methods but, based on his record-smashing success rates and the rave reviews of his patients, they had conceded his superiority in the field.

His drive and passion for helping others outshone his

piercing eyes in her estimation. The gentle care and devotion he lavished on his patients when assisting them in resolving their issues had made him her idol.

A million tiny things along the way had gradually shaped her case of professional infatuation into a deep caring for the man behind the doctor. From his easygoing personality, to his effortless problem solving and the natural insight he had into the way people wanted to be treated, Rebecca admitted her attraction to him had never been stronger.

Which made him perfect for her proposition.

"Your respect means a lot to me, Dr. Foster."

"You've earned it."

"Well, then, I also wanted to inquire about the ad for an experiment subject you assigned me to place in the paper."

"Um...the ad?" For a moment he looked lost, as if he had no clue what she referred to. Before she could clarify, he recovered then asked, "Is there something wrong with it?"

Rebecca paused, gathering her courage before answering. "No. That's not what I meant."

Last chance, Rebecca. Say it or leave.

"I'm interested in participating in the study myself and wondered if volunteering would be against office policy."

He blinked, not responding immediately to her statement, so she continued. She'd gathered her facts in anticipation of convincing him.

"You have a very competitive fee listed here but, no matter how much money is offered, finding volunteers for this type of personal, sensitive experiment is often a long and painful process. In the six years I've worked here, I know of eight promising studies left untried due to lack of willing participants. We both know no amount of theory will substitute for praxis."

If she could assist in Dr. Foster's experiment, she could repay some of the selflessness he'd shown her as a mentor. Her arguments seemed to work. He leaned forward, setting aside the case folder he'd been reviewing. He cupped his chin, a gesture she'd come to recognize as his thinking posture, while he studied her across his expansive mahogany desk. She tried not to shift but failed beneath the weight of his stare.

What did he see when he looked at her?

Compared to the elegant, tailored suit conforming to the defined lines of his torso and great ass, her bargain-bin outfit must seem frumpy at best. Fancy clothes didn't make the cut in her student's budget but she made sure to dress professionally, if not always fashionably.

For a moment, they assessed each other.

Rebecca couldn't help but note the way his unruly hair feathered across his brow in contrast to the neatness of everything else in the room. When the silence stretched a little longer than comfort allowed, Rebecca's uncertainty grew. She began to stammer.

"I understand. You know, if it's not okay for me to participate. I just thought it might be hard for you to find subjects or something." *God, this is unbelievable!* She was an articulate researcher used to communicating detailed observations but she couldn't form a simple sentence around him sometimes.

Dr. Foster smiled up at her. Rather than soothing her nerves, the expression filled her with desire and fuddled her mind further. The edges of his full mouth turned up until she glimpsed his brilliant white teeth. The thrill of anticipation his wicked grin caused reminded her of the way a mouse might feel right before a hungry cat gobbled it for a snack.

Why didn't he say anything? This had to work. The study could solve several problems all at once. Efficiency appealed to her.

"Have a seat, Rebecca." His careful, modulated voice gave no indication of his acceptance or refusal as he gestured to the heavy wingback chair in front of his desk. When she perched on the edge, with her back straight and ankles crossed tight beneath her, he continued. "There's no rule against staff participation so long as you are fully informed of the requirements and demands of the experiment. Though, I have to admit, I don't know if you're right for my study."

Her stomach pitched at his reservation. She had to get this assignment. Stoically, she sat still as a statue while he took his time observing her reaction. If he wished to gauge her commitment, he wouldn't find a crack in her resolve.

"My research will get quite personal. I'd need you to be open and honest with me in order for the trial to be successful."

Rebecca hid a blush, recalling the times she'd copied over notes for the doctor's case files. Although she'd tried to concentrate on typing the erotic words scrawled in his hasty masculine script, she couldn't quite block out the detailed stories recounted to him by successful patients on follow-up visits.

Most of them had required standard treatment involving discussion and counseling but, on occasion, a case called for a more unconventional approach. The doctor had been known to observe couples having difficulty in order to provide objective, real-time feedback—witnessing an experience, he contended, neither party could be objective about relating in a traditional session.

"I can handle it, Doctor," she said, not quite able to confront his steely gaze.

"Rebecca, I'm not trying to dissuade you. However, I need to be frank just as I would be with any other candidate. The study will test a new invention I've created. I believe the Dream Machine has the potential to revolutionize the field of sexual therapy. There are so many people who live their lives without realizing their sensual potential because they're too afraid to tear down the boundaries imposed by society and be free enough to experience what they desire."

As he explained, it seemed as if he spoke of her instead of a generality. Did he suspect her underlying reason for volunteering? Her face flushed and she hoped he couldn't detect the telling reaction in the diffused lighting. Somehow, she knew he did. After all, he was a trained observer, noted for his attention to detail.

"My invention taps into subconscious desires by capturing dreams. During the study, I'd monitor your REM cycles using the device then discuss your fantasies with you. Are you prepared to do that with me?"

Rebecca shifted in his desk chair, which engulfed her,

while she contemplated the ramifications of participating. Trying to still the subtle hints of her trepidation, she met his gaze head on.

"Yes, Doctor, I think I can." Shame flooded her when the simple thought of revealing her fantasies to Kurt began to arouse her. Personal feelings shouldn't be involved in a professional proposition but, from the first day she'd worked at Dr. Foster's office, she'd battled a dazzling attraction. She gripped the black leather arm rest to keep from fanning her face. Moisture gathered between her legs to serve as indisputable proof. Instead of being mortified, she admitted she'd wanted him for so long that this would be a welcome relief.

She hungered for the things he could teach her.

"There's one more thing. I'd need to monitor and influence your arousal level both during the dream stages and during our sessions. This will involve significant intimate physical contact between us. Can you agree to the terms of the experiment?"

"I... I..." The scientist in her wanted to ask for more details but the woman in her was too reserved. She'd been with a few men, boys really, during the first years of college but the brief liaisons hadn't resulted in anything momentous. She'd done it to ease her innate curiosity. None of the encounters had been satisfying. Besides, she'd been much too busy studying and working to spend time on needless pursuits. To be completely honest with herself, she conceded no one but Kurt had ever held her interest.

Afraid she might not live up to his expectations, she hesitated. A vision of him touching her, bringing her pleasure with his skilled hands, overtook her imagination. What if she wasn't all Dr. Foster required? What if her capability to experience passion fell far below the level of normal desire? Her unease hung in the air as the pause lengthened.

Kurt sighed.

"Becca, it's all right if you've changed your mind. I understand if you can't do this. I won't force you to do anything you don't want to do." The supportive words couldn't mask the disappointment resonating in his voice. The fact that he'd called her by her nickname, a name her mother and sister used, made his assurance cut to a more personal level. She recognized it as another test of their evolving relationship.

Instead of confessing her deeper reasons, she took the easy way out.

"No, Doctor, I want to participate. And...well, I need the money right now." It embarrassed her to admit it. He compensated her well and she didn't want to seem ungrateful or careless with her finances. But, even if she did, that was easier than admitting how desperately she wanted him to tutor her on more than clinical depression or the scientific method.

"My sister is coming to the university next year. This morning we were notified of an administrative error in the financial aid office. The scholarship funds were overdrawn and hers got cut. If I don't do this, Elsa can't enroll." Rebecca hated to admit her need for assistance. Her pride rebelled.

"This isn't about *money*, is it?" Though he sounded reluctant to ask her, his eyes seemed almost angry. Afraid she had made him uncomfortable, she worried he might dismiss her as a participant because of his inherent morality. "I'm more than willing to give you an advance on your salary instead. You can always come to me for help."

"No!" she protested, a little too loud for the quiet intimacy of the office. She'd have to give him more of the truth to assure his acceptance. "I want to help you. You've supported me for years. Without you, I'd never have learned so much. I want to do this as a favor."

"You don't owe me anything. You're hands down the best assistant I've ever worked with. Having you here has been my pleasure." His sentiment seemed sincere. Slight dimples accentuated his cheeks when he smiled. Every time she saw them, it spawned an insane urge to lick the delicious indentations. Reining in her impulse, she focused on their discussion.

"I think an apparatus like yours could be a beneficial tool. I would love to see it become a reality. I'd feel honored to know I had some part in its development. Look, I know you've given me raises when you didn't have to. You pay me a lot more than you should. Any student would love to work for you, to learn from you, for free. And finding another subject might be impossible.

Please, let me do this to repay you."

Some of the jovial reassurance faded from his expression. His professionalism slipped for an uncharacteristic moment. "Understand this or our discussion is over right now. You worked your ass off the last few years. You earned every bit of your way. I've never seen someone try as hard as you have. Hell, you push yourself to exhaustion half the time. You even fell asleep at your desk two nights ago!"

Oh crap. She'd never seen him get pissed off.

"Dr. Foster, I'm sorry about that. I was studying for finals the night before and I had a few cases I wanted to catch up on before I left the office." Mortification zinged through her. She didn't think anyone had noticed.

On most occasions, she could operate effectively on less sleep than the average person could. With the recent culmination of her education, she'd had to make do with the time left after work and school, which was less than she could handle on a routine basis. She counted on the sacrifices she'd made paying off as soon as she finished her degree.

"Shh." Dr. Foster waved off her excuses, his features relaxing again. "You misunderstood me, I'm not angry with you. I only meant it as an example of how far beyond my expectations you constantly go. In fact, you work too hard sometimes. If I thought for a second you'd listen, I'd order you home for a nap right now."

She wondered why he glanced away when he spoke. Was he lying about being upset? Before she could ask, he continued.

"Let's try a little test. If you can't see it through, you can quit at any time. All you have to do is say you're done and we'll stop with no repercussions. Look at me, Becca."

She met his stare. His eyes shone with tenderness and understanding.

"I realize we'll be pushing the boundaries of your comfort and experience. I promise you, I won't hurt you or force you to do anything you don't want. You know that, don't you? In fact, I'm willing to pay you for your participation regardless of whether or not you finish the study. I won't allow money to be a factor in your decision."

This was the familiar Dr. Foster. Her foolish discomfort evaporated. After all the kindness he had shown her, how could she think he would be mad over one tiny slipup? She'd never before met anyone she admired so much.

Picking up his favorite fountain pen, he twirled it between his fingers as he contemplated her proposal. "Let's be clear. I want you to participate. I think you would be an excellent candidate. However, I'll only accept your request if this is something you choose to do of your own free will. I want you to do this for yourself. I think it'll be an enlightening experience for you, though also probably one of the most difficult assignments you've ever had. There are no books to study for the answers here. They have to come from within you."

Of course, he understands. I need this. Her inability to overcome her shyness and articulate the real reason she wanted to join the experiment underscored her convictions. She could never reach her full potential as a sexual therapist when she remained so out of touch with her own desires. This experiment, and Dr. Foster's invention, could be the answer. Her cure.

"So, Becca, what will it be?" Leaning back in his chair, Kurt steepled his fingers over his trim abdomen while he considered her. He paused, giving her a moment to mull things over. The space should have been a relief but his self-assured posture compelled her to accept.

"Will you be my subject?"

Rebecca gasped beneath the intensity of his stare, so persuasive it drew her in until his regard consumed her consciousness. She could detect his rich male scent, so strong and spicy in this room, and she shivered in response. Before she knew it, an answer escaped her lips.

"Yes, Doctor. I'm yours."

Chapter Two

As Kurt thought about things to come, the sharp teeth of the zipper on his slacks started to dig into his rock-hard cock. Thankful for the bulky desk, which hid the evidence of his desire from Becca, he soaked in the contrasts of her nature while she perched as prim as a Sunday-school teacher on the chair before him.

Petite, with brilliant green eyes, she made a striking image. The aura of responsibility and somberness surrounding her aged her beyond her mid twenties in direct contrast to her dewy appearance. Several shades of color ranging from chocolate brown to blazing red entwined in the lustrous stands of her hair. It was a look many women tried to procure from a salon but failed to match with half the vibrancy of Becca's natural shades.

As usual, she dressed conservatively. She wore a black, skirted suit with a double-breasted jacket buttoned all the way to the top despite the heat wave scorching the city. When he surveyed her, she crossed her arms in front of her chest, blocking the caress he longed to bestow. He imagined her nipples hardening beneath that damned jacket. The boxy garment might as well be a suit of armor considering its bulk and the lush curves it obscured. His gaze continued to roam over her, inching along to her feet, saving the best for last.

The moment each morning when he discovered which shoes she wore had become the highlight of his day. It always made his cock swell to see her stiletto heels, high strappy sandals or lace-up confections standing out in such drastic contrast to her stark wardrobe. Today's footwear didn't disappoint. The four-inch heels made of simple black leather had delicate straps that coiled around her fine-boned ankles in a seductive spiral, bringing to mind lascivious visions of her bound before him.

The hints of passionate woman lurking beneath her controlled façade intrigued Kurt. Her selection of shoes designed to give any man an instant hard-on provided just one example of those rare insights. As an expert, he believed Becca needed a push in the right direction to relax her inhibitions and unleash her true sensual nature.

Now they had no choice but to test his hypothesis. If only he hadn't been called away to the hospital on a patient emergency two nights ago, he could have watched over her when she gave in to exhaustion and drifted off at her desk. He should have protected her. Maybe he could have driven her home and started the foundation for the new relationship he'd hoped to build as soon as she graduated and was recognized as his equal. Then they could have tested the waters without the taint of the board's involvement.

Kurt couldn't think of that now.

She had approached him like his greatest fantasy come to life, practically begging to explore, with a request mirroring his own primal needs. And, unlike his sultry assistant, he wasn't used to repressing his needs. Certainly not for years upon years. His cock twitched in excitement and he couldn't resist testing her immediately. He flashed her a broad, disarming smile, then moved from behind his desk.

She also stood, expecting him to dismiss her as in typical training sessions they'd had before.

"Good, then it's settled. Let's get started with that trial run, okay?" He grinned.

"What? Right now?" The uncommon sound of uncertainty from her only reinforced his determination. Her eyes widened in shock and she took an instinctive step back from him.

Kurt didn't intend to let her run far.

"Yes, Becca. You know there are some things we need to take care of before we can commence the study. You need to have a preliminary screening to ensure you're in good health and can proceed safely with the experiment. I also need to know of any preexisting conditions and some background information in order to verify the results of the study are due to the effects of my invention. Standard procedures. Plus, we'll see if you can handle my touch."

He didn't give her time to falter over her decision. She wouldn't be able to resist his challenge. Over the past six years, he had come to realize her dedication never wavered. She had been focused on the attainment of her goal to obtain her psychology degree for so long everything else vanished from her awareness as though she had tunnel vision. With the difficulty level of her studies ever increasing, she had thrived on the challenge, mastering new skills and abilities with ease.

As the magnitude of her drive to excel in their field became evident, Kurt found himself becoming more and more intrigued. Every day he worked near her increased his curiosity about the woman behind the perfect academic and ideal protégé who scholastically mastered the science of human interaction yet kept the world at arm's length in her personal life.

Her separation from emotion prevented her from being the top graduate in their field. It also worried him. What if she wasn't ready to explore her sexuality with him yet?

When she'd begun her apprenticeship, she'd been a young woman. At first, she was just a girl, an incredibly mature and responsible girl, but too young for any honorable man to touch.

Back in those days, he'd thought her youth, and the power of her excitement as she discovered new things in their profession, fed his attraction. He identified with her need to excel. Part of him had enjoyed reliving his own journey as he introduced her to some of his favorite works, guided her in conducting experiments and watched with pride as she developed into an amazing therapist.

Becca's growth toward her personal goals had been rewarding for Kurt. Over time, he'd watched her progress and develop, but still, the appeal hadn't dimmed. Rather, it had strengthened. Today, she was a grown woman, fiercely independent, intelligent and loyal but he feared pushing her. She possessed an underlying fragility, which she masked well but couldn't prevent him from glimpsing on occasion.

Lately, he'd sensed her iron will cracking as she neared the completion of her studies. Now, she prepared to graduate, hovered on the cusp of embarking on a new phase of her life, and Kurt wanted to be a part of it but not only as her employer.

He approached relationships with women as a lighthearted interlude both parties could enjoy for a while before moving on. But, instead of initiating any of those fleeting associations in recent months, Kurt lingered in his office most evenings, content to listen to Becca working diligently, happy knowing she sat right outside his door.

He had waited years for her to entrust him with the true sensual nature he sensed lurking inside her reserved character but, if she still wasn't prepared, then somehow he would continue to wait. To hell with consequences and the board. The problem was, he found her more enticing every day and each passing moment dropped like a grain of sand from an hourglass marking the time before everything changed.

If he didn't act soon, the opportunity to guide her through this last lesson would never arise. The board's insistence on the experiment might be the perfect opening for both of them. He prayed something good would come of this clusterfuck after all.

As long as she never found out he had let her down, allowed Dr. James Wexford to steal her most private dreams and share them with the world...

Kurt crossed to her, still not breaking eye contact. She was too wrapped up in her own anxieties to notice his obvious arousal. Good thing, since the swollen head of his dick pushed above the waistband of his underwear and made him wonder how far he could take her this first time. Deciding to test her limits while she teetered off balance, he stalked toward her.

Becca retreated until the backs of her knees bumped into the chaise lounge he reserved for patients. When she stumbled, he reached out to steady her. Observing her pupils dilate at the contact, he aimed a disarming wink in her direction.

"That's right. We can take care of this right here in my office." He spoke to her in a soft croon, like a wild animal. The fear mixed with awakening desire in her bright green eyes caused them to turn glassy as he watched. His stabilizing hands lingered on her arms and pushed with gentle but insistent pressure until she sank onto the sofa. "There's no need to go down to the laboratory. You'll be more comfortable here."

"Kurt, I mean, Dr. Foster..."

"During the experiment things will be different but, for now, please call me Kurt. I've always felt Dr. Foster was too formal."

"Kurt."

He loved the sound of his name on her lips.

"I had a physical a month ago, I could call my doctor and have her fax the results to you."

The flare of arousal he detected in the dilation of her eyes betrayed her. He pressed on, ignoring her offer, certain he understood her true desire.

"No, I need to do the exam myself." There. The flash of relief manifested in her features with the slight relaxation of her jaw muscle and a deep breath. She must have felt obligated to offer him a way out, but would have been disappointed if he'd accepted.

The fact that their extensive time together had taught him to read her well delighted him. Every passing moment cemented his belief in the purpose and success of the experiment.

Despite what had to be tricks of the board, considering he'd placed no paper on her desk this morning, and the sudden coincidence of her sister's monetary distress, it was clear to him Becca craved this experience. Still, he could tell he made her tense and nervous. He promised himself he'd go as slow as the need inside them both would allow.

Kurt turned his back for a moment as he mimed note taking and closed his eyes. He hadn't imagined it would be this hard to keep his self-control. It never had been before. He wanted nothing more at this moment than to push her back on the couch, rip open that heavy jacket, shove up her skirt and bury himself in her wet warmth.

He prescribed himself a few steadying breaths before turning back to her.

Dr. Foster pivoted from the table where he had been taking

notes. The sudden movement made Rebecca wary but his touch communicated tenderness when he leaned over her. Seeming even taller from this position, he smoothed her hair from her neck with one hand while the other settled on her back, holding her in place. She reached out to steady herself by placing a palm on his solid chest and could have sworn he jerked in response. Then again, she noted the fine tremble in her own fingers so maybe she had projected the motion on him.

"Easy." He murmured as he placed two fingers to the base of her neck, igniting a shiver that ran down the center of her body, ending in a sharp clench of her pussy.

She barely subdued a whimper.

"I need to take your pulse." For a minute they stayed still, watching each other. She didn't need his fingers over her artery to detect the heartbeat hammering through her. His touch was a dream come true. Sure, there'd been times they'd brushed against each other while working but he'd never reached out with intent to make skin to skin contact no matter how many times she wished he would. After a minute, he moved away then made a few more brief notes on the pad beside the couch.

"Get undressed now, Becca." Although she tried to conceal her shock, she knew the slightest motions could communicate as much to Kurt as the most expressive gestures did to other men. Her cheeks grew warm as she flushed and she knew he'd be able to detect the signs of her uncertainty.

Torn between the promise of what she wanted most and the hesitancy stemming from her lack of experience, she tried to calm herself. He was a doctor. This would be no different from her annual visit to her physician. *Yeah, right.*

She reached for the top button of her jacket. Expecting him to turn around and leave her to undress alone, as her usual doctor did, he surprised her by continuing to observe her with a strange look in his eyes. He almost appeared hungry, but surely he couldn't be interested in anything other than the study. Even for him, this was an extreme endeavor. The project he'd outlined to her a minute ago surpassed any of his previous work, which usually involved standard therapy but sometimes extended to witnessing, instructing or assisting struggling lovers.

While lost in thought, she removed the jacket and revealed the outline of her hard nipples to his unflinching stare. Right then she remembered what decorated her skin underneath the conservative suit.

"Kurt—" she paused to clear her throat, "—is...is there any way we can wait until tomorrow to do the exam?"

"No, Becca, it has to be today. The actual experiment procedures will be much more intimate. If participating is too difficult for you, we'll forget this ever happened and I'll find someone else for the study."

"No! I can do this. I *will* do this." She cursed the collection of exotic underwear that constituted her one extravagance...well, second, if you counted shoes. But shoes were really a necessity.

The thought of Kurt conducting this experiment with some other woman sickened her. Beautiful women constantly vied for his attention. She'd helped him avoid more than a few who called him at the office, refusing to take no for an answer. All the while, she tried to ignore the sense of satisfaction she got from driving them away when he'd asked her for the favor, or the pangs of jealousy that rolled through her when she'd heard him arranging to accept one of their invitations through his open office door. Funny, at the moment, she couldn't remember the last time he had.

Kurt must be able to see traces of her lacey bra through her demure white blouse by now. Peeking up from behind her lowered lids, she searched for any indication of his reaction. Would he think her promiscuous for her racy choice? Rebecca shivered harder and fumbled the uncooperative buttons on her top.

"Here, let me help you." He reached out and began threading the slippery discs through the holes with deft flicks. The heat of his fingers against her collarbone caused a wave of need. The backs of his hands trailed down her chest. Her shirt parted in their wake, revealing her pale skin. His fingers were long and thick, steady but gentle.

Standing there, exposed and vulnerable, the potency of her reaction to Kurt paralyzed her. The rational segment of her brain struggled to recall the professional intent behind their encounter. He peeled her shirt off her shoulders and untucked it from her skirt before she recovered from his proximity. He couldn't have known how many times she'd imagined a scene like this while peeking in at him from her desk across the threshold.

She came to her senses in time to stop Kurt as he lingered at the waistband of her skirt, his thumbs brushing up her sides. Though he probably intended the gesture to be soothing, she had to move away when passion started to bubble inside her. She didn't think she could stand his touch on her sensitized flesh any longer without making a fool of herself. Already, she feared he could sense her arousal.

Rebecca averted her eyes to keep him from stealing the secrets she held there.

"Don't be ashamed, Becca." Kurt needed to ease the doubts reflected in her eyes. It was odd for her to hesitate. In their work together, her natural confidence made her efficient and competent. "I think you're beautiful. Don't ever be afraid to show me how you feel. You'll have nothing to hide from me when the study is complete."

Her chest expanded as she drew a deep breath, gathering her courage, and then rose to slide down the zipper of her skirt. With one hand, she guided the fabric over her legs while shielding herself from his view by turning away then wrapping her arm around her waist.

Encircling her dainty wrist with his fingers, he tugged it free. He couldn't keep himself from touching her, even so fleetingly, as he took in the matching lace-top garters, bra and flimsy silk panties covering her mound. The glistening damp spot on them betrayed her excitement. She hesitated, looking to him to begin the exam, her breasts rising and falling in rapid bursts beneath his hungry eyes.

"As hot as you look like this, you'll need to take off your underwear, too." Kurt couldn't believe how much she tempted him. He'd always been very controlled with his lovers, enjoying the thrill of the chase, teasing them and making them desire him until they couldn't stand it anymore and begged him for release. Never before had he been this close to the edge himself, not after watching a beautiful woman undress.

The tone of his voice, jagged with strain, forced him to admit his best fantasies didn't live up to the reality of this moment.

Now committed, Becca stripped off her bra and panties before settling on the chaise to roll the sexy garters down her sexier legs. Kurt watched as the motion separated her thighs. The swollen folds of her sex parted, moisture glistening in shimmering strands between her labia, and he yearned to taste her.

"Good girl," he murmured as he moved closer. He pressed her shoulders back, guiding her down on the cushions. He struggled to keep the encounter clinical in an attempt to ease her into heightened intimacy with him through familiar routines.

"First, I'll need to see how sensitive you are." Resting on the edge of the sofa, he stroked his index finger along the side of her face. He dragged the pad to her glossy lips and brushed it across them. She gasped at the sensation, which caused his finger to slip inside her mouth, moistening the tip. He pulled it out and circled her lips again, making them shine.

"Do you usually respond this quickly to foreplay?" He tamped down the jealous twinge causing him to wonder if she blossomed like this for other men or for him alone.

"I-I don't really know."

Stupid college kids, he thought. No one had ever seduced her?

Kurt brought his other hand up to frame her face. Pushing his hands through Becca's hair, he allowed the strands to fill the gaps between his fingers. The warm satin tendrils infused him with longing but her thigh muscles relaxed against his on the couch as he massaged her scalp. His hands drifted toward her neck with leisurely but methodic strokes. A shaky sound somewhere between a whimper and a moan escaped from deep within her.

Every inch he explored was a delight as he discovered she felt even better than he had imagined. He couldn't resist trailing his hands below her collarbones now, dipping onto the top swells of her breasts, as he savored the heat and silkiness of her skin. She shifted beneath him in restless motions as though the light contact wasn't enough for her. His eyes raked an impassioned trail down her body, more beautiful than he had anticipated. Her full, round breasts complemented her smooth, but not too skinny, stomach which flared out to hips that enticed him with their sensual curves.

"Do you do self breast exams?" Kurt whispered as he improvised on his original plan. Beneath his inquiring gaze, she closed her eyes and shook her head. From a professional perspective, she would understand this had no bearing on the study. Her willingness to accept his touch, their newfound intimacy, regardless of logic inspired his wish to reward her with pleasure.

"Let me, then." He smiled down at her scrunched eyelids, hoping she suffered as much as he did. He couldn't bear to weather this pain alone. His cock had never been this hard. Already, pre-come leaked out, dampening his trousers. His balls nestled tight to his body.

Very soon, she could be his.

He started at the outside of her plump breast, walking his fingers in a shallow spiral. As they grew closer and closer to the center, her nipples gathered until they stood straight out. He brushed the palm of his hand over them as he made his way toward the goal with his fingertips then watched the rosy peaks darken when she flushed with excitement. Becca lay so still beneath his touch he realized she focused on maintaining the posture, withholding her desire from him.

She had so much to learn yet.

"It's okay to feel pleasure. Remember, this study will be about your sexuality. Determining your limits will mandate exceeding them. You won't be able to avoid ecstasy. Enjoy it. I will."

The intensity of her reaction impressed Kurt. She attempted to speak but had to try twice before her voice would cooperate. When it did, her words tumbled out as though angry with her body for betraying her. "This isn't easy. You're my boss!"

"Not here, not now. We're in this together. Go with it, let it take you." Kurt's fingers made their way to her nipples, rewarding her for her candor. A strangled moan burst from her. He redoubled his efforts, intent on driving her wild. He let the desire raging inside him be evident in his expression, to soothe her obvious yet misplaced embarrassment.

When she noticed the lust in his stare, the tension in her muscles melted away. Rubbing her nipples harder, he graced them with light pinches, conditioning her to respond as he commanded. The initial step away from her ultra-professional bearing would be the hardest for her. He found it difficult to push her, but his dominant instincts declared it the right course of action. Meanwhile, he reminded himself no matter how much he reveled in her pleasure, it was all for the study. For Becca. Her career, but not personal.

"You're doing great." He stroked her breasts one last time before sliding his hands to her hips. Instinctively, her pelvis lifted toward him but he avoided direct contact, moving lower until his hands cupped her feet. He massaged the sole of each with firm strokes to keep from tickling her. Another sigh of pleasure rewarded his efforts. Those wicked heels couldn't be comfortable to wear. He rubbed her feet bit by bit, working his way from her toes to her heels and ankles until she lay pliant before him.

"You're so sensitive. You react intensely to tactile stimulation." He showered her with reverent whispers, causing her blush to deepen. "It's nothing to be ashamed of. Passion is a normal emotion and you have so much of it in you. Don't hold anything back from me. You will let me know how you feel at all times." As he spoke, his hands glided up her legs, pausing to stroke the sensitive skin behind her knees before moving up the inside of her thighs with excruciating patience.

Her skin scorched him now. The waves of heat from her core warmed his hands. He could make her beg for his touch now that desire seared away all her inhibitions, but he refrained. With every contact, the professional shell cracked further and revealed more of the tantalizing woman beneath.

The transformation stole his breath, a thousand times more seductive than watching her undress. The juices running down her slit into the valley of her ass made him wish he could bury himself balls deep inside her welcoming grasp.

"How many lovers have you had, Becca?" It wouldn't be many. She'd smothered this side of herself. Besides, she spent most nights right here, working cases with him at the practice, or completing projects for her studies. He needed to know how careful to be with her. "When did you last have sex?"

By now, he suspected she was too involved to balk at the directness of his questions. When she panted out her answer, a purely male part of him cheered. "I had sex before winter break last year with my date to the end-of-the-semester banquet. That was the third time."

Kurt's fingers quaked on her upper thighs at the thought of her innocence. He couldn't stop himself from touching her pussy. He cupped her, enjoying the light weight of her tender flesh and downy hair against his hand. The slickness of her secretions allowed him to glide his palm over her. She arched into his hold and moaned.

Her trust had been a requirement to go this far but he needed to know her faith in him was absolute. The experiment would require her to go beyond anything she had ever experienced before. It would only work if she placed herself in his control. He would settle for nothing less than her total surrender. He would invest the patience necessary to earn it.

"Do you enjoy touching yourself like this?"

Kurt watched the muscles in her abdomen flex upon hearing the suggestive words he used. He'd never made a woman come just by talking to her but Becca tempted him to try it. These were the kinds of ideas being near her inspired.

The ripples of desire contracted the visible portion of her pussy in rhythmic pulses. He imagined her vaginal walls attempting to milk an imaginary cock. The pleasure had to be overwhelming her senses now.

"Yes," she gasped. Pressing against her inner thighs with his forearms, Kurt urged her to spread her legs wider. She complied. He began moving his hand in a slow circle while he pressed the base of his palm against her. When the sweet scent of her arousal filled the air, he gritted his teeth against the urge to take her rough, quick, now.

To make her his.

"Have you ever had an orgasm?" He continued in his most mesmerizing voice, inviting and soothing.

"Never with a man." She admitted it without hesitation now, her body strung tight around the pressure building inside her. Kurt dipped his fingers into her slit. He ran them up and down, accustoming her to his touch, before teasing them both by pressing one against the entrance to her pussy.

"Are you ready for me, Becca? I need to see how tight you are. I need to feel you around my fingers."

"Yes, Doctor. Kurt."

He groaned when his name fell from her lips, low and husky with need.

"Open your eyes. Watch me. You won't be able to avoid it during the study." He waited for her to comply, loving the cloudy look that proclaimed she had passed beyond her inhibitions. With firm and steady pressure, he pushed one finger inside her to the first knuckle before drawing it out again. She bucked beneath his hands then cried out her pleasure as he reintroduced the digit to the second knuckle. Kurt was so turned on his cock throbbed in his pants. He feared he might embarrass himself.

Focus. Today is about her. About proving she can trust you, taking the first step.

His finger, coated with Becca's desire, shuttled in and out of her clinging passageway. Her muscles stretched to accommodate the intrusion as it bored deeper on every stroke. He concentrated on her pleasure, tucking a second broad digit inside her. Her flesh gripped him, so hot, tight and slick he could hardly believe it.

Making good use of all his studies in human anatomy, Kurt drove his fingers in further until they brushed her G-spot. He bent them until he pressed the sensitive bundle of nerves inside her womb against her pelvic bone. She writhed beneath his hand.

Turning back now would be impossible. For both of them.

"That's right. I want you to come for me if you can. Do you

want to, baby?" He began moving his second and third fingers in and out of her, still slow but building the tempo now. He withdrew until they poised on the very cusp of her entrance before burying them as deep as he could reach. The knuckle of his index finger, curled into his palm, rubbed against her clit. She gasped, squeezing her eyes tight, as though trying to ward off the explosion he could feel gathering deep inside her.

She was his.

"Oh! Yes, Kurt, please don't stop. Please."

"That's right, sweetheart, come in my hand. I need to see how much you can feel. Don't hold back."

He bent low over her, chanting encouragement in her ear. His fingers thrust faster now, nudging the sensitive patch of nerves on each pass. He rubbed his knuckle against her clit in a firm rotation. "Come for me, Becca."

"Ah, Doctor. Kurt!"

He growled in triumph as her delicate tissues spasmed around his hand. His eyes followed her hips as they thrust against him. His own release loomed near. Though he tried to abstain, her pussy squeezing him, the hot juices running between his fingers, the musky scent of her arousal and the sound of her orgasm stripping away the last of her reserve shoved him over the edge. He ground his erection against her hip on the couch in an attempt to stop the inevitable.

It wasn't enough to keep the hot come from shooting out of his dick in an earth-shattering release.

"Oh God, Becca." He groaned. "You're perfect."

Rebecca feared things would be awkward afterward. They lay still for a moment, catching their breath. Then Dr. Foster stood, looking down at her, making her conscious of her flushed cheeks and tangled hair. *What have I done?*

All rational thought had fled her mind the first moment he'd touched her. Waves of pleasure had battered her body, making her helpless to do anything but flounder in the tide, all the while struggling to keep her head above water lest she drown in ecstasy.

But she still had to work with him every day. She'd hoped

he would hire her after graduation and maybe even advance to working her own cases soon. Had she destroyed any chance of her dream coming true?

"You can get dressed. We'll start work on the study tomorrow. Your normal duties are suspended. The project is most important now."

Disappointment zinged through her. That was it? He was going to let her walk away?

Of course he was, their encounter hadn't been personal to him. He'd simply needed to examine her. She'd nearly forgotten.

Hadn't he come, too?

In the heat of the moment, it had seemed so but maybe she mixed fantasy with reality.

As she reassembled her clothing, he treated her with the same respect and professionalism he always had. While that should have eased her nerves, it only made them more ragged. She hadn't comprehended the depth of her longing until now.

Had she imprudently risked her emotions by getting involved?

He'd promised to let her stop at any time but her honor would make her see this through regardless of how vulnerable it made her to explore her sexuality with him.

Rebecca finished dressing and walked to the door but, as she opened it to leave, she sensed him close behind her. His warm breath feathered across her shoulder and his hand, his wonderful hand, covered hers on the door. She turned to look at him with questions she couldn't voice written in her expression. Bridging some of the distance between them, he bent down to kiss her cheek.

"Thank you," he whispered.

She started to reply but he had already turned and headed back to his desk.

Chapter Three

When Rebecca awoke to the orange light of morning, she blinked several times then tried to remember the cause of the exquisite tenderness in her muscles before it all came back to her in a rush. Oh, God! Had she really been such an idiot?

The mental image of herself in Dr. Foster's office, contorted on the patient's chaise, muscles tight and straining under his dexterous ministrations, snapped into focus. Lying in the comfort and security of her warm bed, she could admit the episode had nothing at all to do with her altruistic commitment and everything to do with her long-unsatisfied daydreams of Kurt.

For the past six years, Rebecca had watched the way he helped his patients face their fears and attain their dreams of sexual freedom. But, as maturity enhanced her discerning vision, she had begun to see through his easygoing mannerisms. He had an innate sense of how to dominate and cut to the heart of someone's desires even when they remained oblivious to their own secret longings. Like a maestro playing a well-tuned instrument, he also knew when to back off a patient who'd reached their limits. He was gentle but demanding, quietly insistent, a combination that had stirred her imagination for years.

Groaning, she rolled out of bed, disgusted with herself. She'd cast herself in the role of one of Dr. Foster's patients, which couldn't be conducive to advancing her career. Entranced by his smoky eyes as he peppered her with questions about her sexual history, she had detected his unspoken conviction. Kurt thought she was repressed. Hell, it might be the truth but her single-minded focus had been necessary to achieve her goal.

Rebecca didn't regret the path she'd taken. It was just that the idea of her mentor perceiving her as weak or constrained disheartened her. While she dreamed of exploring her fantasies with him, she would never accept his pity. She'd seen him convince recalcitrant patients often enough to realize he'd used some of his infamous charm to get her to proceed with his unusual experiment protocols but it didn't matter because he'd coerced her to overcome her inhibitions and reach for something she desired.

He'd presented her with a golden excuse.

She planned to snatch it and run but she wished it didn't mean he considered her, in some way, lacking. Applying her scholastic knowledge of emotions to the feelings swirling inside her proved more difficult than she would have imagined. Logic couldn't solve this problem.

Following the completion of her dissertation, Rebecca had arranged to work fulltime at the clinic until graduation. She had been thrilled but now apprehension infringed on her glee. How could she maintain professionalism when the rules of the study required her total abandon? What if she disappointed Kurt? What if she exceeded his expectations?

Could they continue to work together or would there be no going back? She hoped the unbiased empathy he demonstrated on a daily basis would extend to her as well.

Head swimming with questions, she trudged toward the shower, both dreading and eager for the day ahead. She flicked on the water and gathered her clothes while the temperature in her apartment's antiquated water heater crept toward lukewarm. After selecting a suit from her closet, she rifled through her underwear drawer.

Should she opt for a modest, matching cotton set because he would see it? Immediately, she discarded the idea. She was no cowering wallflower in need of his help. When she volunteered for the study, she saw it as a way to experiment a little herself. She needed experience. Who better to give it to her than the sexy man who made her feel safe, who was an excellent teacher and who attracted her as no other man ever had before?

She refused to betray his request for open and honest communication by changing her normal behaviors or hiding the heightened reactions he'd inspired. With a grin, she grabbed her most provocative lingerie, a see-through lace teddy, and her highest pair of heels. She'd noticed how often he appreciated her shoes, and the steamy look in his eyes when she'd revealed her sexy undergarments during his exam the day before.

Dr. Foster had taken her by surprise yesterday. Today, she would fight fire with fire.

℃

Rebecca had known yesterday's encounter would alter her relationship with Kurt but when she entered the office and stared at the dents in the carpet marking the space her desk used to occupy, she panicked. Her palms grew sweaty and she struggled to control her labored breathing.

She loved her job at the university clinic. Despite her earlier bravado, the reminder of how her participation in the Dream Machine study could jeopardize her career terrified her. Her only solace lie in her conviction she'd never excel in her field until she understood passion firsthand. Plus, her sister's education was worth risking her career, her pride, everything she'd ever worked for. Elsa relied on her alone.

Even if she didn't get a job in Dr. Foster's office, her academic record ensured a prestigious position elsewhere. With the added benefit of the sexual experience this project would give her, she would be a stellar candidate. Reaffirming her earlier commitment to stay strong, she drew a deep breath and willed herself to ignore her doubts. Many obstacles had littered her path to success. She'd smash this one like all the others.

Fortunately, she didn't have much time to brood about the situation. Kurt appeared in the doorway to his office, leaning one hip on the jamb in the relaxed pose she'd come to know so well. He looked amazing in his crisp black slacks and silk shirt with the sleeves rolled up to his elbows. The loosened collar gaped, allowing her a glimpse of the dark hair sprinkled on his chest.

Closing her eyes to block out the vision, she tried to resist the immediate reaction of her body. Sensing Kurt's gaze roaming over every inch of her, she stilled her wringing hands. She willed herself to square her shoulders and meet his stare. Drawing a deep, calming breath, she opened her eyes. When she did, she watched a slow, sweet smile of approval spread across his face.

Without a word, he held out his hand. She obeyed his silent command. Crossing to him, she closed the gap by sliding her palm across his. The arc of the electric attraction between them caused her to gasp. He entwined their fingers before leading her down the corridor behind his office. As they made their way deeper into the facility, she concentrated on his hand wrapped around hers. His fingers were long and strong, warm and supportive.

It seemed right.

She'd never been back to this part of the clinic since he reserved it for his personal study and experimentation. A separate branch of the building housed the general labs, leaving this area secluded. With each step, they drew further away from the bustle of the main practice and deeper into the solitude of the restricted area.

Kurt paused before the door at the end of the hallway to punch in a combination on the keypad next to the door. When the light flashed green, he turned to face her.

"Last chance, Becca. Are you sure?"

Without hesitation, she rotated the knob herself, pushed open the door and took the first step inside his private laboratory.

She hadn't expected this. The whole room gleamed, bright white and clinical, compared to the subdued colors and indirect lighting of his office. Some distant part of her mind registered the ominous *thunk* of the closing door then the snick of the lock engaging as she surveyed the environment.

In the center of the room rested a large padded table similar to the one she had relaxed on when Kurt and their colleagues had treated her to a massage at the local day spa for her birthday last year. Surrounding the table, several mechanical objects beeped and whirred. A few she recognized as standard medical equipment but most remained a mystery. In addition to the machines, whiteboards covered with notes and designs for the new invention lined one whole wall. Imbedded in another, a large reflective window she recognized as a one-way observation mirror flung back the picture of her wide-eyed stare and open jaw.

Absorbed in the surroundings, she didn't notice the doctor approaching behind her until he caressed her hip. She flinched beneath his searing palm. He'd always been so careful not to touch her when she studied with him.

"I've dreamt of this for a long time," he whispered in her ear.

Rebecca assumed he referred to the development of the Dream Machine. If it was as monumental a breakthrough as he anticipated then it would aid thousands of people, guarantee his professional success and, no doubt, make him a very rich man in the process. Otherwise, why would he be so desperate to find a subject that he risked the participation fee if she didn't complete the study? She forced her brain to untangle the problem as she would on any other assignment.

"Tell me more about the Dream Machine. How long has it been in development? Will you show it to me?" She vacillated between curiosity and apprehension as she thought about what was to come. "What will it feel like? What will it do to me?"

"You'll have all the answers in time." Catching his intense stare, she watched Kurt's grey eyes darken. He refused to be rushed. "We need to establish some rules and get you prepared. First, while in the lab you will address me as Dr. Foster or Doctor. Do you understand?"

Rebecca comprehended the importance of proper procedure and documentation for the success of an experiment, even one as personal as this. Trying to ignore the tingle of anticipation spreading through her at the prospect of submitting to his authority, she gave him a tentative smile and answered, "Yes, Doctor."

"Good girl. Second, to maintain the integrity of the experiment, once we begin the official proceedings tomorrow, all of our time here must be witnessed." Although she recognized the standard procedure, she cringed at the thought of anyone but Kurt having access to her innermost desires. Revealing them to him would be difficult enough.

"I thought the intrusion of other people might be difficult for you given the nature of our study so I made a case to the review board that it could skew our results. As head of the board, Luke convinced them to agree." He shot her a conspiratorial smirk.

A sigh of relief escaped her parted lips. She'd always liked Dr. Malone.

"Therefore, I arranged to have our initial sessions videotaped instead." Moments ago, she would have balked at having her first attempts at passion captured on film. Yet, now, gratitude flooded her senses on hearing their sessions would be recorded. Pushing away the potential embarrassment, she focused on the bright side. If nothing else, she would always have the memories of her time with Kurt in the experiment archive.

She communicated her assent with a slight nod.

"Finally, whenever we are in this room, you will be naked."

When she began to object, he expounded. "My interactions with you will vary during the study. You might not always understand my reasons but I expect you to act without question. Too many specifics could alter the outcome of our research. You have to trust me even if what I ask is intimate or unexpected. If you are unwilling to continue, remember you only have to say the word."

He led her to the edge of the examination table. The genial man she thought she knew so well had transformed the moment they crossed the threshold to this room. Laying down the rules, he wielded indisputable control, making clear the extent of the leniency he had granted her while training in the field. There, he had been a mentor demonstrating ways to become a successful colleague. Here, she was clearly his subject. She had not only accepted his terms but also petitioned to be involved, granting him the right to demand her obedience.

Isn't that what you wanted? To give up control, to let

someone else take charge for once?

He reached forward. Cupping her chin, he raised her face with steady pressure until she couldn't avoid the heat smoldering in his eyes. "Becca, I've seen all of you. I loved every inch. Now, get rid of your clothes or I'll do it for you."

A mental image of the doctor tearing her skirt off fuzzed her mind. When she paused to consider it, he slapped her ass with enough warning to make himself understood. The contact shot sparks of desire up her spine. She yelped in surprise...and arousal. No one had ever played with her like that before. She found herself eager to see what it would be like to push him further.

"Get going," Dr. Foster growled. Suddenly, her rebelliousness in selecting the revealing lingerie that enhanced her provocative shape didn't seem like such a good idea. She debated testing him for one more moment before she chickened out. Unlike yesterday, she stripped off her suit without hesitation to stand proud before him in the lace teddy, matching stockings and heels.

"Damn. You have amazing taste in underwear." Kurt exhaled a harsh breath. She slid her feet out of her shoes then bent to roll the stockings down the toned muscles of her legs. Selling her car for textbook money had some side benefits. When she shifted, his eyes fixed on the slender strap of the teddy tucked between her thighs.

"Stop," he demanded.

With her foot in mid air, poised to draw off the stocking, she froze.

"I want to look at you." The nylon sheathing fluttered to the floor as he placed a hand on her collarbone. Firm, steady pressure from his fingers encouraged her to turn a circle before him.

When her back faced his front, he halted her progress with a squeeze on her shoulder. Bending nearer, his lips hovered over her ear as he whispered, "This drives me crazy."

Her head dropped onto his shoulder when he traced the line of fabric along her crack. She imagined the way it presented the exposed globes of her ass for his enjoyment.

"You have a perfect ass." The explicit words shocked her nearly as much as they turned her on. They also set the stage for this new facet of their relationship. Kurt wasn't the kind of man to do things halfway. By entering this room, she had approved this intimacy. Little did he know, she craved this dark sexual journey and had for a very long time.

His touch broke her from her thoughts. Fitting his palms to her, he cupped her buttocks. What she had always considered extra junk in the trunk seemed to please him.

Rebecca glanced over her shoulder, satisfied with her boldness, as she unclasped the crotch of the sexy garment, deliberately disobeying his instruction to stay still. He indulged her by letting her goad him but it reassured her to see she had his rapt attention.

Feeling secure and sexy, she continued.

She tugged the tight fabric over her head, drawing a sharp breath when the lace rasped against her sensitized nipples, which grew harder by the second. As soon as she dropped the lingerie on the floor, Kurt pounced from his rigid stance. His left arm clamped around her waist like an iron band as his right hand splayed high on her back, forcing her to bend over. She braced herself with her palms on the table in front of her a moment before he spanked her ass again.

The crisp sound reverberated in the room. As the shockwaves of pain and pleasure flew through her, she was relieved he hadn't treated her like a fragile patient. Before she could figure out what he expected of her, he scooped her into his arms only to deposit her on the inviting, terrycloth-covered table.

"Enough teasing. Let's get started. Don't test me, Becca. I *will* punish you and you aren't ready for that yet."

She squirmed a bit on the platform although it was more comfortable than she had imagined. She tried not to glance up at him, knowing he would detect her arousal, but she couldn't take her eyes away from him for long. Turning her head, she realized her mistake when the bulge in his slacks shifted, with heavy thumps corresponding to his heartbeat, a mere inch from her face. She longed to reach out and discover how firm and hot his shaft must be. Judging by the size of the tent forming in the front of his pants, his erection would be huge—far bigger than either of the men she'd been with before.

When Kurt stepped back, she wondered if he could sense her hungry stare on his crotch. Eyes fixed on hers, he began to unbutton his shirt. The sight of his well-muscled body mesmerized her, confirming all her daydreams. He was more than halfway done when some semblance of her intelligence returned. Her gaze shot to his and she asked, "Dr. Foster, what are you doing?"

The trembling in her voice dismayed her.

"It's only fair you see me too. I hope it will help you relax. You don't mind do you?" As though she would object to the dark golden muscles revealed to her. The ripple of sinewy flesh along his chest and abdomen and the light trail of hair leading into the waistband of his slacks fascinated her. His fingers worked the fly of his pants with deft movements while she checked to make sure no drool escaped her salivating mouth.

Face flushed with heat, the first bead of moisture pooled inside Rebecca's womb. She focused on burning every detail of this scene into her memory for the lonely nights ahead. His fingers slid inside his bulging boxer briefs. When he nudged them down, she thought it proper to avert her stare but found she couldn't. His long, thick erection sprang free and bounced against his flat stomach.

The whimper that escaped when she wished she could taste him brought her back to her senses.

She jerked her eyes away, causing Kurt to chuckle. "Go ahead and look. If we can't be comfortable with ourselves, how can we help others with their intimate issues?" She couldn't bring herself to gawk at his hard-on even though it was the object of her obvious desire. Instead, she focused on his feet then followed the trail of silky charcoal hair, admiring his powerful legs until she realized she'd ended up right back where she'd started.

His testicles drew up tight against his body, leaving his scrotum wrinkled and a shade darker than the rest of his skin. She wanted to trace a finger up the prominent veins making his cock throb.

The physical evidence of his arousal comforted her. He couldn't fake this reaction. Last night she had begun to doubt that the chemistry between them affected him as it did her. She even wondered if she'd imagined the desire in his expression while he'd examined her on the couch in his office.

But she'd been right. He wanted her, too.

Disappointment zinged through her when he pivoted, took a lab coat from a hanger on the wall and threaded his arms through it. With sure, efficient motions, he knotted the belt around his tapered waist. The gesture accentuated his broad shoulders. The coat highlighted his hard, throbbing erection, which parted the fabric in the center, standing out, framed in white. Kurt bent over her prone form. For a moment, she thought he would kiss her. Instead, he engulfed her wrist with his hand then stretched it above her head. She chastised herself for forgetting this was his job.

"Dr. Foster!" A fuzzy band wrapped around her wrist, pinning it in place.

"Shh, it's all right. I just need you to stay still. Today's session will ease you into the experiment. I'll prepare you, accustom you to the environment and test out some equipment. Baby steps." He fastened the fur-lined cuff then attached it to the peg above her head before moving on to repeat the procedure with her other hand. Arms crossed, the position forced her breasts to stand out, drawing attention to her engorged nipples.

Kurt trailed his fingers along her torso until he found the two straps on either side of her waist then drew them through the buckle in the middle. He rested his palm on the supple skin of her abdomen, causing her muscles to jump beneath his fingers. He rewarded her with a tight smile, then cinched the belt until he struggled to remove his hand from beneath it.

He brushed his palms across the sensitive skin below her belly button, then down her legs, accustoming her to his touch. Finally, he clasped her ankles in his firm grasp before strapping them to the table as well.

Rebecca couldn't still the instinct to struggle. She wriggled against the bonds, testing their strength, and discovered she couldn't move more than a fraction of an inch. She'd never done anything like this before. The fear and thrill inside her competed for dominance.

Panic threatened to wash over her but she fought to subdue it. She had always looked out for herself. The thought of lying back, passive, accepting whatever he chose to do to her, terrified her.

"Breathe."

His voice drew her away from the edge. Glints of anticipation sparkled through the fear. She battled her initial reaction, reaching for the exhilaration underlying her apprehension. Trusting anyone other than Kurt would have been impossible. With him, though, she was aroused and surprised to find her senses heightened. Glancing up with a nervous flick of her eyes, she met his gaze as he observed her reaction. His appraisal forced her to concentrate on convincing her muscles to relax and allowing the straps to cradle her.

Immediately, they felt more comfortable and less restrictive.

"Good girl. That's right, I'll take care of you." The gentle croon lulled her while he stroked her hip, petting her, soothing her. His approval flared inside her soul. Every beat of her heart strummed though her clit. The slick wetness of her passion dripped from her so steadily now it ran down her ass, onto the table.

Kurt moved to the bottom of the platform. She heard the clink of metal as he released a mechanism located somewhere under her feet then her legs shifted with a lurch that corresponded to the noise. He looked up at her as he grasped an ankle in each hand then yanked them apart. The table split down the middle, between her legs. The pieces rotated outward before locking in place, leaving her stretched and totally exposed to his view.

Primal reactions drove her to thrash once more, to curl her legs back in close to her body. Or, at least she tried, but the restraints held fast. Her breath came in several large, sporadic gulps. She wrestled her shock until Kurt's comforting strokes on her skin registered on her mind. She focused on the tone of his voice as he murmured reassurance, attempting to accept her complete vulnerability. She tried to relax, tried to focus on what he was doing and soon she regained some composure.

Once satisfied, he circled the table, observing her from every angle.

"Hmm... We're almost set. But there's one more thing I think we need to do," he muttered, almost as though thinking aloud. Stalking around her, he continued handling her, prodding her, applying firmer pressure in some spots as though testing her resilience. "Yes, just one more thing."

Standing in front of her once again, he raised her head and shoulders using a control that elevated the section of the table her torso rested on, tilting it forward so she could observe his actions.

"Have you ever shaved your pussy, Becca?"

She had to try several times before she could make her voice audible. "N-No, Doctor."

"I'll have to trim you so the camera can get a clear recording of the experiment." Her eyes went wide as he stepped over to the sink against the far wall then began filling a bowl with lukewarm water. When he returned to the table, he set the container on a stainless steel rolling tray positioned between her legs then scooted his chair beside it.

Rebecca heard a heavy drawer in the base of the table open with a squeak. The noise of several unknown objects clanking together echoed through the laboratory as he rummaged among the contents. Straightening, he laid a razor, shaving cream and several towels next to the basin of water on the cart.

Embarrassed, she realized sitting close between her legs he couldn't miss the signs of her arousal. Her thighs flexed as she tried to close them.

"You're so stunning like this. I love the way your cunt looks, spread wet and clenching." Whether he said it to alleviate her self-conscious anxiety or because it was true, he put her at ease. He specialized in human sexual reactions and, if she believed rumors, had extensive personal knowledge of the subject. If he could maintain professional detachment from a physiological response, she would try too.

As he talked, he grabbed a pair of latex gloves off the counter then made a production of tugging them on. With a diabolical grin, he let them snap against his wrists. He couldn't know it would make her even wetter, could he? Excitement infused every cell of her body. She lost track of their purpose and nearly cried out for him to touch her, sure she could come with one swipe of his gloved finger against her clit.

"Ask me to do this for you," he instructed, his voice deep and sensual.

Why did he want her to ask? He could do whatever he wanted, she couldn't stop him.

"Admit you're curious. Ask me. Not because you have to but because you wonder what it will feel like, because you want me to."

"Yes. Please, Dr. Foster, shave me." she begged.

Chapter Four

Triumph flared inside Kurt. The sweet honey dripping from Becca's pussy made it clear the setup affected her. The environment excited her. He'd absorbed her look of hunger when he'd reached for the latex gloves, drawing them on though they were unnecessary props. More certain than ever she yearned to submit to him as much as he wanted to take her, he had pushed her further than he intended by demanding she confess her desire.

Now he would reward her.

Using all of his natural ability and experience, he prepared to give his delectable assistant a taste of what she needed. Even if she didn't understand it yet. He prayed he could maintain control, which threatened to elude him around her.

He shook the can of shaving cream then shot a ball into his palm. He paused, his hands hovering above her hips for a fraction of a second. Her eyes dilated in anticipation. After a few moments, he smeared it across her pussy.

Becca gasped.

The contrast of the cool foam with her building heat must have been startling. His eyes locked on her, engrossed in every motion. The soft band holding her hips to the table thwarted her attempt to thrust her pelvis at him.

He kept his touch light, the contact too subtle for her to gain any relief at all. Apprehension warred with desire in her eyes as the blade lowered toward her. Her struggle enchanted him. She jerked, what little she could, when he increased the pressure of his hand immobilizing her flesh then drew the razor away from her, removing the first strip of hair.

Kurt worked over her with the precision and focus he applied to all of his research. He studied her pretty pussy twitching with the alternating chill of the cream and blade followed by the warmth of the water as he wiped her clean. When the razor dipped lower, skimming the sensitive flesh between her vagina and anus, she moaned out load.

His laugh strained with his own desire, "It feels good, baby, I know. That's why I had to tie you down. I wouldn't want to cut anything off by mistake."

Finishing with her, he removed the gloves, pushed the cart out of the way and then stood back to observe his handiwork. "Do you know the best way to test for a perfect shave, Becca?"

She shook her head.

"By feeling with your tongue. Let me show you."

Delighted, he watched her grit her teeth to keep from calling out for him to touch her, though she didn't object to his personal inspection methods. When he cranked another handle in the side of the examination table, a padded platform extension slid out above the drawer in the table base. Kurt lowered himself to the bench and knelt between her legs.

Leaning in closer he asked, "Can you feel my breath on you?"

She only moaned in response, but he knew she could. The sensation would be evident on her ultra-sensitive skin. He ran his fingers around her swollen lips with the barest of contact, awed by the slick, smooth texture.

He nearly caved in and tasted her before she begged but he forced himself to wait. She had to acknowledge she needed him. He wouldn't let her revert to the mental comfort of excusing her behavior for the sake of the experiment when she wanted the intimate contact as desperately as he wanted to taste her.

Kurt blew warm air across her clit. The mouth of her pussy quivered in response. From this distance, he could observe every detail. He looked at her face in time to witness the strain and pleasure overtaking her at once. "Do you enjoy the sensitivity of a shaved pussy?"

At her hesitation, he raised one eyebrow in silent question

then started to retreat.

"No! I mean...yes, I like it. Please, don't leave me like this! Doctor, please help me." Her cheeks deepened from rose to maroon. She'd spoken before her brain could stop the words. He loved watching the color rush up her skin from her chest to her face.

"You want me to make you come?" He paused until she affirmed it.

"Yes. Please, please make me come."

Groaning, he leaned forward to eliminate the fraction of an inch between them then buried his face in her wetness.

Becca's hands curled into fists where bound above her head on the examination table. He savored her exquisite cry of pleasure when his tongue swept along her slit. He wanted to drown her in pleasure, her escape impossible with her hips bound to the table. As his tongue swirled around her clit, he brought his hand up to brush against her opening.

He used one finger to test her moist heat. It began to slide inside. Even as slick as she was now, his finger did not easily penetrate. The firm but sure pressure of his thick digit invading her snug channel drew a whimper from her before her passageway stretched to accommodate him.

Her pliable flesh clamped around him.

"God, Becca, I've never felt a woman so tight before," he mumbled against her skin, unwilling to separate from her for a moment. He might have worried about hurting her but the sounds bursting from the depths of her chest didn't result from pain.

With two fingers buried in her now, he felt her climax building. As her rings of muscle clenched in rhythmic pulses around him, he marveled at the searing force of her reaction. She lay beyond reasoning, moaning uncontrollably, eyes shut, head thrown back. When her orgasm began, he slid his pinky down to the tiny hole below and rubbed her wetness over it.

She gasped but didn't flinch from his exploratory touch.

Kurt feared all his plans would fly out the window. If he didn't get moving with his agenda for the day, he wouldn't be able to stop himself from finding out how tight her pussy could wrap itself around his throbbing cock the old-fashioned way. The sweet look of pure longing in her eyes when she glanced up nearly undid him but he forced himself to hold strong. He wrapped his lips around her clit then sucked with tender pulls. Her eyes fluttered closed as she surrendered to sensation. Becca must have been seeing stars, her eyes clenched shut as she reached for the summit.

"Tell me how you feel."

"Never. Felt. So… Good."

Then she tensed beneath his hands as she plummeted over the edge. When the first spasms ricocheted through the tissue deep inside her, Kurt nudged the very tip of his finger inside her ass. Part of him roared. He knew he was the first to take her this way.

Screaming, she crashed through the last barrier, falling into a long, powerful orgasm. "Doctor!"

He stared in awe as ecstasy consumed her.

While she caught her breath, Kurt slipped his fingers from her still shuddering body. He drew fresh water to wash her. His instincts urged him to give her a moment to collect her thoughts before pushing on. He tended to her, then encouraged her to rest for a few minutes before placing the base of the Dream Machine's arousal sensor into the slot he'd incorporated in the table's design.

The probe was a complex electronic measuring device based on a myograph, used to measure muscle contractions in the vaginal wall. He'd modified it by coating it with a firm but stretchy flesh colored material with properties similar to skin, which he'd invented to make it more comfortable. In addition, he'd updated the circuitry with wireless technology, enabling it to network with the Dream Machine. This allowed its use in more diverse applications such as embedding it into probes like the one he used today. He wanted to test out the equipment to ensure it functioned as he expected.

At its current setting, the probe had a one-inch diameter. The instrument fit onto an attachment arm, which contained the transmitters that communicated the data gathered about pressure, heat and moisture to the monitoring unit beside the examination table. Currently, the probe connected to a revolving arm, which would insert and retract the device into Becca's pussy, mimicking sex.

Kurt couldn't wait to try his latest toy.

By the time Rebecca became aware of her surroundings, the probe hovered outside her pussy. Coming to stand beside her, Kurt stroked her hair. "You're doing very well."

Weak, with waves of contractions still sloshing through her, she peeked up at him. Although she'd just had the best orgasm of her life, it only took one look at the passion on his face and the pearly pre-come oozing over the head of his engorged cock to be ready for more. She never would have believed she could feel the least bit unsatisfied after that experience but she wanted him buried inside her.

Was that part of their game? He'd just devoured her like a starving man at an all-you-can-eat buffet. His cock stood hard and ready. He'd told her repeatedly to be honest about her desires.

In a voice scratchy from screaming, she asked, "Doctor, will you fuck me?"

"No. I don't want to distort our results. Today, I have to test some equipment. I'll take readings with this probe while your pussy is at its regular size."

Damn it, think! This is his job. Your job.

Disappointed, she turned her head away from him. She didn't reveal that nothing about this experience was ordinary for her but she certainly had never reacted like this before. Just being here with him aroused her more than any fantasy she'd ever had.

"I set a tool I'm going to use to gather data just outside your pussy. In a moment, I'm going to insert it. Then we'll start taking measurements. I need to verify the machines are functioning as intended."

The thought alone made her muscles clamp. *I am so screwed.* His clinical narration couldn't disguise the erotic nature of what was about to happen. Her body strained toward him. More of her come pooled below her ass on the table.

"Though, I have to admit, the sight of you like this is making it very difficult for me to concentrate. Would you like to assist me?" His legendary virility couldn't be suppressed. His reaction would be the same independent of the subject but, unlike her, Kurt didn't feel the need to hide his nature. It would be no hardship to ease his discomfort. In fact, it would be a dream come true.

"Yes, Doctor. Tell me what to do," she whispered.

Sliding his fingers into her hair, he tugged until she turned to face him.

"Have you ever sucked a man's cock before?" Though tempted to lie so he wouldn't think her naïve, the power of his smoky eyes demanded an honest answer.

"No." She rolled her eyes when her voice came close to squeaking. She wanted to know what he tasted like, what his stiff flesh would feel like against her lips. She wanted to make him experience even a fraction of the longing she did when he came near. She wanted to make him burn, too. "But I want to know how. Teach me?"

Faster than she thought possible, Kurt lunged closer. Holding the base of his cock, he teased her by rubbing the head against her lips to spread his salty moisture over them. When her tongue nipped out and stole a sample, he moaned. Loving that she had the power to affect him too, she reached her tongue out again and licked the purple tip of his cock.

"Open up." He moaned again, and then thrust between her lips.

Absorbed in her explorations, Rebecca ran her tongue around the ridge of flesh near the head then traced the most prominent vein to his balls. She loved his tangy flavor and the clean, earthy scent of his skin. She tugged him deeper with her unpracticed suckling, letting his groans and sighs guide her. He seemed content to let them both indulge for a moment.

Then, keying the remote in his lab jacket, he triggered the probe's forward motion.

"Ohh!" She moaned around his shaft. The steady pressure built on the opening of her pussy. She struggled to concentrate on his cock as the smooth device impaled her, driving her wild.

"I can feel the vibrations all the way up my spine when you do that." Kurt's low encouragement filled her with smug satisfaction. He fucked her face with careful, shallow strokes since her bound state limited motion.

The probe bottomed out, fully embedded in her. The base tucked against her sensitive vulva. The monitor across the table from her began drawing a glowing line, measuring the clasp of her channel as the device tunneled into her at a deliberate pace. The whir and low clanking of the moving parts contributed to her arousal. The probe was thicker than Dr. Foster's fingers but nowhere near as wide as the erection overflowing her mouth. She wondered what it would feel like to be stretched so wide.

He initiated the cyclic motion of the probe. It entered then retracted from her hot hole before beginning again. Kurt's growl drew her attention.

"It's working. The monitor is confirming the passion I can see on your face. Damn, that's hot." When he pressed his shaft further into her mouth, the line on the screen jumped. With a wicked grin, he teased her, "I see you enjoy it when I make you take me deeper. How far can you go, Becca?"

She opened her mouth wider, inviting him to find out. His tempo matched the measured strokes of the probe fucking her. She gripped the machine with her inner muscles, loving the rough friction it generated when it forced its way back inside her. Kurt fondled her breasts as he continued to slide his dick in and out of her sucking mouth. First, he brushed his fingers against her nipples with glancing strokes of his fingertips. Then he pinched them with a gentle grip.

He tested her to see what she liked.

"Mmm." She moaned around him wondering if the green line climbed on the printout behind her. Surprise filtered through her arousal. She hadn't expected to enjoy pleasuring him this way. The wet sounds of the probe entering her repeatedly mixed with the slurps she made as she swallowed around Kurt's dick.

"This is amazing. The way you surrender to passion is incredible." He panted now. "Damn it, Becca, ease up. I won't be able to stop myself from coming in your mouth."

At his words, the beeping got higher pitched.

"The probe readings just spiked. You want my hot come on your tongue?" Again, the sounds escalated. His primal shout echoed in the stark room as his cock grew firmer and longer, the ridges gaining definition against her tongue. His revelation must have driven him beyond control.

"Drink it. Every last drop." He shuddered then growled a moment before the first rush of seed coated the back of her throat. Swallowing instinctively, her own orgasm crashed inside her while the probe continued fucking her with deep, steady plunges.

Flames engulfed her, burning her preconceptions to the ground. Nothing had ever felt this good before. Her muscles shuddered in pulse after pulse of blinding ecstasy. Screaming around his dick, she let the moment carry her away until the probe slowed and, finally, stopped outside her.

In a haze, she felt Kurt withdraw his softening shaft from her mouth despite her continued lapping.

"I'm sorry, baby. That's all there is for now." Smiling, he squeezed her hand before moving away. He disengaged the probe then released her bonds. She remained where he had placed her on the table, unable to move. When he returned to her side, he cradled her, dazed and sated, in his arms for a moment before he picked her up. Arms winding around his neck, she snuggled against his firm chest and sighed.

Kurt opened a door on the far wall, opposite where they'd entered, then carried her into the next room. Familiar with the dark space, he strode through the shadows to lay her on a huge bed in the corner.

"Rest for a while." He pressed a kiss to her forehead before tugging a downy comforter over her.

Within moments, she slept.

Chapter Five

Rebecca awoke to a faint scratching sound. She blinked several times to clear her eyes while trying to place her surroundings. A buttery yellow glow illuminated the small room while a man bent over the desk opposite the bed, making notes in his journal with a raspy mechanical pencil. Kurt! She couldn't help but sigh as she remembered the decadence they'd indulged in.

Lying still, hoping he wouldn't notice she had regained consciousness, she used the opportunity to study him. He'd pulled on a pair of sweat pants but his lab coat had vanished. He must have left it in the laboratory. With no shirt covering his bronzed skin, the flicker from a few candles he'd lit highlighted the broad expanse of his well-muscled back. She wanted to run her hands down the furrow of his spine.

When she shifted to relieve the pressure between her thighs, she must have made some small noise.

Setting aside his notes, Kurt turned. His smile expanded when he realized she was awake. "How do you feel?"

"Mmm, good." She blushed a little at the way her voice sounded husky from the mix of satisfaction and sleep. Gathering the blanket around her, she sat up, dangling her feet off the edge of the oversized bed. This must be his personal study, a place for him to crash after working long hours on involved research projects. He had a reputation for burning the midnight oil when motivated.

She had often wondered what compelled him. What was he searching for?

Plenty of women called him at the office hoping to occupy his free time but none of them could distract him from work for long. It didn't make sense to her. The man had to care for something other than the pursuit of science.

She noticed a small bathroom including a shower off to the side. In addition to the bed and utilitarian desk, a dorm fridge and a television occupied most of the remaining space. The room should have been cramped. The king-sized bed hogged one whole wall. But, instead, a cozy atmosphere permeated the room.

Kurt crossed to the bed. The mattress dipped when he settled beside her. The motion forced her to brush against his side as he stroked errant curls off her face. She soaked in the intimacy of the moment even though she knew it contained no romantic significance for him. His renowned expertise as a lover was only exceeded by his reputation for never involving his heart in his affairs.

"You're all I could have hoped for."

"Thank you, Doctor." Her pulse hammered until she looked away, afraid he might discern her desperate wish for his words to be personal instead of professional. Suddenly, she sat altogether too close to him. Unsure of how to proceed, she began to fidget. Should she get up and leave? Where were her clothes?

Sensing her awkward restlessness, he asked, "Would you like to take a shower? I left your things in the bathroom."

Rebecca nodded then rose, taking the comforter with her to shield her body from view. When she shut herself inside the compact, tiled restroom, leaning against the door, she wondered what she'd gotten herself into. What cost would this experience come at?

She rushed through a shower then threw on her clothes, driven by the urge to escape any possible emotional pitfalls. As she reentered Kurt's study, her mind hoped he'd be gone already while her heart yearned for him to be waiting, to provide reassurance their professional relationship remained intact.

He looked up from his notes, re-dressed in the clothes he'd worn earlier.

Damn. So much for getting away while he changed. He must have guessed she would bolt but didn't intend to give her the chance. His muscled body infringed on her personal space when he stood, placed his hand in the small of her back then escorted her into the hallway through yet another door.

Rebecca thanked every divine presence she could conjure when they avoided the laboratory. She couldn't stand the reminder of what they'd experienced together while pretending it didn't affect her outside of the experiment. She assumed he would show her to the door but, as he handed over her purse, she realized he also prepared to leave. How long had she slept?

"I'm sorry if I kept you later than you intended, Dr. Foster."

"Out here it's Kurt, remember?" Opening the front door, he ushered her onto the sidewalk and locked up the office. A beautiful night, warm and cloudless, allowed a handful of the brightest stars to shine through the haze created by the city lights.

"Wow, I must have been out for a while." She spoke to herself yet he heard.

"I would have stayed with you all night but, I have to confess, I'm craving a nice dinner out." As if on cue, his stomach rumbled. She couldn't stifle a giggle as he rubbed a hand over his ripped abdomen.

Since when did she giggle? Then again, she couldn't remember the last time she'd been so relaxed.

"Have dinner with me. I know you work late after classes but it's past even your dedicated hours. I should've gotten you up earlier but I got into my observations and you appeared to be sleeping well." Kurt reached out to brush his thumbs under her eyes, tracing the pronounced shadows, more visible after having washed off her concealing makeup.

Somehow, the tender, innocent contact riled her senses. Odd considering the intensity of their earlier session but he'd never touched her in all their years working together. Her resistance melted, becoming malleable to his suggestions.

"You don't rest enough, Becca. Always working so hard. Don't you think it's time to loosen up a little?"

Without waiting for her answer, he maneuvered her to his

Jayne Rylon

car. He had to know she'd walked to the clinic as usual. Opening the door of his sleek black sports car, he tucked her into the passenger seat before joining her.

"Really, Dr. Foster, I should be getting home." The weak protest was automatic.

He made a soft sound of warning that reminded her of a growl. "Kurt. It's Kurt now and I don't want to let you go. Stop trying to back away from me, from what we did today. I won't let go." He appealed to her sense of responsibility, the reference to her *paid* participation in the study a sure tactic to keep her there. She couldn't tell if he did it intentionally but she figured he did. He didn't seem ashamed, though, just determined. Then again, the experiment could be the breakthrough of his life work. He wouldn't want to lose any progress they'd made.

"I'd like to talk about what happened. I'm guessing our session might have been overwhelming for you. I don't think you should be alone yet. Besides, you're done with all your courses now. You should have some fun for a change."

"You're not going to give up until I go with you, right?" She sighed, snuggling deeper into the supple leather seat, too exhausted to maintain their usual stiff formality when it seemed so pointless. A few short hours ago she'd taken his cock in her mouth.

She wanted to spend time with him but hated the idea of an evening filled with extended case discussion. Or worse, introspective analysis of her earlier reactions. He was right about one thing. She needed to relax, not prolong her work for the night. She wished for one bright second he sought her company for more personal reasons.

"No, I won't give up," he affirmed.

Rebecca couldn't deny she'd aroused him during the experiment, but what healthy man wouldn't get horny watching a naked woman orgasm in front of him? It wasn't that she thought herself unattractive but she had nothing in common with the flashy, sophisticated women Kurt dated. Therefore, the only reason he could have for requesting her company involved the experiment. As much as she wanted to, she would never shirk her duty.

"All right, then. I could go for some food." A hot meal from a restaurant without a drive-through window *did* sound amazing. This afternoon's adventure had sapped her energy. She'd been too nervous to eat beforehand.

Two of the most violent climaxes of her life, the rare luxury of a long afternoon nap, and the struggle with her emotions left her boneless and out of place. The day had altered her reality because, without a doubt, she could never return to such disinterest in sex with her newfound awareness of how magnificent it could be.

Hell, she hadn't even had sex with Kurt. Technically. Still, it was by far the most important encounter of her life. On the down side, she faced the daunting task of seeking employment elsewhere when the experiment wrapped up.

Despite her earlier conviction, she doubted she could regain her professional composure around him. Every time she looked at him, she had flashes of his broad hands lashing her to his examination table, his velvety tongue licking her pussy and the ecstasy that had been chiseled on his face as she sucked his impressive cock while his invention fucked her.

They rode to the restaurant without speaking. The cockpit of the roadster filled with lyrical jazz as Kurt navigated his way through heavy traffic toward a restaurant she'd heard him recommend often. She'd wanted to try it but couldn't justify the expense when she could cook a week of dinners for the cost of a single entree.

He left her to her thoughts, though she sensed him studying her out of the corner of his eye. With weakened, if not obliterated, barriers, Rebecca should have attempted to shield herself from his prying eyes but she couldn't shake herself from contentment long enough to care.

It wasn't until he rounded the hood and opened her door to hand her out of the car that she realized they'd arrived. She caught the valet's wink and could have sworn she heard him say, "Nice one," a moment before Kurt tucked a crisp, large-denomination bill into the young man's hand.

Then, a second man addressed them from the entrance to the restaurant. "Dr. Foster, how nice to see you tonight."

Without asking his preference, the host showed them to a quiet corner booth as sheltered from the main dining area as possible in the busy restaurant. The man had mistaken her for one of Kurt's playmates. She tugged on her rumpled suit jacket, trying to restore some semblance of order. Kurt directed her to the bench seat on one side of the table, courteous as ever, before taking his place across from her.

Modern-styled geometric paper lanterns lit the restaurant. Dark wood tables, tarnished copper sculptures and slate tiles lent the room an ambiance rife with male strength. She felt sheltered and diminutive in comparison. Kurt, however, fit right in.

The atmosphere suited him. She flushed with appreciation as the flickering lights danced in his eyes and glanced off his glossy charcoal hair. When she realized he peered back at her with equal intensity, she looked away, embarrassed.

Breaking the long, but not awkward, silence he reached across the table to wrap his fingers around hers, pressing her hand against his strong palm. "Trust me to order for you? I come here enough to know all the best dishes."

"Of course, Dr...Kurt."

One side of his mouth kicked up in a smile over her correction. She couldn't prevent an answering grin. "It does take some getting used to, you know? I've always thought of you as my boss."

Something flashed in his eyes.

She might have figured it for hurt if it hadn't been such an obvious point.

Before he could respond, though, the waiter arrived. Kurt made his selection without consulting the menu. They slipped into their usual easy companionship, avoiding the discomfort she feared would linger after their passion had faded. But now, as a pleasant side effect of their intimacy, their roles were less formal.

He only mentioned the study directly once.

They laughed together when a rogue noodle escaped her fork and splashed a few drops of sauce on the back of her hand. Before she could wipe it off, Kurt brought it to his mouth and licked the savory paste from her skin.

She gulped.

"Are you okay with this, Becca? I know some of what happened today might have shocked you."

She simply nodded, the words stuck in her throat.

"Good." He wrapped her hand around her fork again then smiled. "I can't always tell you why I'm doing the things I am during the study but I'm glad you're enjoying the experience."

She wanted him to continue, to discover the extent of his desire but the waiter visited again to refill the empty breadbasket. When he left, the moment had passed.

Dinner flew by in a blur as they consumed the delicious meal. The waiter removed their empty plates then placed two glasses of dessert wine before them. Rebecca hesitated. The most she'd ever drunk consisted of a few beers at one of the frat parties she'd gone to last year. Even then, she'd only done it to get her courage up to have sex with her date. She hadn't cared for the way it stole her self-control.

Nonetheless, she could use some help staying relaxed right now so she imbibed a cautious sip. The wine trickled across her tongue, cool and sweet. She swirled it around her mouth before swallowing.

"This is great, it's so smooth." Her tongue reached out to lick a drop off her lips.

Kurt imagined the swipe of her pink tongue affected him like an electric shock on his nerve endings. His dick stood at attention, recalling the way she'd explored every inch of him earlier. He wondered if she had any clue as to what a sensual creature she was.

The way she responded to his every touch and all manner of stimuli impressed him. He noticed how much lighting, colors, textures, physical touches and, now, tastes affected her. It pleased him to observe her trying new things and enjoying them.

Considering the immense effort it must have taken her to lock away those natural tendencies behind the driven, chilly demeanor she affected all these years, there must be a reason she remained so committed to her goals. Kurt found he desperately wanted to understand why.

He needed to know her better.

"Becca, what made you want to be a psychologist?"

She looked up from the half-full glass of wine then blinked a few times before she appeared to focus on what he'd asked. "Hmm? It sounds clichéd, but I thought it would be a great way to help others."

He could tell she'd given him the CliffsNotes version but she stopped as though finished. Luckily, ferreting out information from people hesitant to share came naturally to him. He leaned back in his seat, prepared to enjoy the hunt. Discovering the inner core of a person had lured him to this profession. He'd learned at an early age to be suspicious of people's motives. Even those you knew well could have hidden agendas.

Humans, and what drove them, fascinated him. It just seemed that once he got to the heart of a person, he'd never found one who captivated his attention the way the mere thought of Becca did.

A complex woman, with so many layers, she inspired him to peel them back until he unwrapped the gift buried beneath them all. Private to a fault, it had taken six years for her to trust him to the point where he could begin this exploration. When she had first come to him, she would freeze at any casual touch from co-workers or other students and only responded to direct questions. Always serious, she never initiated frivolous conversations, focusing on communication related to their work and her studies. He had adapted to respect her comfort zone and allowed her needs to shape their interactions.

Back then he never would have believed her capable of the wild abandon she'd demonstrated earlier. Becca performed her duties with flawless execution. She was open and generous with patients, diligent and hardworking, but the personal distance she wedged between them had driven him crazy with curiosity. Women never responded to his interest with that kind of automatic cold shoulder.

Hell, he hadn't even known of her sister until she

mentioned the girl's education as one of her reasons for volunteering for the experiment. Kurt had recognized the sudden scholarship "error" as a ploy on the part of the board as soon as she'd spoken the words. If it had been true, the aid office would have appealed to him for help. After all, unknown to her, he'd augmented Becca's scholarships for years. He wouldn't have allowed financial hardship to lure her into something she didn't want.

Don't act so noble. Guilt crawled through his gut, urging him to reveal the true circumstances behind the experiment's initiation. Again, he found he couldn't do it. At first, he had thought to exorcise his interest in his sexy protégé by crashing through her emotional barriers. He'd planned to appeal to her sense of responsibility to rescue his career and satisfy the board. Now, he realized the smoldering need inside him to know her, possess her, went deeper than carnal interest.

He'd waited years for her to complete her studies, to become more than his student. Although it wasn't a hardship to sit across from her—the warm light, the wine and her satisfied body made her skin glow—he couldn't wait a moment longer to discover what made her tick.

Becca's fingers tightened on the delicate stemware. She shifted in her seat, avoiding eye contact, but he promised them both he'd figure out what had forged this marvelous woman, help her heal, and then set her free.

Therefore, he didn't mention she'd had enough wine. If it helped, he didn't mind her getting drunk. He resigned himself to dealing with the consequences later. Answers dangled within reach. She didn't share this side of herself with anyone.

He wanted to be the first, the only.

"Tell me about your family," Kurt demanded.

He'd always honored her privacy before so Rebecca assumed he needed background information. Disappointment rushed over her. She'd been enjoying the dinner without any obvious continuation of the case study. For a moment, she considered refusing to answer but the liquid courage flowing through her veins, and his compelling tone, convinced her it would be better to pretend—for one night only—his interest in learning more about her stemmed from a personal desire.

The alcohol in her system weakened the filter between her thoughts and her mouth. Her curiosity escaped before she could reel it in. "Are you asking me for the study, or because you want to know?"

He hesitated as though considering what answer to supply. In the end he settled for a terse, "Both."

Good enough to delude herself he cared at least a little.

"Well, it's just me, my mother, and my sister. My sister, Elsa, is coming to Elembreth next year." Though she didn't speak of her family much to anyone, she wanted to do everything in her power to validate his research. Even if it meant being vulnerable.

In any case, now that he'd reminded her of Elsa, it would be best to satisfy his curiosity in order to earn the healthy fee. But, the reminder of her obligation didn't shatter the illusion of her imaginary date as much as she'd have liked.

Rebecca bolstered herself for the unpleasantness of the discussion ahead by touching the glass to her lips again. It was easier to speak of, think of, her sister than her mother even with the alcohol blurring her vision.

Kurt seemed to understand her reluctance to talk about her mother and didn't push her. Yet.

"You mentioned Elsa's plans to attend school here yesterday. Why are you so protective of her?"

"Who says I'm protective of her?" she snapped.

Eyebrows raised, he waited in patient silence until she realized the implications of her tone.

She blushed. "I suppose I do look out for her, but that's what big sisters are for, right?"

"No, that's a parent's job, Becca."

Taking another fortifying taste of the fragrant amber liquid, she braced herself to confide in him things better left unsaid. She didn't have any dark skeletons in her proverbial closet, but she preferred not to discuss the topic with others due to a survival instinct honed during childhood. Trusting him with her past proved infinitely more difficult for her than yielding to his touch had been. There, her body had betrayed her by shutting off all thought. The freedom had allowed her to give in to the secret desire she'd held for him all along.

Case history may be important to my reactions in the study.

Her upbringing had molded her into the person she was today. Even as a trained psychologist herself, old habits died hard. The stigma surrounding mental illnesses made it difficult to air her private business. She'd spent most of her adolescence trying to project an image of the perfect home life to the outside world. Irrational as it seemed considering their profession, she still worried the truth might change Kurt's perception of her.

"Becca?" He leaned closer then stroked her knuckles with the tips of his fingers. The gentle caress made her warm all over and, before she knew it, she poured out her secrets.

"I guess, looking back on it now, my mother has always battled clinical depression. Of course, as a child, I didn't know the terms to explain why she acted the way she did. She wanted to be a dancer. I know she had talent. Pictures of her dancing are the only places I've ever seen her happy. Completely alive."

Pausing, she peered into the empty glass she twirled between the fingers of her right hand while Kurt squeezed the other in reassurance, encouraging her to continue.

"I don't know exactly what happened, but from a few tabloid articles I found and things I've heard her say in her sleep or...other times." She thought of all the days she'd returned from school to find her mother abusing the pain medication she'd kept on hand. "I know she went to an audition for the ballet in New York. She couldn't have been more than eighteen at the time. When she got a call back, the director told her she could have the part...as long as she agreed to sleep with him."

Grateful for the waiter pouring a refill from the towel-wrapped bottle, she swallowed another mouthful. Kurt watched with the quiet thoughtfulness of a seasoned listener. He probably absorbed every nuance, as her gaze skittered around the room, across the table, to her glass, but never meeting his.

Still, she couldn't help herself. With the telling begun, the words flowed out like water gushing over a broken dam, eager to be free once and for all.

"She got pregnant. With me. Of course, the director denied everything and she didn't fight. She had to quit dancing, get a job..." Her breath hitched so she took a steadying gulp of wine.

"She never recovered, Kurt. Sometimes, I would come home to the old pictures scattered on the table and my mother passed out on the kitchen floor or sitting with a blank stare fixed on the wall. It wasn't always terrible, I don't want you to think that, but it came and went. Every day I feared it would be a bad day. For a while, her condition seemed to improve. She met Joe—Elsa's dad—but, when she got pregnant, her depression worsened and he left her. Then, it never lifted again.

"I took care of Elsa from the day she was born, tried to hide the tough times from her and help her with friends and school. Hell, even now, I check in several times every day to make sure she has what she needs—at least as much as I can give her—and is doing all right. It's been so damn hard to be away, to trust in the way I raised Elsa. The first year I almost gave up and went back, but I've always known I needed to help people like my mom who looked healthy but needed assistance, counseling, with nowhere to go."

Rebecca swiped at her cheeks when a tear slipped free. "I abandoned them for *my* dream, for a greater purpose. I have to do well. It has to be worth it. This is my only chance."

Kurt stroked her hand. "I'm sorry, baby. Don't cry, you did the right thing. Thank you for sharing with me. Your story explains so much. You're mature for your age because you had to grow up fast. Elsa had her big sister to look out for her but who was there for you, Becca?"

"I am capable of taking care of myself. I learned from my mom's experiences. I know what I want and I won't let anyone budge me from it no matter what. I will be a psychologist. A damn good one, too!" She plopped her re-emptied glass down a little too hard.

Had the table been so close a moment ago? The smooth weave of a cloth napkin soaked up the tear tracking down her face with a few dabs. She flushed with the pride she rarely allowed to seep out. She'd struggled all these years and now the finish line loomed ahead.

The position in Dr. Foster's office would fulfill her aspiration. She refused to lose it now.

Chapter Six

With the key to Becca's psyche in hand, Kurt backed off. He didn't want to cause her any more pain. His heart went out to the child she had been so briefly. Growing up fast, she'd never had anyone to turn to. Where would he have been without Luke, who'd been his best friend since high school? Without someone he knew could be trusted absolutely during the blackest moments of his life?

"Come on, sweetheart, I think you've had enough for one day." Wrapping his arm around her waist, he supported her as she rose from the booth. Then he guided her from the restaurant.

She dozed on the ride home but roused when he helped her up the stairs to her apartment. She tripped on the first step, breaking into a fit of laughter when her shoe fell off and dropped through the open rise.

"Oops."

He couldn't stifle his amusement at seeing her this way, relaxed and open. The controlled side of her would be aghast. Somehow, that made her antics twice as funny.

He made a mental note to grab her shoe on his way back, then pulled her into his arms before scooping her up. Her slender body rested in the frame of his arms as he carried her upstairs, savoring the way they fit together like two pieces of a jigsaw puzzle. The bend of her knees and curve of her neck rested on his flexed biceps.

"Mmm." She burrowed deeper against his chest, flinging her arms around his shoulders. Pressing her face into the crook of his neck she said, "You smell good."

Kurt ignored his body's reaction to having her so close and pliant. He juggled the keys in one hand, balanced her on his hip, then nudged the door open with his elbow. Flipping on a nearby light, the coziness of her small apartment surprised him. He hadn't expected her to take the time from her busy schedule of work and studying to make this place a home.

Rich cobalt walls surrounded him with a soothing influence. Fabric accents of all textures littered the room. Puffy pillows, downy rugs, blankets and even tapestries on the walls contributed to the inviting ambiance of the room. He should have known her sensual nature would require this stimulating environment but, she suppressed her needs so often elsewhere, he hadn't anticipated it.

Distracting him from his insight, she squirmed in his arms then licked a line of pure lust up the side of his neck. The resulting shockwave radiating through his nervous system almost caused him to drop her.

"You taste good, too" she breathed.

"Becca," he rasped out a warning, heading toward her bedroom to get her safely tucked in for the night.

She misunderstood his intent and continued to worm closer, rubbing her firm nipples against his chest with a low whimper. By now, his cock felt ready to explode. The eager flesh jumped as he put her down, her body sliding across every inch of his front. Gritting his teeth, he started to strip off her suit while he summoned all the reasons why he shouldn't lay her on the bed and take her right now.

Head back, eyes closed, she seemed to revel in the heat of their bodies smashed together.

"I want you for myself. Not some experiment or duty." Though her words slurred, the intent was clear. He needed her the same way. Just not like this.

"I feel you." She must be referring to his aching arousal, which throbbed in heavy beats against her belly. Her candor and abandon caused him to tense further. The stiff flesh prodded her delicate skin as she undulated against him.

"God, Becca, you're killing me here." He groaned then

peeled her shirt from her shoulders, unveiling her naked breasts. She hadn't bothered to replace her underwear after their encounter this afternoon, which added to the insanity rising inside him. If he'd realized her bare pussy lie exposed under the table at the restaurant, he wouldn't have been able to stop himself from slipping his hand between her sweet thighs right there.

Probably best he hadn't known.

Kurt hurried. He had to put her to bed then get out of there before he took advantage of her inebriation. Several soft pops made him aware of a seam about to give way. He gentled his motions to avoid tearing her skirt in his haste. She moaned and arched toward him. When he had her stripped naked, he clenched his jaw then tugged her into his arms again for a blissful moment before dumping her, less gently than he intended, between the sheets.

She writhed on the bed, reaching for him as though to pull him down beside her. When he fluffed the fresh linens over her, she turned stiff and still, realizing her error. The stricken look she shot him, when she opened her eyes to witness him backing away with deliberate steps, hurt like a rusty knife twisting in his gut.

"You're...leaving?" Incredulity caused her voice to crack.

"Now is not the time, Becca. Not like this."

Angry heat rushed to her face as well as the swath of smooth skin visible above the sheet draped across her upper chest. She became shy, withdrawing behind an emotionless mask that did nothing to hide her embarrassment from him.

She spoke in a broken voice so low and distraught he knew she hadn't intended to utter the words aloud. "How could I have forgotten? Tonight wasn't about bonding with me. It was about research. He won't touch me outside the laboratory."

Witnessing the anguish on her face, Kurt couldn't abandon her.

"Shit, I'm sorry, Becca. I didn't mean to give you the wrong idea." She never drank, he'd overheard other students joking with her about it a few times in the halls. He should have realized she wouldn't understand her body's reaction or the fact that he would never take her in this state, not when she could use it as an excuse for her actions the next day.

When he finally claimed her, she would have to admit her desire was more than a chemical reaction or an obligation during the experiment. Kneeling beside her bed, he grasped her hip in one hand then rolled her to face him. He couldn't stop a mental grin at her hard nipples thrusting against the sheer covering.

Even after suffering mortal humiliation, her body still burned for him. She turned her head into her pillow but the feeble attempt couldn't muffle the whimper escaping her lips. The unfulfilled promise of release had to be painful. He angled her face toward him, praying for the strength to do what she needed.

"Go home, Kurt," she choked out. She blinked, as though desperate not to let the tears filling her eyes leak out. One delicate hand rose to block her vision. "I don't want your pity."

"I won't leave you like this. I'm sorry, Becca." Stroking the hair from her face, he wrapped his fingers through hers then disengaged her hand, forcing her to see the truth in his eyes.

"I can take care of myself." Her voice hardened, falling back into the stony mask of independence she had perfected over the years.

"But this time you don't have to." The compulsion to provide her with one small gift flared inside him, overwhelming all inhibitions. "Do you have any toys, baby?"

When she leveled a blank look at him, he continued the calming, downward path of his hand rubbing her back. The pain in her eyes banked the throbbing need inside him. As bad as he wanted her, he could give her relief without taking his own as long as he did it fast then left before his libido could take over.

"A dildo, maybe a vibrator? Come on, help me out here."

As though the contact of his skin against hers added to the muddiness of her thoughts, already addled by the wine, she didn't speak right away. He continued to caress her, encouraging the nervous tension to leech from her muscles so she could surrender to the flames he stoked higher inside her.

"Beside table, top drawer." She moaned.

Kurt reached, slid the drawer open then withdrew a blue, hard plastic, sparkly vibrator. If he wasn't so aroused he feared he might come in his pants *again*, he would have been amused. The device seemed slender and short but, when he considered the extreme tightness of her pussy, he figured it would be plenty for her. He hoped that when he did fuck her, she would adjust to his oversized cock. The last thing he wanted was to cause her true pain. Well, unintended pain, anyway.

He massaged her flat stomach with featherlight touches, then slid his hand lower until he brushed her smooth, fresh-shaven mound. Her hips thrust upward in an instinctive arc. With his other hand, Kurt rubbed the head of the vibrator against her lips. She opened her mouth, taking it inside with hungry sucks. He remembered the feel of her lips, hot and insistent on his rigid flesh. He closed his eyes, giving himself a silent count of ten to calm down.

Then he withdrew the toy from her mouth and shifted his attention to her warm, wet folds. Her arousal coated her now smooth labia, making them shine when her thigh muscles tensed and relaxed in rhythmic pulses as though riding an imaginary lover. She wouldn't last long. Overwhelmed by her display of passion, especially considering their work in the lab earlier, he rubbed his palm over her hard nipples, before placing the vibrator against her clenching entrance.

"Please," she begged. "Now." With her eyes closed, he imagined the world around her retreated until everything but the pressure building in her core faded. Thrusting, he buried the dainty instrument inside her, turning it on high with a twist of his wrist. When his fingers brushed against her swollen clit, she screamed. Surprised, he gaped at her instantaneous climax. He held the vibrator inside her pussy as she came so hard her tight rings of muscle tried to force it back out.

"Kurt!" He stared, in awe of her intense reaction, until it faded. Then she drifted off into unconsciousness, her whole body going limp.

Kurt's chest heaved with the breath sawing in and out of his lungs. When he slid the vibrator from the grasp of her still-clutching pussy, he couldn't resist bringing it to his mouth to clean the taste of her from it. He'd never been with someone who climaxed with a single touch. She slept—or had passed out—so he stood but he couldn't force himself to leave. His feet rooted to the floor while his gaze refused to stray from the amazing woman in front of him.

He peered down at her resting against the now rumpled sheets, hair strewn around her face, flushed body sparkling with a fine coat of perspiration. She was the most beautiful thing he'd ever seen. While he may not be able to take her tonight, his flesh, harder than it had ever been before, demanded satisfaction.

Releasing the fly of his slacks, he set his cock free of the confining fabric. The vibrator dropped onto the bed beside the siren. He brought one hand up to cup his balls while the other wrapped around his cock. At the first touch, his sensitized nerves jumped, eliciting a groan. He couldn't believe he had this little control over himself. It was as though he were sixteen again.

He couldn't make it home like this. Instead, he began to stroke the length of his shaft. It seemed longer and harder than he could ever remember. Kurt spread the pre-come dripping down the head of his cock around in his palm, jerking himself faster. He listened to the wet, fleshy sounds as he thought of Becca. Scenes flashed through his memory. He recalled the submission and trust she'd given him when she'd allowed him to tie her to the exam table this afternoon, the way her lips had stretched around him and her eagerness to learn about the boundless passion she possessed.

With such vivid fuel, his balls tightened in his other hand within seconds, his orgasm building. He must have moaned, because she stirred. She her lashes fluttered, then she peeked up at him through sleep-hazed eyes.

"Are you going to come on me?" she whispered.

He froze in mid motion. *What the hell am I doing?*

But, instead of sounding horrified, she smiled her encouragement.

"I want to feel it." Turning towards him, she reached out, cupped the back of his thigh then tugged him closer.

Before he realized what he intended, he knelt on the bed next to Becca. His pants fell around his knees as he touched the tip of his erection to her breasts. She cupped one luscious mound in each hand, sandwiching his cock between them. The heated silk of her skin was more temptation than he could resist.

The liquid seeping from his cock eased the way when he began to stroke through the luxuriant valley. His balls brushed against her belly as he slid, long and slow, between her perfect tits. After a precious few heavenly strokes, his climax demanded release.

With one final pump, he exploded, sending his seed shooting out across her chest. Watching the first strand decorate her nipple made the orgasm intensify until he feared he might burst a blood vessel or have a heart attack.

Either way he'd go happy.

Spent, he half collapsed. His hands braced on the far side of Becca, preventing him from crushing her while his hips thrust in a shallow path across her chest. His cock glided through the hot ejaculate covering her, drawing his balls across the globes of her breasts.

Kurt dragged himself away from her even as his still-hard cock begged him to return, to bury it balls-deep inside her, to claim her once and for all. He stared, transfixed, when her tongue darted out to steal a quick taste of his cream off her own nipple. Then she massaged the rest into her chest like the most extravagant lotion on earth before nuzzling deeper into her pillow and closing her eyes, drifting off to sleep once more.

Now *that* was the hottest thing he'd seen in his life.

He retrieved the vibrator off the bed, headed to the bathroom, cleaned it—and himself—before returning to wash away the evidence of his lack of control. Swiping a damp cloth across her beautiful chest, Kurt couldn't believe this had happened. No woman had ever affected him like this before.

Feeling bewildered, and more than a little guilty, he knelt to ensure she was okay one last time. He tucked the sheets around her, brushed his lips over her forehead and whispered, "Sweet dreams, Becca."

Chapter Seven

The mother of all headaches greeted Rebecca in the morning. She considered the amount of light pouring in the windows with her slit eyes and determined she had overslept. Turning on her side, she reached for her clock radio to assess the damage but her hand bumped into a tall glass of water, spilling a few drops on the note pinned beneath it.

Becca, take these aspirin and drink all of the water. I have a nine o'clock appointment but I'll meet you in the laboratory around noon.

—Kurt

She froze in mid motion to stare at his familiar scrawl as hazy images of the night before resurfaced. *Oh, God!* It hadn't been a dream. She struggled to push aside the fog of confusion that had surrounded her on waking the last few days. Her ability to tell dreams from reality had become faulty with the stress of finals and her upcoming job search taking its toll.

She swung her legs over the edge of the bed, dropped her head in her hands then concentrated on remembering yesterday. The experiment! For a few minutes, the sexual adventure seemed like a dream, if an oddly familiar one, before she conjured details even the best nighttime mirage hadn't rivaled. Details too vivid to be fantasy including the velvety texture of Kurt's erection on her tongue and the enthralling scent of his skin.

The blurry recollection of divulging her family troubles

alarmed her far more than the exploration of her long-subdued physical needs. Worst of all had been her naiveté in pretending he cared beyond some damn footnote explaining her reactions during the study. Had she really told him all about her mother?

In the full glare of morning, with the flickering light and his gentle support removed, the harsh implications of her actions staggered her. She'd worked all this time to prove her unsurpassed aptitude for both her job and schoolwork, to show Dr. Foster she deserved a chance in his firm. Now she may have jeopardized it all because she couldn't think straight when he was near.

Just like her mother.

Disgraced and ashamed, she recalled the way she'd assaulted Kurt the night before. He'd been working a case. Instead of remaining calm and detached while communicating the necessary data, she'd demonstrated her inability to handle the pressure by getting drunk to cope. Still, he'd been kind enough to see her home. Then, to top it all off, she'd begged the man who'd been her mentor for years—the man she hoped would continue to be her boss—to fuck her. Again.

He'd been too nice to say no outright. *Not like this, Becca.*

Crap! He couldn't stand to touch her in a personal setting so he'd used her vibrator instead. She sneered at her overdramatic thoughts in self-disgust but she couldn't deny he'd contained the more sexual aspects of their relationship to the study proceedings. His mechanical solution had maintained impersonality. When the spotty memory of him working the device into her made her pussy start to get wet all over again, even as she berated herself for wanting him, she debated giving up and climbing back into bed. She couldn't imagine him ever taking her serious as a professional again.

But she couldn't quit now.

I'll be more focused than ever. Unwilling to watch her dream fall apart so close to realization, she vowed to pull herself together. Today, her attraction to Dr. Foster wouldn't affect their work together. She would demonstrate to them both she could remain detached regardless of the pathetic crush he must now know she had on him.

Please, God, don't let him laugh in my face.

⚃

Kurt hadn't slept at all. His release in Becca's apartment hadn't soothed the need raging inside him. He'd spent a restless night in a futile attempt to ignore his painful arousal. Two cold showers this morning hadn't solved the problem either. He'd seriously considered canceling an appointment for the first time in his life, but Dan counted on their sessions. The man had started making real progress in recent weeks. Kurt would never jeopardize his patient's health.

In the end, duty won out over selfishness.

The thirst clawing at his throat would only be quenched when he saw Becca again, even if he had to pretend the experiment necessitated their interaction. Confessing the depth of his longing wasn't an option, not if he wanted to preserve their working relationship and definitely not if he wanted a successful experiment. If he didn't see this through, the board would have him banned.

The truth would destroy everything.

An eternity passed between each heavy tock of the second hand, until the hour freed him from his patient. Finally, he could begin work on the Dream Machine for the day. He grabbed Becca's lust-inducing shoe off the table in his office, his dick filling again at the sight of it. On the way toward his laboratory, he chuckled, recalling the classic fairy tale, Cinderella.

If claiming his princess and convincing her of their perfect fit could be so simple, he'd slip the spike heel on her right now. But her stubborn streak, and lack of self-awareness, prevented such an easy solution. Hell, he didn't know what to make of things himself. The potent energy between them shocked him. It had taken all of his willpower to walk away from her last night. He grinned at the thought of continuing their journey while he opened the door to the laboratory.

He had so much to show her.

Her innocence drew him but he was man enough to admit

it scared him, too. Without practical experience, Becca might fall victim to society's propaganda promoting romantic ideals of love in relationships. She might forget her training, her understanding of science, and believe a relationship between two people consisted of more than compatible hormones and animal magnetism. But, he didn't have a choice.

If he wanted to compile official data in support of the Dream Machine by the council's deadline, he had to act now. However, if he came clean with himself, he'd have to admit his primary goal had transformed from proving his invention worked, to using the Dream Machine to draw Becca out of her rigid confinement.

Besides, he had no doubt about the functionality of the Dream Machine, thanks to the fucking bastard who'd stolen his invention in the equivalent of taking it out joyriding for a night. He'd preyed on Becca as she dozed at her desk while Kurt had been called away on an emergency.

Then, soon-to-be-ex-Dr. Wexford had shared the privileged view into Becca's delectable dreams with the board. Since every last one of her fantasies featured Kurt, they'd insisted he recreate the scenes and measure her responses to see if they truly comprised her greatest desires, as long as she consented to intimacy with him. Which she eagerly had, even seeking him out before he could propose the arrangement. She'd provided all the confirmation necessary with her sweet approach.

No, the Dream Machine worked. He just had to verify it for the review board.

He entered the private workspace, pleased to see Becca waiting for him. Following quick on the heels of his elation, a surge of disappointment burst through him at her clothed state. The insolent glare, which pronounced her intentional disobedience, ratcheted his irritation to the next level.

He had a reputation for being laid-back in the classroom and at work. He enjoyed the company of women, especially strong-willed women, but a streak of dominance ran deep through his soul.

In private, he craved the thrill of the chase and the eventual surrender of an independent woman. Those he pursued had never resisted his will for long. His sexual preferences compelled him toward submissives. Therefore, when he saw Becca—the one woman whose compliance he coveted—clothed, hands on hips, with pure defiance radiating from her expression, something inside him snapped.

He couldn't suppress his nature around her.

Kurt crossed to her with two powerful strides then fisted his hand in her hair. Tugging the silky strands with enough force to sting, he compelled her to meet his gaze. Today she would get more than the patient teacher. Even he couldn't disguise reactions this intense. He prayed she could handle the extremity of his temperament because he wouldn't stop now unless she quit the study. Their own version of a safe word.

"Have you forgotten the rules so soon?" He spoke with a quiet command more forceful than a raised voice. The beast inside him yearned to run free after years on a leash. Close enough to see his expression reflected—a little wild—in her eyes, catching her scent, he focused on controlling the need to tear off her clothes.

He'd like to teach her another kind of lesson right here and now.

Kurt watched excitement flare in the beautiful jade depths of her eyes as he studied them for hints of panic or discomfort. Though the shock and miniscule pain of his grip flickered across her expression, her arousal overrode the other reactions. Becca arched closer to him, her nipples growing tight where they poked his abdomen. Then she held still, never looking away but ceding to his challenge, allowing him to keep her close.

A shiver ran through her. So connected to her, each minute movement advertised her needs like a giant, glowing neon sign. She tried to hide but he understood pleasure, not fear, drove her response. If frightened, she wouldn't hesitate to knock him back. Knowing she enjoyed his control only fueled his desire. Still, she wasn't giving him anything for free today.

"You weren't here yet. I didn't feel like sitting around nude while I waited, *Doctor.*" She paused long enough to make the bastardization of his title apparent. While he demanded the use of his title in this room, he couldn't construe it as a sign of respect or deference when it launched off her lips like an insult.

Damn! They'd made such good progress last night. Now, despite her body's betrayal of her obvious arousal, she'd returned to the cool distance and impenetrable formality that drove him insane. Kurt had to breach her resistance before she could withdraw further. Her retreat tested his control like a deer running from a wolf, but she couldn't absorb the full force of his disposition yet. He had to earn her trust first.

Fortunately, he held all the cards in this situation. Hell, he'd always enjoyed a challenge. Whatever barrier held her back, he would find and destroy it. Tormenting Becca with desire until she begged for relief at his hand sounded like one of the most gratifying things he could imagine.

"Resistance is a waste of energy." Dr. Foster's voice, rough and graveled, raked across Rebecca's senses. "Get those clothes off so we can begin."

She hadn't wanted him to think her eager although, in truth, she might have died if anything had delayed him. Sheer determination veiled her desire. She refused to let herself get sidetracked again. Proving she could be professional in all circumstances, especially in their business dealings, was of utmost importance.

She stifled a gasp when he abruptly released his hold, attempting to ignore the pulsing ache left in its wake. She stumbled back a step. A thrill of excitement raced through her, mixing with the tingling in her scalp that reminded her of his authority. She focused her attention on the task at hand in an attempt to distract herself from her body's traitorous reaction.

With efficient precision, Rebecca removed, folded then stacked her clothes before scooting onto the examination table. Though she couldn't prevent her skin from blushing under Dr. Foster's observation, she concentrated on relaxing her fists at her sides when she reclined.

She braced herself, meeting his direct stare when ready. "What's the objective for today's session, Doctor?" she asked, proud no tremble or breathiness betrayed her arousal.

"We'll get to that. First, I need to explain something."

A frustrated sigh came from his direction. His regard

etched her skin as he studied her. In fact, she could practically hear the gears in his mind turning as he debated the best way to crack her charade. They both knew that's what it was but the power struggle only heightened her arousal. Way out of her league, his experience would lead to her certain defeat in a test of wills but she refused to give in without a fight. Her anticipation multiplied.

What is wrong with me?

The rustling of fabric reached her ears as he removed his clothes with careful deliberation, daring her to watch, before replacing them with his lab coat. His words came calm but stern. "Becca, I'm not sure what's happening here, but..."

When he stood beside her, the waves of heat radiating from his hard-on scorched her outstretched arm. His throbbing erection filled her peripheral vision, tempting her to peek, but she remained as still as a statue. Kurt grasped her chin then pivoted her head toward him until she couldn't avoid his steel-grey eyes.

Once he captured her full attention, he continued, "But... I think the truth will work best in this situation. One truth anyway." He spoke to her with the measured phrasing he used when analyzing problems in their casework, seeking out a solution by lining up the pieces. Before he could reach the correct conclusion in this instance—discovering her personal feelings for him—and chastise her for her conduct the night before, she tried to head him off. Maybe then, they could both move on.

"I understand about yesterday evening, Dr. Foster. I'm sorry for the way I behaved." She gathered a breath to force the rest out but had to close her eyes to finish it. "It's no excuse, but I don't drink alcohol. I realize this is a professional exercise and I won't forget it again. I apologize."

She prayed he would overlook her foolishness but too much rode on his response for her to witness the pity or disgust that might be lurking in his expression now.

A millennium passed before he spoke again.

"I refuse your apology. I will never forget what happened last night."

Shock caused her eyelids to pop open and her head to jerk, breaking his hold. Her worst nightmare had come true. Sure she'd lost her chance, it took a while for his comforting tone, and the fact that he was still talking, to seep into her consciousness.

"—have no concerns about your career. I see it's holding you back. I know this is a lot to happen all at once for you, Becca, but there are things you need to learn." Prohibiting her response, he laid his hand over her lips when she would have objected. "First, this experiment is about more than testing the Dream Machine. I want you to be the best psychologist you can be. I understand now why it's so important to you."

Shame bubbled inside her again at the thought of her outburst in the restaurant. She swallowed hard before focusing on his face. When she did, she didn't glimpse the pity she feared but, instead, she saw understanding and concern. That almost frightened her more.

"I can't express how much I respect your commitment, but how can you expect patients to trust you with their problems if *you* can't trust others? How can you discuss their sexual fears and needs if you don't know what your own are?"

Reeling from the turn of conversation, the direction of his reasoning confused her.

"Wh...what? You're not upset with me for last night?" Her trepidation snuck out in a squeak before she locked it away again. It didn't escape his notice.

"Of course I'm not angry. You're so damn innocent, Becca. Yet, starving for this..." He stroked his hand across her bare midriff. If he intended the gesture to soothe her, he failed miserably.

"Look how you respond to the slightest touch. You pretend to be indifferent but your body doesn't lie. I didn't plan to tell you so soon but your perception of me as your boss is getting in the way of honest reactions."

Her mind scrambled in a million directions as it attempted to decipher his meaning over the clamor of her body, screaming for him to touch it again.

"Listen to me. Feel me, know what I'm saying is true."

As though she could focus on anything else at the moment. He mesmerized her with the euphonic timbre of his voice. His fingers paused on her stomach as he lingered in his speech, punctuating the important points with caresses and squeezes that left her as entranced as a charmed animal.

"I want to teach you. I need to show you what it means to trust, to be open. Only then can you reach your potential in this profession." Peering down at her with a sly smile, he added, "And *my partner* needs to be the best."

"Partner!" If not for his hand pinning her to the table, she would have bolted upright.

Laughter rumbled from him as he savored her reaction. "Of course, Becca. You have to know I want you to stay on here after graduation."

Kurt's eyes shone with pride and longing he didn't bother to shutter from her. Overwhelmed, her vocal chords refused to function.

He continued, "I'm sorry I didn't tell you sooner. You deserved to know my intent to promote you. You deserve recognition. You earned it. I assumed you knew and that's my fault. I won't let you go."

His faith returned her voice, but she found it impossible to convey her emotions. "Dr. Foster, really, thank you. I don't know what to say. I mean, I hoped. I dreamed, but..."

Rebecca couldn't believe it. A partnership. She'd half expected him to fire her after the way she'd acted last night. Not even in her wildest dreams did she expect such a high-level position this early in her career. She wouldn't ruin this second chance.

She would learn what he needed to show her.

With that, her awkwardness vanished, proving his instincts had been correct as usual. As the tension drained from her body, Kurt bent over her—brushing his lips against hers—until she melted under his touch. Her body responded automatically to the tender kiss, opening to him. He traced her teeth and gums with his tongue. With infinite care, he rubbed his lips over her parted mouth, indulging for a moment before separating them.

Her heavy eyelids fought their way open when he switched directions, resuming his speech as though their conversation hadn't touched them both.

"Now, I want you to realize your full potential but I feel you're holding back. Therefore, I'm going to assist you." For a moment, the feral gleam off his bared teeth had her wishing she could retreat one tiny inch but he kept her tight against the table.

"We need to complete this experiment, Becca, but our time here will be about more than that. You confessed a need for experience the other day in my office, yet you were so wrapped up in your goals you neglected to see it as a component of your education. I understand why, sweetheart. I really do, but you've missed some important lessons. Not the kind you find in a book, either. I'm talking about the kind you learn from living."

As he spoke, she noticed his cock throbbing. Glistening liquid seeped from the tip.

"What do you get out of this, Doctor?" she whispered.

"Can't you tell how much I enjoy sharing this journey with you, guiding you?" He wrapped his free hand around the thick base of his shaft, then stroked himself with long, sensual motions. She had to bite her cheek to keep from reaching her tongue out to taste him. "I believe in you, Becca. I want you to be my partner. You're amazing now. You'll be even better once we're done here. Plus, our mutual physical attraction will increase the strength of the research. This works for us, Becca."

Her heart tripped in her chest. After all this time, her dream was coming true. His repetition helped it to sink in. The trembling of her arms and legs made her glad she already lay down. She wouldn't have been able to stand beneath the intense weight of her bliss, shock and yearning.

"I'll teach you. I won't ever let you down, I swear, but I need you to promise me something in return."

Her reservations had melted away with the ultimate demonstration of his faith. As quick as that, the last of her barriers disintegrated. Respect, attraction and gratitude ensured she would grant him whatever he desired. She nodded.

"Yes, Doctor, anything."

"For the duration of the experiment you're mine."

Kurt struggled to rein in his elation as he lost himself in her adoring gaze. Never before had he taken such pleasure in another person's joy. He would give anything to see her happy. He made a silent vow to satisfy her desires for a mentor, a lover, and a man who valued her beyond belief.

Until now, the demands he made on women had eventually proved too much for them to handle. He had tested their desire until they reached their limits, then set them free—no matter how much they begged him not to. He was always dissatisfied. With Becca, he'd discovered a woman whose sensuality had no bounds. Her appetite to learn, her curiosity, matched his own. If only she would liberate herself.

"I require your complete submission."

She froze, blinking at him while she considered his words. While she hesitated, her nipples pebbled, and her legs shifted in an attempt to relieve some of the pressure between them.

"I don't know what to say." She opened her mouth as though to answer but closed it again with a snap.

Allowing her to compose her thoughts, he waited. This had to be her choice, given freely.

"I've already agreed to be open with you during the study, to share my fantasies. I've consented to letting you touch me, be intimate with me, teach me about passion, measure my arousal, and record all of my responses. What more can you want? What more can there be?"

Seeing the genuine confusion in her eyes, Kurt smoothed the lines on her brow. "It's easy, Becca. Give yourself to me. I'll instruct you. I'll be here for you through every step of the journey. I won't push you further than you can go, but you have to trust me to know what you can handle. Trust me to know what you need. Make one decision now, to give me complete control."

He wondered if she realized the way her face tilted to maintain contact with his fingers, like a pet begging its master to keep stroking it, as he spoke.

"Will you do this? No excuses now. This is not for your

sister, not for the study, not for our partnership, not for your career, not even for me. Do this because you have to explore this part of you. Because you've hidden yourself away for so long. Because you need to feel."

The words had barely passed his lips before she replied.

"Yes, Doctor."

"From now until the end of the experiment you'll stay here with me. You'll be under twenty-four-hour observation. I'll monitor your dreams at night with the Dream Machine, run sessions during the day. Together, we'll work to see how far you can go."

Kurt grinned when she whimpered at the thought. His breath fanned her temple when he whispered, "I'll show you pleasures you've never imagined. I'll tutor you in what it can be like. You will trust me. You will be mine."

He couldn't wait any longer. Turning away from her enticing body before the need to claim her overwhelmed logic, he stepped to the equipment cabinet against the wall behind Becca's head. From her angle, she couldn't see what he was doing. Instincts prevented her budging from where he'd left her, despite her innate curiosity. Signs like this made him confident she was a natural submissive.

He placed the video camera he'd taken from the cabinet on the platform he'd designed to support it. Then he attached it to a rigging system fixed to the ceiling of the laboratory. Using the control box, which also contained the switches for every other mechanical device he'd created in this room, he raised the unit. It hovered above the examination table to capture the action below in crisp detail the standard surveillance equipment couldn't match.

The buzz of the pulley system caused Becca to twitch on the table. He sensed her uncertainty but chose to let the suspense build instead of reassuring her. He watched as her body stiffened. Her nipples, already hard as diamonds, stood out from her breasts. While her fingers fisted in the terrycloth covering the exam surface, her chest began the rapid rise and fall of elevated respiration. When she spotted the camera staring down at her, she moved her hands in an automatic attempt to cover herself.

"No." Kurt had been waiting for her to falter. He stood beside her in an instant, his hands wrapping easily around her wrists. As he dragged her arms to her sides, he instructed, "You will make sure the camera has a clear view at all times. The review board requires complete documentation of our proceedings, remember?"

For a moment she balked, her skin blanching. He laughed but little humor infused the sound. "Are you thinking of our colleagues watching you with the infamous Dr. Foster? Don't pretend you dislike the idea. I won't let you hide your desires anymore. Is your sweet pussy soaked thinking of those men and women at the shiny boardroom table watching you beg me to show you more? To take you higher? Is it, Becca?"

She didn't answer.

Kurt didn't need to touch her to be sure. Her spicy arousal perfumed the room. He placed the tip of his index finger on her slick labia before bringing it to her lips. When she moaned, her hips rising off the table, he slid it inside her mouth and forced her to sample her arousal. The eager laps of her tongue ingesting the proof from his hand provided answer enough. Still, he couldn't resist teasing her.

"It's either this or I go get one of my other assistants to watch. Would you prefer that?"

The thought had Kurt's hard-on thumping against his abdomen but she wasn't ready for that level of play yet. Becca flushed a deep burgundy, then whimpered, clenching her thighs together as though she could smother her physical response. Her reaction had him considering it a moment longer, wishing the probe was embedded in her now to supply objective feedback. The readings might prove interesting. He made a mental note to record this in his journal for further deliberation.

Perhaps, when she was more comfortable...

"No, Doctor. Please don't."

"Then forget the camera. All you need to worry about is me. Give yourself over, do as I command and I won't let anything bad happen. Remember my promise. You can stop at any time. Just say the word and it will be over. No hard feelings." Though true, he would never keep her against her will, Kurt would be so fucking disappointed he didn't think he could ever try again. If she couldn't satisfy him, then no one could.

"Enjoy, Becca."

Chapter Eight

Rebecca watched the green recording light flash on. Her face flamed now that it documented their session. For the record, Kurt stated their progress to date. She strove to convince herself the anticipation building in her stemmed from fear or outrage when pure lust dampened her thighs, betraying her excitement.

"We have now completed all of the preliminary reviews including the initial examination of the subject, the gathering of background information and an equipment test run. Today we will establish a baseline reaction to compare the results of the dream sessions to."

While he set the stage for the review board, she tried to make sense of her swirling emotions. Elation at securing a partnership in Dr. Foster's practice battled with the desire heating her body to distraction as she watched him stalk around the table. She recalled vulnerable patients he had treated over the years in an attempt to squelch her apprehension.

He's a good man, you can trust him—give him control. For so long now she had segregated herself from others, depending solely on herself. She wondered if she could do it. Could she let go?

"Stay with me, Becca," he murmured in her ear, breaking her out of her thoughts. His mouth tucked close under the cover of her hair, ensuring the privacy of his guidance even from the panoptic lens. "All you have to worry about is pleasing me."

Straightening, he adjusted the table. Once again, the restraints encircled her ankles and, oddly, she felt comforted and secure. The joy of being bound surprised her but, as with yesterday's session, she found the immobility imbued her with an ironic sense of freedom. She couldn't waste energy on avoiding the situation or denying her passionate response. Instead, it focused her on the things happening out of her control.

Today, however, Kurt left her arms unfettered. After splitting the table then shoving her legs wide open, nearly to the point of discomfort, he bent the middle section beneath her knees. They rose, drawing her legs close to her chest. Then, he reattached the probe to the connector welded between her thighs.

Rebecca's pussy clenched at the memory of the machine stroking inside her. The metallic clink of the attachment locking in place triggered instant hunger as though she were affected by the classical conditioning made famous by Pavlov's subjects.

Her low moan cut the silence as the blunt tip of the instrument notched against her opening. Kurt flashed his reassuring smile and patted her leg, exercising his innate bedside manner. Somehow, it didn't alleviate her nervous energy.

He raised another segment of the table, this time under her shoulders. The comfortable position left her half-reclining, half-sitting, knees bent and legs spread. Kurt ran his fingers beside her calves, uncovering slots in the face of the platform. From each, he withdrew a retractable strap that reminded her of a seat belt. He worked his way up from her ankles, stretching the bindings around her legs every four inches or so until her striped shins, knees and thighs were glued to the table. The flexible nylon warmed against her skin, cradling her as it conformed to her curves.

Now high up on her thigh, his hand bumped against her steaming core. She moaned as her hips lifted an inch or so, seeking his touch, before reaching the limits of the restraints. Kurt evaded her with a nimble shift before strapping her waist to the table as well.

"I won't touch you. Don't do that again." He landed a light

slap on the flesh of her inner thigh, startling her. "Today's session is about a baseline, no interference from me. I need to know what your normal levels of arousal are."

Rebecca grimaced as she turned her head to avoid the censure in his eyes. *Get a grip*, she scolded herself. *Keep it professional.* More important now than ever, she slammed a lid on the impulse to beg him to touch her, kiss her, let her taste his long, thick cock. She licked her lips as it, already so engorged and rigid it had to be painful, bobbed in time with his heartbeat. At least he wanted her, even if his control outstripped his desire.

She winced at the clear demonstration of his priorities. Though he found her attractive, little, if anything, mattered more to Dr. Foster than his work. This was a monumental project. As partners, he would expect her to respect their research as much as he did. She would do whatever it took to ensure the successful development of the Dream Machine, but fighting her raging need seemed impossible.

"You're quite a sight, Becca."

She squirmed, testing the bindings. She reached out but couldn't remove the straps due to the angles and the distance.

Satisfied, Kurt stepped back to admire her. His compliments soothed some of the sting of his refusal. "I wish you could see what I see. To me, you look like a gorgeous but decadent masterpiece. Between the black lines across your fair skin and the innocence in your eyes, I can't stop staring."

Seductive power raced through her despite her defenseless position. He studied her for the space of several ragged breaths before shaking his head as though to clear it.

"I have one other attachment I'd like to test today. Do you mind being the first to try it? I can assure you it won't hurt you." Before waiting for her answer, he reached into his lab coat pocket then withdrew two silvery rings, each attached to a thin wire. The rings appeared firm but shifted beneath his fingers.

Hesitant, Rebecca watched as he plugged connectors like those you'd see on a set of headphones into the monitor that had tracked the probe's readings the day before. Moving even with her chest, Kurt whispered in her ear again.

"Don't refuse me now. We've just begun." He lingered, nibbling her earlobe while his head blocked the camera's view. Sensation rushed along her nerves like a shockwave. Instincts compelled her to turn her face away, exposing her neck. With a moan, Kurt surged forward to nip the sensitive spot before soothing it with his tongue.

She would do anything he asked. When she inclined her head in the slightest nod, the corners of his mouth curled up in a triumphant smile against her throat. He lifted his head then brought the silver circles to his mouth, licking first one then the other. Her eyes widened at the sight. A hiss broke from her clenched teeth when his fingers guided the tool around her nipple where it adhered.

On contact, it constricted of its own accord to form a snug circle around the outside of her areole. He stroked the flesh, testing the area to ensure a proper fit, then repeated the gesture with the other appliance, making her back arch at his light touch.

It wasn't nearly enough.

"These measure size and density, providing another indicator of your arousal. They'll expand and contract to outline your nipple, tracking the circumference as a data point." His eyes never strayed from the rings, which made constant adjustments to conform to her body.

"Fascinating," he murmured.

His intense scrutiny reinforced the safety of the environment. Kurt's careful monitoring wouldn't allow anything to go wrong. Of course, her faith in him along with their smoldering attraction only made the rosy peaks tighter. The circlets shrunk further.

"How does that feel, Becca?"

She struggled to describe a sensation so new and glorious. "They're amazing, Doctor. Mmm, they're shifting to match me. The pressure pinches a little. It almost hurts, but it's so good."

Turning from her, Kurt dragged his desk chair about ten feet from the examination table beyond a bold red mark slashing the floor. She gauged the angle before figuring the placement ensured he remained out of the camera's line of sight. When he adjusted the height of his seat, she blushed. He must have a perfect view of her shaved pussy, dripping with natural lubrication. The way he'd positioned the probe at an angle, on the verge of penetrating her, permitted him full visibility.

Assured of the attachment's proper functioning, Kurt tore himself away. He retreated to his outpost. Otherwise, he wouldn't be able to resist touching Becca, to hell with the experiment. He concentrated on sinking down then keeping his hands steady when he placed the remote control on the wheeled tray next to his journal and pen. One ankle resting on the knee of his other leg, he balanced the open notebook in his lap to jot a memo to himself for later study.

Subject responding well to stimuli as expected. Elements present in the original dream research seem to evoke the strongest response in accordance with my theory.

He reclined while observing her eyes haze. He didn't need the readings from the machines to detect her extreme arousal. Perhaps this wouldn't be a clean trial. Maybe he'd have to run several rounds of testing to desensitize her to the excitement her surroundings enhanced.

Glancing up from his writing, he witnessed her straining at her bonds while her hips struggled to thrust forward in a subtle rocking motion. Her heavy-lidded eyes prevented her from noticing him admiring her perfect tits, nipples now fully erect and gleaming with the encircling silver rings.

"Are you ready to begin?" he asked, surprised by the husky tone of his voice.

"Begin?" She sounded distant, almost dazed, as though she wasn't sure what he meant. "Haven't we already begun? What's all this?" She gestured to the machines, the camera, the restraints.

"Yes, Becca, begin. The best way to establish the baseline is through self-stimulation. This would demonstrate your ordinary state of arousal and method of fulfillment. I realize some factors might skew the results in this case. For example, the equipment, as well as being observed, appears to heighten your arousal. However, those things will also be true when we progress to the dream stages so the effect will cancel out in the long term."

She blinked once, then twice, before comprehension dawned in her lust-clouded mind.

"You want me to masturbate for you?" Her bright eyes went wide as her voice flew up an octave.

Rocking back in his chair, Kurt rested his palms on his thighs then met her incredulous emerald gaze head on.

"Yes. Touch yourself. Make yourself come for me."

She blushed, scrunching her lids closed as he watched another drop of liquid squeeze out of her tight slit. She was so wet now her sweet juice trickled down her crack, leaving a trail of heat between her cheeks. He wished he could taste her.

"Pretend I'm not here. Imagine you're alone in your bed. Can you do that, Becca?" He focused on regulating his voice, keeping it smooth and gentle when he wanted to bark out his demands. He locked away the intensity of his longing by reminding himself of her innocence. She was untried and needed to ease into this.

"Yes, Doctor. I'll try."

Though she kept her eyes closed, Kurt angled the notebook in front of him to block her view of his hand wrapping around his dick in case her long lashes fluttered open. He didn't want the visual stimulation to throw off the readings.

"Good girl. It's going to be all right, you'll see. I'll start by inserting the probe at its smallest as I did yesterday." His cock jerked in his hand, recalling how even that meager intrusion had stretched her flesh. "I'm going to measure how tight you are, what your normal reactions are, so we can compare the results to your body's feedback during your fantasies."

"Relax, Becca. Let it inside you." She gasped when he initiated the forward motion of the machine. The tip of the probe pressed, insistent, against her pussy. From his optimal vantage point, he watched the muscles first contract then slowly, so slowly, begin to part. The relaxation allowed the machine to furrow deeper inside her.

As soon as the wicked but delicious attachment breached the ring of muscle at the opening of her pussy, a line appeared on the monitor beside Rebecca. She didn't know where to look, nowhere was safe.

The sight of the instrument forcing its way inside her flooded her veins with arousal. Yet, the irrefutable proof of her desire and depravity in enjoying this procedure—drawn in the neon green line blazing across the monitor—tempted her, too. However, Kurt's expression as he witnessed her possession ultimately captured her attention.

When she saw her own passion reflected in the strain on his face, her swollen pussy clamped around the probe. The quiet beeping of the monitor increased.

She tried to obey his command by imagining she lay in her cold and lonely bed but she couldn't resist licking her lips as she remembered what his flesh had tasted like or the slick heat of his semen coating the back of her throat.

Again, the beeping increased tempo. Kurt groaned.

"Baby, are you so hot you're going to make yourself come just sitting there thinking? Come on, Becca. Touch yourself. Show me how you take care of yourself. Focus on the feel of your hands on your luscious body."

Little did he know, just being in the room with him shifted her into overdrive. She wanted to ease the flames burning inside her to the point of pain but, still new to shared intimacy with him, her shyness reared its head.

At least she didn't have to worry about lack of interest. One guy in her past had accused her of being frigid because sex with him couldn't quiet her worrying mind, always focused on school, her job and her goals. Of course, she'd known he was full of crap but she had never expected pleasure could swamp her like this.

The desperation of her need paralyzed her.

"Dr. Foster..."

"I don't know what's going on in your mind but if you don't want to talk it out with me then let it go. You're tensing up."

The lines traced on the monitor had dipped and the beeping had slowed. What if she couldn't do this in front of the one man she wanted? What if she failed him?

"Becca, you're analyzing too much. Do it. Now."

Something inside her loosened. Her hand shifted where it rested, rubbing the outer lips of her pussy. They were so smooth now that he had shaved them. Every featherlight brush of her fingertip, and the cool breeze blowing across the exposed skin, echoed in her core as she spread the wetness around her swollen folds.

"That's it." His approval raced through her, prompting her to grow bolder. Increasing the pressure of her fingers, she stroked a slow path along the outside of her lips. When her inner muscles gripped the smooth probe, she thought she heard a sound from Kurt's direction. A groan?

Rebecca couldn't think much about it as ecstasy began to overwhelm her. Pent up for so long, her passion steamrolled her logic now that he'd given her permission to let it out. As soon as she started touching herself, her eyes closed and pleasure overtook rationality.

Her mouth opened, her chest fluttered with uneven respiration, and her thigh muscles slackened, scooting her down a fraction of an inch. The motion lodged the probe in her to the hilt.

A moan burst out of her at the intrusion. Her free hand flew to her chest. The rings alternately chilled then heated against her breasts. She had to rub her nipples or the sensation would drive her crazy. Using a finger on either side of her slit, she massaged herself, trapping her clit between her fingers. The rippling of her vaginal walls triggered another wave of honey, which coated the probe before leaking from her.

Restless, she tried to impale herself further but the straps prevented her forward motion. The tug reminding her of her bound condition inched her closer to release. She wished the probe were fucking her as it had yesterday. Hell, she wished *he* would fuck her.

With that single thought, her orgasm loomed near. As she

teetered on the edge, the pitch of the machine recording her responses crescendoed.

"Yes, Becca. Just like that. God, you look gorgeous."

Rebecca sighed when she heard his reassurance. She concentrated on clenching the probe so it stroked her as she needed. Her muscles milked the foreign object, straining to wedge it further into her body or, maybe, to eject it. She wasn't sure which. The nipple rings tightened again. She couldn't last much longer under the unrelenting waves pounding her.

Usually it took her a while to orgasm, even when she used her vibrator. She only got quick relief when she woke in the middle of the night from a dream of Kurt's powerful frame moving in heavy thrusts on top of her.

She'd barely acknowledged the fantasy when she flew over the edge. The whir and escalating beeping of the machines didn't register on her mind as they recorded her climax. All she was aware of was the rapture rushing through her with every heartbeat, the invading probe she shuddered around, the restraints—tight but comforting on her skin—and, somewhere in the distance, the guttural sound of Kurt succumbing to his own needs.

"Doctor!"

She drifted in a strange combination of satisfaction and yearning. The orgasm had been titanic. Yet, more than ever, she craved Kurt's cock. She wanted him to dominate her, force her to surrender to both of their desires. She huffed out a breath. He'd refused her twice already. She didn't have the courage to make her request only to be denied again.

Rebecca peeked out. She admired his broad back as he soaked a rag in the sink. He came near, then bent over between her legs with a wooden stick similar to a tongue depressor clasped in his hand. The collector scraped across her tender tissue with rapid strokes, eliciting a shriek. She couldn't stop herself from squirming against the restraints in an attempt to relieve her hypersensitive flesh while he removed copious dollops of the feminine come still oozing from her.

"Shh, Becca, I need to measure how wet you were." He continued scooping her secretions into a large vial with mLs marked in red slashes up the side. When satisfied, he placed it in a metal stand on the counter. His hands found a clasp beneath her ass then disengaged a similar collection reservoir. She hadn't noticed the discreet plate and funnel earlier.

Adding the contents together, he made note of the volume in his journal, humming with appreciation at the final figure. He swiped the warm, wet cloth across her thighs and crotch to remove the last bit of stickiness from her skin and ensure her comfort.

"Baby, you're amazing."

She expected him to remove the probe and nipple rings but, instead, he ran a finger over her pussy, around the side of the inserted device. Her hypersensitive nerve endings rebelled. The ferocity of her reaction startled her, as it had when her orgasm had made her a victim of spontaneous combustion.

"I'm sorry, Doctor. I couldn't help but come so quick."

Anger flared in his usually easygoing expression as he drew himself to his full height. "I told you never to apologize for your nature. If you do it again I'll be forced to punish you."

She tried to ignore the jump on the monitor indicating an unexpected clench of her pussy at his threat but a man as observant as Kurt couldn't possibly have missed it. "Besides, that's why we have several trials to establish a trend."

She treated him to a blank stare until her relaxed body reawakened at his implication. With him standing so close, distracting her, she wasn't certain she'd understood him.

"Several?"

"Yes. We'll try this again, maybe four or five times, to obtain an average reading." As though he expected her to accept the decree instead of rebelling at the idea, he patted her head. Before she could object, he gave her a quick peck on the cheek then headed back to his chair.

"Now you've had a chance to rest, let's start over."

"What?" Her incredulity shone through once she found her voice. She couldn't come again so soon. He couldn't expect her to when every nerve still tingled, resonating with violent relief.

"Again, Becca. You know it's impossible to create a reliable baseline from a single data point."

"Doctor," she objected, trying to think of an explanation to make him understand. "I'm very sensitive right now. I can't..."

"You've never had more than one orgasm in a night?" Peering over his shoulder, he scrutinized her reaction, making it impossible to obscure the truth.

"Never before yesterday." She flinched at the suggestion of her deficiency then averted her eyes, turning her head away from him.

"Still hiding from me, Becca?" He returned to her side, reached out and gripped her jaw between his thumb and strong fingers, forcing her to face him. "I asked you a question. You promised to be open. Remember, total honesty? Nothing you tell me will make me think less of you. If anything, I'll pity the men who were too inept to deserve you. I'd never judge you. There's so much I can show you, sweetheart." He stroked his thumb in a shallow arc over her cheekbone.

"Starting with this..." Reaching down, he gripped her forefinger then dragged it to her pussy, tapping it against her clit. A startled yelp escaped her throat. He only grinned.

"Don't worry, Becca. Keep rubbing. It'll start to feel good again, I promise."

Kurt guided her finger in the slow circle she had traced around her clit earlier until her muscles relaxed and the probe readings began to climb once again. With a wink, he took his seat for act two.

Chapter Nine

After the fifth orgasm, Kurt admitted he couldn't stand anymore even if Becca could have. Her limp body collapsed, exhausted. The straps alone held her on the table. Eyes closed, oblivious to the world, her breath sawed in sexy little pants through parted lips.

He was dying to sample her sultry slickness wrapped around his aching erection. Several rounds self-gratification behind cover of his clipboard hadn't diminished his arousal in the face of her utter abandon to her passion. She'd always been his best student.

Unable to help himself, he'd soaked in every detail. Like the way she feathered her fingertips on her clit for a moment before stroking along the side of the bundle of nerves then around the bulge of the probe. He'd studied every movement, tucking the knowledge away for the time when he could take her.

He wanted to discover every way possible to please her.

By a comfortable mile, today had replaced the time during his wild college years he'd spent the night with three very willing bisexual women as the highlight of his sexual experience.

Once he'd provided a safe environment for exploration—free of recrimination in her career—and a dash of control, she had blossomed. Self-imposed restraints had melted before his eyes. Her abandon stirred wicked ideas of what to show her next.

But he had to be patient.

Restricting himself to a snail's pace, he refused to risk overloading her senses and frightening her away. He'd waited this long already. He'd continue to be patient until the time was right to escort her into deeper waters.

Kurt collected the last of her fluids, still marveling at her responsiveness. He disengaged the probe and nipple rings, placing the equipment in the cleaning bins according to protocol. Then he restored the table to its base configuration before releasing the bonds cocooning Becca's legs. She rolled onto her side, curling into the fetal position with a weak moan.

"Come on, baby." He lifted her from the table, savoring her blissful trance. "We need to get you cleaned up, then you can take a nap. Not too long though, I need you to sleep well tonight."

"Am I awake now?" Her scratchy whisper was a side effect of her earlier vocal responses.

He chuckled, taking absurd pride in her repletion, though he hadn't had much to do with it. Like a cat, she nestled against him, ensuring the highest possible percentage of her skin made contact with his bare chest. His cock stirred. In total disbelief, he wondered if he'd ever have enough of her.

"You were starving, weren't you?" he whispered into her hair, inhaling her floral scent. She nuzzled her face against the side of his neck but didn't answer his question.

"You're so strong. You'd never drop me, would you?" Becca's complete transparency, both physical and emotional, made a drastic change in the guarded woman he'd come to know so well. The fierce emotions her reliance instilled made him swear to protect her, fulfill her longing for security, no matter what the future held. "Never."

He fanned his fingers across the cooling skin of her back and around the ultra-smooth spot under her knee. Though she wanted to relax now, she'd be sore tomorrow if he didn't take care of her as he should. Kurt refused to let her suffer.

He brought her into his adjoining studio apartment then set her, like a priceless vase, in the steamy bathwater he'd started running before he released her. The tenderness seeping through his heart as he bathed her unsettled him. Desire, he understood. Even caring was a part of his normal interactions with women, but never before had the urge to shelter and nurture overwhelmed his rationality.

As a rule, the thrill of the chase and the eventual submission of a spirited woman brought him complete satisfaction. Now, he'd developed a sudden, infuriating craving for Becca to turn to him, to trust him, to want *him*—the man behind the doctor, the mentor and the boss.

What the fuck? Kurt didn't believe in this shit, or anything he couldn't generate conclusive proof of for that matter.

Emotions are symptoms of complex chemical reactions, which science can't yet explain. Nothing else. Don't make this more than it is.

His rationalization rang false but the vision in front of him derailed his train of thought.

Becca lounged in the water lapping across her torso, blissfully unaware of her destructive impact on his lifelong hypothesis. He empathized with the confusion Einstein must have endured when he postulated the existence of black holes and their capability to distort the laws of physics.

Her eyes remained shut but the goose bumps dotting her skin faded when the heat, and the restorative ions of the bath salts, soaked into her delectable body. He washed her with his bare hands, lathering the soap across her smooth skin and pebbled nipples, scrubbing her more than necessary for hygienic purposes. All the while, he spoke to her in a stream of calming nonsense. Unsure of the words himself, he knew she heard but didn't understand his soothing litany.

Kurt didn't need a response to comprehend the implications of the moment. She would never let him care for her this way if she didn't have absolute confidence in him, if he hadn't reached some part of her psyche previously locked away.

Her surrender was a touching gift. It threw him off balance. That had to be the reason for the emotional vertigo disrupting his judgment.

He dried her silent, pliant body with a plush towel before returning her to his personal quarters. He placed her on the bed, taking a moment to light a few of the candles scattered around the room before moving to her side. He folded back the comforter then positioned her on her stomach on the flannel sheets. She rubbed her cheek against the fuzzy fabric but didn't rouse from her sensual daze. Popping the lid on a bottle of oil, he began to rub the mild muscle relaxer into her creamy skin.

He stared at his hands spanning her back with ease. Though she had a petite build, he'd never thought of her as such a little thing before. Her eagerness to learn, her confidence in her abilities and her determination to succeed made her seem larger than life despite the vulnerability he'd sensed lurking within.

When he cupped her voluptuous hips, massaging the joints he'd kept stretched earlier, Becca groaned. Unwilling to break the spell of their shared calm, he leaned over her back to whisper in her ear.

"Are you doing okay?"

"Mmm." She managed a tiny nod.

He finished kneading her legs, working her thighs until the knotted muscles beneath his fingers slackened. Accepting his reward, he lay down beside her then tucked her back against his chest. He brushed a stray lock of hair off her face, wondering why he hadn't seen how beautiful she was from the first moment they met. Drowsy himself, he murmured, "You did so well, Becca. I knew you would be amazing but today surpassed my highest expectations."

"Thank you, Doctor," she mumbled from the murky fog between sleep and waking. She placed her hand in his, which engulfed it, where it draped across her subtly rounded abdomen.

"Kurt," he corrected, nipping the side of her neck. A sigh slipped from her lips. After holding himself distant all these years, he fought the exhaustion sweeping over him. He wanted to relish this rare time but he couldn't stay awake much longer.

He set his alarm clock to ensure they didn't take more than a brief nap before arranging the downy comforter over them. Only then did he allow himself to drift off, holding tight to Becca's lax form beside him.

BEEP BEEP BEEP

Rebecca startled awake from a deep, disorienting sleep then crashed into a solid wall of muscle in her attempt to locate the source of the racket.

"Calm down, sweetheart."

Kurt?

She blinked then realized several things at once. She was naked, in a bed other than her own and he had dragged her close, wrapping his arms around her flailing limbs. From the searing heat of his flesh branding her with his obvious desire, she assumed he didn't have any clothes on either.

"Where are we? What happened?" Her hoarse voice attested to the depth of her sleep. After running on so little for so long, she was exhausted. Her mind struggled to restart as she desperately thought back.

"My quarters, off the laboratory." The mellow timbre of his sexy voice reassured her. When she looked up, he met her questioning gaze with a satisfied smile. His hands still stroked her back, soothing her.

"You had an intense afternoon. Your body isn't used to it." As he spoke, his palms traced a route down her spine, then up her sides, pausing to circle her hips as though he enjoyed outlining the dip and curve there. "I'm sorry I can't let you doze longer, Becca. I have to make sure you sleep well tonight."

"I don't think that's going to be a problem." She almost purred in contentment.

Her mind began to function. The details of their intimate situation became clearer. While she wanted to enjoy it, she was too nervous about the newness of the relationship and how she would avoid the potential awkwardness between them. Lounging in the crook of Kurt's leg, the brush of his aroused cock against her hip startled her. She froze. Uncertain of his expectations, she didn't want to appear to be encouraging him or inviting a more personal encounter.

Where did this afternoon leave them?

Before she could decide what to do, he withdrew his hands,

pushed up from the bed and effected his usual charm, giving her space to sort things out and catch her breath. She flashed him a smile of appreciation for his intrinsic understanding.

"Come on. Let's grab something to eat then we can come back here and discuss what's going to happen tonight so you're prepared."

Trying to clear the distractions from her mind, Rebecca swiped her hands over her face. When she opened her eyes, Kurt stood before her dressed in a pair of sweatpants, looking as rumpled as she felt.

She couldn't prevent the laughter from bubbling out of her chest.

"What's so funny?" The uncharacteristic moment of insecurity had him glancing down at himself to make sure everything was in order. The gesture inspired her mischievous streak. He didn't look anything like his usual, confident, unflappable self. Their earlier work had affected him too, which reassured her in some odd way.

"I've never seen you have a hair out of place before." She grinned and couldn't remember the last time she'd been this lighthearted. "You look cute."

He grimaced at her declaration. For a moment, she wondered if she'd overstepped her bounds but Kurt returned her grin.

"Normally, I don't think I'd be all that happy with cute." He shrugged. "But letting you tease me seems a small price to pay to see *you* like this."

She drew the covers up over her breasts. The mention of her wantonness still unsettled her. Her humor faded. No longer a matter of professionalism, she scolded herself for entangling her affection in this crazy experiment. She couldn't afford to care for him.

"Don't hide from me."

"But, I'm naked!" The sense of outrage filling her didn't result from being displayed in front of him. Not physically, anyway. She feared he would laugh again. After all, an hour ago she'd been bare, pleasuring herself and going wild before him. They both understood they'd moved past those barriers.

He refused to let her disguise her discomfort. Stalking to the side of the bed, he didn't give her the chance to avoid him. As she picked up the edge of the blanket to mask herself further, he yanked it out of her grasp then flung it onto the floor behind him.

"I will not allow you to chastise yourself for your reactions earlier or how they make you feel now. I've told you how much you pleased me. I enjoy the new facets of our relationship and your honest reactions. That should be all that matters to you at this point. Act accordingly."

Harsh breaths echoed in the otherwise quiet room as Rebecca stared at him in shock. This was not the man she knew. His authority compelled her to slide into acceptance of his will, to embrace the luxury of being at his command. Instead, she forced herself to remain aloof and protect her heart when he spoke only of passion or professionalism.

"I'm not ashamed of my performance in the study. Sleeping naked next to you in our off hours, Kurt, is another matter. I'm going to get dressed." With all the dignity she could muster, she brushed by him then swept into the bathroom, leaving him gaping in her wake.

She perched on the side of the tub while the water from the shower drummed the other side of the curtain behind her. Though clean and relaxed from her earlier bath, she'd needed to buy some time to reflect. This would have qualified as the longest shower in the history of the planet.

She had a lot to think about.

With her dream to become a partner in the university clinic realized, she floundered without purpose. The next step on her life path was uncertain. She struggled to separate her experiences during this exercise from her emotions for Kurt. The more they progressed, the more she worried she wouldn't be able to do it. Could she hide her feelings from him forever?

The way he'd cared for her today swamped her with affection and longing. The magnitude of her desire to submit made her feel weak. It would be too easy to let him take over all the time. Her mother had taught her better than that.

A loud bang on the door startled her from her thoughts.

"Are you okay?"

"Yes!" she yelled from behind her hand to maintain the illusion of her fictional shower.

"I know there isn't that much hot water in there!" Kurt bellowed, hopefully to make sure she heard over the noise of the spray and not because he was angry.

She didn't answer.

"Waking up next to me must have really turned you on to make you freeze yourself in a cold shower for damn near thirty minutes."

His arrogance almost inspired her to abandon her stronghold. Instead, she breathed deep and concentrated on suppressing her initial reaction. She didn't want him to get the wrong idea.

After a pause, he yelled again. "If you're not out of there in five minutes, I'm going to rip down the curtain and lick every drop of cold water from your—"

The mental image destroyed her resolve. Now she'd never get it out of her head. She wrenched the door open, cutting him off before he could make the threat any more vivid. The infuriating man grinned.

"You *were* hiding. Damn." He backed away from the door, ushering her out with a swing of his hands. "Since your grand exit didn't seem to indicate a desire to go out to dinner with me, I took the liberty of ordering a pizza. It's getting cold."

The smell of fresh dough and gooey cheese punched her in the gut as she emerged from the bathroom bundled in a luxurious robe she'd found laid out for her. Kurt had stocked the small area with almost everything they'd need for a few days. With the exception of her clothes.

Her stomach rumbled.

"Dig in. I got your favorite."

As she debated refusing, he went into the bathroom and shut off the shower. She thought she heard a low chuckle but chose to ignore it.

They'd indulged in the all-American dinner more than a few times while working late nights. Those evenings comprised some of her favorite memories as they chatted about open cases or school. The rare, relaxed occasions accounted for most of the breaks she'd allowed herself since beginning her training. The reminder of their easy companionship put her back on level footing. Accepting the plate he offered, she served a slice onto it then turned, searching for somewhere to sit.

"Sorry, it's a tight arrangement but I have to be with you at all times. Go on, take the bed. I need to finish up a few things." He waved her toward the other side of the room with an absent flick of his hand before carrying his dinner over to his desk. As he sat down to resume work on his notes, he turned. "I know this is hard for you, Becca. But I won't let you hide. Remember, *I* decide what your limits are unless you want to quit. And you're stronger than that."

Then, he let the matter drop.

She watched him become engrossed in the documentation, wishing she could assist him like usual to calm her tumultuous blend of fear and anticipation. Of course, she couldn't be involved as anything other than the subject but it reminded her again of her changing role. Gathering up her plate, she shuffled onto the bed.

Rebecca attempted a few positions but, no matter how she arranged herself, she couldn't find a way to sit that didn't require two hands to hold her robe for full coverage. Kurt appeared engrossed in the records, his dinner lying mostly forgotten next to him on the desk. He'd write furiously for a few minutes then reach over, scoop up his pizza, take a large bite and keep going.

Sure he wouldn't notice her exposed state, she scooted across the bed until her back bumped the wall. She sat cross-legged, tucked the fabric between her legs, tugged it across her chest, tightened the belt as well as she could, then rested her plate on her thigh.

She flipped on the TV then cycled through the channels, watching bits and pieces of shows that caught her attention but she didn't have a favorite program to tune into. In fact, she didn't own a TV and wouldn't have been able to pay for cable if she had. Always busy, it was an unnecessary expense. So, instead, Rebecca studied Kurt as she dug into another slice of pizza.

He dwarfed the standard-sized desk, about half the size of the mahogany monstrosity in his office where he worked during regular office hours. She sighed as she recalled several vibrant dreams she'd had about him laying her back on the glossy surface and sliding his cock into her...

She hadn't realized she'd gasped when he appeared at her side.

"What's wrong? Did you burn yourself?"

"N-No, I'm fine. I..." Her mind raced in frantic circles as she tried to work out the details. *Why didn't I think of this before?* She had dreams of Kurt often—extreme, detailed, erotic dreams.

"You what? Are you sure you're all right, baby?" Concern etched his features as he observed her. "You're pale and your pulse is racing. It's been a stressful day for you, I know. Tell me if you don't feel well."

Blushing furiously, she couldn't see a way out of this uncomfortable situation. Kurt set her half-eaten dinner on the table beside the bed then pulled her onto his lap. The closeness increased her discomfort.

"This relates to the experiment." It wasn't a question. When she didn't deny it, he sighed. "Becca, your training makes it clear you can't keep secrets from me about our research. I need full disclosure. Tell me what's going on here."

He was right, of course. Besides, she'd given her word to be open and honest no matter how embarrassing it might be.

"I just realized you're going to see my dreams tonight." Comprehending how moronic her admission must sound, she added, "I mean, I knew you would. That's the whole point of the experiment, right? But I didn't think it through all the way."

"What's there to think about?"

"I dream of you."

She confessed so softly that even straining he might not be able to make out the words. She knew he had though when his arms tightened around her and his hardening cock nudged the globes of her ass.

"Thank you for your candor. I'm flattered and grateful. Because, when you didn't object to me witnessing your dreams during my outline of the study, I thought it might not be an

113

issue. I admit, I hoped you were so worried about exposing yourself to me that you hadn't considered the content of your dreams."

"Why would that concern you?" she asked, hoping to hear what her rational mind figured couldn't be possible.

Tilting his head forward, he let it drop until his brow rested on hers and his raptor eyes focused like lasers on her own.

"Because I dream of you too, Becca."

The bolt of energy his words generated electrified her exhausted muscles. She jerked back. "I meant I've had *sexual* dreams about you."

"I know what you meant." He gathered her close once more.

Kurt didn't volunteer any details so she reasoned he'd dreamt of her in a platonic way, which wasn't unusual since they interacted every day. People often make cameo appearances in the dreams of individuals they're close to, she reasoned. But he was about to find out she hadn't referred to such a normal occurrence.

Even if he'd had the occasional lurid dream about her, she bet he'd never had the ones where they were emotionally involved. Nothing she could do would prevent the mortification her future held because sleeping next to him would only enhance her active imagination. Each breath tinged with the intoxicating scent of him would be sure to trigger her most daring dreams.

Resigned, she rested against him. Suddenly, it seemed as though the day had sapped all her strength. This one last outburst had drained any residual energy. Even the thought of finishing her dinner couldn't entice her to move.

Kurt massaged her scalp with slow circles. The motion, as well as his heat and strength, combined to suffuse her with lethargy. *When did he start touching me?*

She couldn't stifle her yawn.

"You're exhausted, aren't you, sweetheart?"

"Mmm. Who wouldn't be after a day like today?" She could hardly believe the episode in the laboratory had happened. It seemed like a fantasy. She never would have imagined pleasure could be so intense or so frequent. And, if tonight's dreams were anything like her usual ones, today's adventure would be a drop in the bucket compared to what tomorrow held.

"Okay, then. Let's get you ready for bed."

Chapter Ten

Kurt would have loved to question Becca more about the content of her dreams. If the glimpse he'd had earlier in the week represented the norm for her, they were vivid and carnal. But she was fading fast. Her heavy eyelids drooped, and he needed to prepare her properly. Then he wouldn't have to ask. He could watch her fantasies unfold. He barely stifled a groan of anticipation.

Although it seemed they'd retire sooner than he'd planned, she didn't have the energy to stay awake much longer. Son of a bitch. Why hadn't he noticed how hard she'd pushed herself lately?

He'd bet she hadn't slept a full night in months. He wished he'd paid more attention and forced her to rest but it could be better this way. Fatigue would drain some of the fight from her mind and make her more receptive to the images put forward by her subconscious. He laid her on the bed then unwrapped her body from the fluffy robe like a delectable treat.

"What are you doing?" She grabbed the lapels.

He enfolded her delicate fingers in his hand.

"I need to get you ready for the Dream Machine. I'll explain the procedure as we go. Then, I'll let you sleep." Kurt didn't want to give her an excuse to flee now but he had to offer one last chance to change her mind before things got intense. "Are you sure you want to go through with this?"

"I think so." Her eyes closed but she couldn't obscure her nerves from him.

"I'll be right here the whole time. I won't let anything

happen to you."

"I know." As soon as her grip slacked, he slipped the covering from her.

"Good girl." He took her robe then draped it over his desk chair. He opened the bottom cabinet section of the nightstand next to the bed before withdrawing a metal unit with an attached display panel, which he put on the surface of the table. The machine was about the size of a briefcase. A simple, plain grey box with a ten-inch, flat-panel monitor embedded in the side housed the advanced electronics.

"That's the Dream Machine?" Her eyebrow arched.

"Yes." Amused he asked, "What did you expect?"

"I...I don't know. How does it work?"

"It's pretty basic. I modified a computer with an oversized hard drive. This unit records the data feeds from diodes. It stores them for later viewing on the attached monitor or you can burn the videos to DVDs for screening on any standard player. The trick comes in converting the dreams from brain waves into images."

Becca loved to learn new things. He often demonstrated technology and ideas for her. She wouldn't be able to contain her curiosity about something so novel. He indulged himself in explaining his invention.

For the past year, he'd devoted all his energy to making the Dream Machine a reality. Having someone to share his success with, someone who could understand the concept, the apparatus and its possible applications, was rewarding. He couldn't wait for her to work alongside him, proposing improvements and generating new ideas. The notion was nearly as exciting as the thought of fucking her. Nearly.

As expected, she suppressed her exhaustion and rolled over for a closer look. He hoped this familiar routine would help to ease her anxiety as professional interest overcame her nervousness. Thrilled she had become comfortable around him, enough that her lack of clothing or their intimate position didn't seem to faze her, Kurt pressed on.

"I found a way to modify a standard diode used to measure brain waves similar to those used to detect heartbeats. You know, the kind you see taped to people on TV emergency room shows?"

She nodded.

"The device transmits the wave pattern to the computer into a special program I built. It transforms the sequence into pictures the same way your brain does for your subconscious."

"So, when I'm asleep, I'll have to wear one of those diodes?"

"Yes, I'll attach it at the base of your neck with surgical adhesive. I've been working on the design. It's comfortable. I've included a wireless transmitter in the diode itself so you don't have to worry about choking yourself at night. Since the diode is tiny, the range is short. Therefore, you'll have to be within ten feet of the unit for it to work."

"So, I'll be sleeping here?" She motioned to the rumpled expanse of sheets.

"Yes."

The machine didn't have to be engaged for her thoughts to come to life. He couldn't suppress a smile, "I'll be sleeping with you, Becca. I told you I'd be with you twenty-four hours a day for the remainder of the experiment. I need to be here in case anything happens. Although, I swear I would never let you do this if I thought there was any chance you could get hurt."

"Okay." Her throat flexed as she gulped. "I'm not afraid of getting injured."

"Just to be sure, I'm also going to monitor your vital signs. You'll sleep naked. You'll be most comfortable that way. The other diodes will need to be attached to your chest to track your heart rate and breathing during the collection phase."

With a soft whimper, Becca shied away from him. He was sure she didn't realize she'd done it. She had always hidden her insecurities, even on the best or worst days she must have had these past years. The glimpse of her emotions encouraged him to probe further.

"What is it?" He gave her the time she needed to gather her courage. She'd promised to be candid with him during the experiment. She would honor the commitment because she valued loyalty and honor. But he craved her admission of what they both understood.

"It's hard enough you're going to see my intimate thoughts. Knowing I'll be totally exposed, and that you'll be lying next to me while I'm having them, makes me uncomfortable."

Kurt nodded. "Let's even things out. I'll sleep naked, too. I always do."

"Um. Th-that sounds fair."

For the first time in a long time, he laughed aloud. Her practical response didn't fool him. The gleam of hunger in her eyes gave her away.

At the suggestion of his hot flesh pressed to hers as they snuggled deep into the lush bedding, her instantaneous and obvious arousal perfumed the air. He couldn't help but tease her a bit to observe her reactions.

In addition to her tongue moistening her lips, her nipples pebbling before his gaze and the way her heart rate kicked up triple time, goose bumps rose on her arms. She chafed them with brisk swipes of her hands designed to eliminate the betrayal of her response. Instead, the motion caused her luscious breasts to bounce beneath her crossed wrists.

He had to touch her.

"Cold, Becca?" He tucked her against his side, which prevented her from glimpsing his grimace at his deliberate obtuseness. He rubbed his hands down her slender arms, sharing his heat. When a hard nipple mashed into his rib cage, he fought to swallow a groan. He supposed it was fitting punishment for getting her riled up. Tonight had the makings of the most difficult night of his life. Only one thought kept him from going insane with lust—tomorrow all his patience should pay off.

"I'm good, thank you, Doctor."

Since they hovered at the start of the dream collection phase of the experiment, he didn't protest her use of his title although it rankled. He wished she would let go and admit she wanted to do this for them, not for the experiment. Although she progressed, her evolution was taking more time than he preferred.

"Okay, then. Lay on your stomach. I'll begin attaching the diodes." Becca flipped over, presenting her sweet ass in innocence as she wiggled to settle herself in a comfortable position. Her breasts plumped beneath her ribs as her arms relaxed and her legs spread until a sliver of her pussy peeked from between her thighs.

Kurt allowed his stare to roam over her. He ached to kiss her, but he had to wait at least one more night. Twenty-four hours had never seemed so long.

When she peeked over her shoulder at him, he leaned in to brush her hair aside. He drew a quarter-sized diode from his pocket, removed the covering on the bonding agent then applied the device to the base of her neck. He wrapped his hand around her fragile throat, pressing down on the transmitter to ensure its sufficient adhesion.

Once again, her delicate frame aroused him. Elated she didn't flinch at her vulnerability, he encircled her neck with his fingers then placed a warm kiss beside the device.

Her muted sigh broke through to him. The faint indention on her skin indicated he'd nipped her neck, though he hadn't realized he'd done it. He couldn't prevent himself from taking one last taste of her skin. Licking the spot, he soothed it.

"Is it not sticking?" Her raspy whisper sounded uncertain as she attempted to rationalize his actions. She still refused to admit how far they'd come in the past two days.

"There's nothing wrong with the sensor." Before she could object or retreat from him again, he helped her roll onto her back then began applying the additional input devices. He might have been angry when she closed her eyes, since the flush creeping across her chest indicated embarrassment caused her to avoid meeting his hungry stare. Instead, her shy acceptance was somehow endearing.

Watching Becca fight her own reactions amused him because she slid closer to him with every moment they spent together. She couldn't ignore the chemistry between them forever.

When his hands hovered a fraction of an inch from her skin, she bowed up to meet them. Deciding to make the most of her response, he took the opportunity to touch her for reasons other than attaching the medical devices.

Kurt's hand cupped her left breast. She arched against his hand, grinding her puckered nipple into his palm. While pleasure distracted her, he attached the next two diodes above her heart and lungs. He stroked one finger around the devices until she relaxed beneath him again. He continued to caress her until her breathing turned steady and deep. The simple contact electrified his fingertip while she slipped in and out of a light doze. He'd saved the last requirement for when she would be the most amenable to the needs of her body.

"There's one more thing."

"Hmm?"

"I've designed a special receptor, similar to the probe in the laboratory. It's much smaller and will be comfortable for you to sleep with. I've also created a harness belt to keep it in place throughout the night." He attempted to soothe her with his modulated voice. Seeing her so relaxed filled him with a sense of satisfaction. He didn't want to disturb her but this had to be done for the experiment to work. The board would require evidence.

Becca roused just enough to question him. She stammered, "Inside me? All night?"

With a firm hand on her shoulder, Kurt restrained her. "Shh, baby. You can take it. In fact, it'll enhance your pleasure. If you have a stimulating dream, your muscles will have something to cradle and squeeze."

After a brief hesitation, she agreed. "Okay."

She fidgeted beneath him as though the suggestion of the device inflamed her. To keep her steady—and prevent her from dislodging any of the diodes—he swung one leg over her hips, pinning her in place. Her reflexive movements drove him crazy. Could he stop himself from taking her if she continued the seductive sway of her hips rocking against him?

"Mmm. I love your weight on me, holding me here."

Her admission shot straight to his groin. The hard-on he'd been keeping at bay throbbed to life. If he didn't move soon, she wouldn't be able to ignore it prodding her yielding belly, even exhausted and half-asleep. And if she begged again, there'd be no stopping him from fucking her right now. It had nearly killed him to deny her earlier.

He reached to the floor below them where he'd staged the harness out of Becca's line of sight. He gripped her waist in his hands, his fingers touching in the middle, then lifted her to slide the fur-lined, leather straps beneath her body. One thin band encircled her waist like a belt while another threaded through it, perpendicular to the first. The sensor and small probe looped onto the strap which, when belted closed, pulled snug between her legs, holding the device in place.

He rubbed the entrance to her pussy, pleased by the wet heat proclaiming her readiness. With a needy gasp, she angled her pelvis higher. Eager to oblige her, he slid his finger inside the welcoming grasp of her moist channel. He scrutinized her face for any hint of pain caused by his invasion. Her swollen labia gave evidence to the lingering effects of the afternoon's activities but he'd been with enough women to know the mewling sounds she made stemmed from pleasure, not pain. Within seconds, her pussy began to slicken further.

"Kurt" she pleaded.

"No, baby. I won't let you come. You're ready now." Although the instrument was modest, he ensured the comfort of her extraordinarily tight pussy. Or at least he'd meant to but he'd gotten lost in the yielding tissue scalding his finger. It would feel like heaven hugging his cock.

He sighed with regret when Becca forced herself to abandon the building arousal, hating to deprive her when he wanted nothing more than to ravage her all night, but it had to be done. Leaving her needy would prime her mind for erotic dreams. A wet slurp accompanied the motion of his finger when he pulled it from her pussy. Then, he lubricated the sensor with her juices.

With one smooth push, he inserted the device inside her before buckling the strap to the belt in front, securing the contraption for the night. "How do you feel?"

"Nice. Comfortable. Horny." Her rueful mumble lightened his heart.

At least he wasn't the only one suffering. Kurt smiled against her hair. "Same here."

Their chests glided across one another as he reached to turn on the Dream Machine. Damn! The contact inflamed every nerve in his body. He suppressed the animalistic instinct roaring for him to act.

Instead, he scanned the instrument panel to ensure the proper functioning of the equipment before he switched off the lights. Comparing Becca's heartbeat tracking across the screen with the gentle thumping on his palm, he was satisfied.

The faint glow of the monitors bathed the small room, making it seem more intimate. Pulsing green illumination draped over them, casting diffuse shadows that highlighted the provocative contours of their bodies lying next to each other.

"Will the light bother you, sweetheart? I have a sleep mask you can wear if you'd like."

"No, thanks. It's like a nightlight. It's comforting." Her observation echoed his own.

Kurt had intended to stay on the other side of the bed but, when she trained her drowsy gaze on him, he couldn't keep even a foot of space between them. Something about this woman called to him, urging him to rest with her. He never slept with women. Not just to sleep. Now, though, he looked forward to closing his eyes with the knowledge she would be by his side when he woke.

Moments away from succumbing to exhaustion, Becca sighed when he tugged her to his chest then stroked her hair. They fit perfectly together. She stiffened when his erection twitched against her thigh but he couldn't let her go now. He prepared to keep her next to him all night by whatever means necessary. So he told her a half-truth.

"I need to hold you like this to make sure you don't move around too much and dislodge the sensors." If he couldn't bury himself inside her, he at least wanted to shelter her in his arms. He'd never been possessive about a woman before but need drove him to stake a claim, to overcome her independence and show her, in some small way, she belonged with him.

"Yes, Doctor," she answered in a relieved whisper before snuggling into his grasp.

Kurt lay awake for at least an hour after she went

completely lax, breathing deeply. He didn't need the sensor readings to tell him she slept. Stroking a repeated circuit down her back, across the upper swells of her ass then along her side, he memorized every inch of her body.

Usually, he'd be untangling limbs and making a stealthy exit about this time. Now he was content just to hold her. He'd always wanted Becca but, before, his desire had been motivated by a need to prove he could make her leave her past behind, discover her sensual nature and strengthen their future partnership.

Now, he wasn't sure what he felt beside confusion. And lust.

As recently as the day before, he'd explained attraction as nothing more than a chemical reaction. He'd argued vehemently with Luke, and in research journals, that love could not be real. Nature used emotions as an evolutionary tool. Lust, friendship, even hate—those reactions were all explained by scientific theories on the development of needs. Convenient tricks of the mind enforced behaviors that would increase humankind's chance of survival.

After all, it had to feel good to reproduce or our species would have died out long ago. Partnerships offered protection, split work—which conserved energy—and provided security. But love? He'd always thought people made themselves believe in a higher order to justify their behavior as more than a primitive reflex.

Kurt had entered the board's charade hoping to convince Becca they would make a great team, a partnership in both the business they excelled at and a life he thought they could enjoy together. He'd tried to justify the decision by assuring himself the board would grant her deepest wish—to become a partner and board member—if she learned to embrace her sexuality and trust others by completing the experiment.

The uncomfortable swelling in his chest refused to conform to his theories.

Hell, he'd pushed his own moral limits, both professional and personal, to the max to steal this experience in the first place. Why had he been desperate enough to use Becca's situation as motivation to explore her nature instead of taking the risk she would deny his proposition if faced with the truth? He'd told the board to go to hell before, why hadn't he this time?

Could it be...?

And, if it was real... If love existed as more than a Hallmark myth, had he destroyed any chance for a future with Becca by keeping the truth of the break-in from her?

Kurt sighed, unwilling to recant a lifelong tenet. He chalked up his wayward thoughts to unrelieved lust, and the perfection of her physical responses having fuzzed his logic. Refusing to think on it further he decided to savor the night and her presence beside him.

Tomorrow was going to be one hell of a day. He needed his rest.

Kurt forced himself to sleep with a sense of anticipation unrivaled since he'd been a kid on Christmas Eve. When he drifted off, a smile graced his face and his arms wrapped tight around Becca, subconsciously keeping her close to his heart.

ભ

Kurt woke early the next morning. Becca still slept, her limbs tangled around him. Gauging by the damp heat pressed against his thigh, there would be a lot to do today.

He glanced at the pattern of polysomnographic waves recorded throughout the night. The general trend of the graph told him his subject had passed through the last likely rapid eye movement stage of sleep. This REM stage would be where her dream activity would take place. Careful not to disturb her, he brushed his lips against her forehead, slipped out from beneath her lush warmth then rolled the desk chair next to the Dream Machine.

First, he flipped to the medical readouts. He scrolled through the findings to ensure everything appeared normal. As he expected, the results showed Becca in perfect health. During most stages, her vital signs slowed within normal parameters for the appropriate phase of the sleep cycle she would have been in at the times indicated on the screen.

The first REM stage occurred around ninety minutes after falling asleep. Tracking a little more than an hour into the recording, Kurt slowed in search of signs of dream activity. *There.* At ninety-three minutes and twenty-seven seconds, her respiration and heart rate began to accelerate then became a bit erratic.

Flipping to the camera view, he ignored the way he looked at peace holding her in his sleep in favor of noting her fingers and facial muscles demonstrating the mild twitches of pre-dream states. Then, about a minute later, her face went slack as the paralysis associated with REM sleep kicked in. Most researchers believed this inability to move accompanied increased brain activity to prevent dreamers from acting out their nighttime visions.

After marking the beginning of the first REM stage, he fast-forwarded the video until her vital signs returned to normal ten minutes later. The first REM stage of sleep was short but each stage lengthened until waking. He expected her to demonstrate the typical five to six dream periods. Each would have grown longer with the final stage lasting up to an hour.

Kurt subdued the need to view her dreams immediately. Instead, he stuck to protocol. He methodically marked the start and end times of each REM stage in his journal before programming the Dream Machine to translate the waves into images, as though his restraint proved he could overcome his raging desire.

If he allowed himself to watch the first scene before finishing the rest of the research, he would never make it to the others. Carefully, he recorded her biometric data as well as the temperature, moisture and pressure readings from the sensor inside her pussy during each stage. The thought of her draped on top of him while her body squeezed the instrument made him shift the uncomfortable weight of his dick. Only one thing could ease the pressure building there.

Willing himself to focus, he finished the necessary work while waiting for the dream sequences to convert. After what seemed like years of waiting, but was only five minutes, the first of Becca's fantasies completed processing. Kurt tilted the display to face him head on, the screen now pointing away from the bed. It took two tries for his trembling hand to click open the file captured the night before.

A vision flickered to life on the monitor. Hazy, incoherent shadows flitted through the darkness. He wondered if the machine would work after all. Then, a minute later, the swirling shapes and forms coalesced.

Becca's dreams came to life before his eyes.

Chapter Eleven

Rebecca's eyelids fluttered open. A long, comfortable night's sleep combined with the sexual release of the day before left her refreshed and eager to start the day. She took a moment to relish the satisfaction coursing through her before blinking to clear her vision.

Oh my God. Not three feet in front of her, at eye level, Kurt's hand wrapped around his gloriously erect cock. The sight filled her with instant longing. The bulbous head and plump veins stood out in relief on his thick shaft, creating ridges guaranteed to delight a woman.

Fascinated, she tried to stay immobile and silent. As she watched, he spread his powerful, muscled thighs wider. His firm ass rested on the edge of the chair while his left hand ran down from its perch on his ripped abdomen to cup his testicles. Massaging them, he groaned then squeezed his throbbing flesh. While his attention was diverted, Rebecca peeked up at his face.

He focused on the screen of the Dream Machine, which she couldn't see no matter how she strained her neck. Kurt wore headphones, so she assumed he listened to the recording as well. Shock rippled through her. *He's watching my fantasies.*

Exhilaration, and a healthy dose of relief, kicked her heart into overdrive. Whatever she had dreamed up turned him on, too. Maybe sharing her secrets wouldn't be as difficult as she dreaded.

A drop of milky white fluid appeared from the slit at the tip of his cock. The memory of his musky flavor tempted her. She wished she could taste him again. Afraid he would stop if he knew she watched his forbidden display, she froze and thanked God for the audio, which prevented him from detecting her panting.

Her conscience prickled for observing him unaware. Then again, he was jerking off to her dreams, so she supposed they were even. She lay enthralled by his animal grace and the raw virility radiating from him.

Taking advantage of the pre-come oozing from the swollen head of his cock, Kurt spread the slippery substance around until his hand glided up and down his erection with a moist, slapping sound. She loved the way his skin flexed and shifted around the solid core of steel-hard flesh.

Rebecca observed his chest heaving and the restless motion of his hips thrusting toward his hand. He would come soon. His head dropped back, his eyes closed, and she couldn't help herself. Before she realized what she intended, she'd slid across the bed, breached the distance between them and placed her hand over his.

He'd made her vow to be open and honest. In this moment, she wanted nothing more than to participate in his passion.

Kurt snapped to attention the instant their skin touched. Eyes open and questioning on hers, he yanked off the headset. Before he could object, Rebecca offered him a hesitant smile then brushed his hand away and replaced it with hers. Resuming the pace he'd set, she stroked him.

"Let me, please." She needed to give him release.

When his dick jumped in her hands at her request, she knew he wouldn't deny her. Sliding closer, she pried his other hand from between his legs then licked a slow path up the center of his balls. The motion jostled the sensor still buried inside her. She moaned.

"Damn, sweetheart, I won't last very long if you do that." His voice was harsh but reverent.

A bold smile comprised her only answer. With her usual modesty burned away by the heat of her desire, she graced his tight, wrinkled sac with another long stroke of her tongue. She wrapped her fingers around his rigid flesh, straining to reach all the way around it. She continued laving the underside of his cock, tracing the vein, then circled the ridge of the head.

Kurt moaned. His hips bucked causing his damp member to slide across her cheek. Possessed by an impulse to shatter his control, she opened her mouth and took him deep inside. She recalled the places he seemed to enjoy her touch from the last time she had sucked him, pleasuring him with abundant enthusiasm if not skill. Curious, she tried to adapt based on his reactions. Learning how to gratify him became her goal.

She was an excellent student.

When his hand fisted in her hair, she whimpered around his impressive girth. Guiding her, he encouraged her to take him in further on each pass. She swirled her tongue around the head of his cock. He tensed.

"If you...don't want me...to come in your mouth...you'd better stop now." His labored breathing broke up the harsh words.

Instead of stopping, she redoubled her efforts, moaning at the earthy scent of him. Once, twice more she bobbed over him before he held her impaled on his flesh. His bunched abdomen rippled in front of her before the first spurt of his come splashed on the back of her throat.

"Becca!"

She still attempted to lave him with gentle swipes when he tugged her into his lap. While he feasted on her lips, his softening erection rested hot and satiny against her thigh.

"Do you have any idea how good you make me feel?" Kurt whispered, their lips still touching.

Aroused, and ready to beg for relief, she rubbed herself against him. Her body burned for his touch. She was so turned on she forgot to be embarrassed about her wanton behavior.

It shocked her system like a speeding train slamming to a stop when he lifted her with a brusque jerk then set her aside.

He knelt in front of her to release the harness from around her waist. The glide of the sensor slipping from her pussy made her knees weak. Empty and hollow, her body mourned the loss. He wrapped his arm around her for support while he removed the other instruments from her breast and neck. Just when she expected him to come closer, he stepped away again. The lack of his presence, his warmth, disoriented her.

He turned her toward the bathroom then smacked her ass, startling her into motion.

"Go take your shower. Afterward, we need to get to work."

This time Rebecca did take a cold shower.

Standing under the freezing spray, she let her head drop against the frosty tile. What had she been thinking? Her traitorous hormones had gotten out of control. Again. She'd wanted Kurt until lust overrode her common sense. She hadn't been able to hold herself distant from him.

Disappointed, she chastised herself for forgetting. The infamous Dr. Foster didn't experience the same personal craving she did when they touched. But how could this longing be one-sided? How could her perception be so skewed? Frustration entwined with her growing confusion.

Was she imagining his sexual attraction to her?

No, she thought with a wry grimace, *I didn't imagine his raging hard-on in my mouth a few minutes ago.*

So, it seemed he would let her relieve him but refused to fuck her. Full-fledged anger began to replace her uncertainty, a rare occurrence. Maybe he could sense her desire to give him more than her body. Kurt had already demonstrated greater insight into her than any other person. He must realize she would struggle to separate these intense physical sensations from the tenderness flaring to life inside her. A notorious bachelor like him would run for the hills before encouraging her affection.

Being near him made her want to discard all her boundaries and rely on him. The natural way he made her submit buoyed her yearning to grant him control. Every time he got near, her rationality, determination and promises to herself dissipated. She could only think about pleasing him. Worse, she abandoned her independence. To be honest, she'd acquired a taste for letting go of her focus on goals in exchange for riding the tsunami of passion he generated.

Rebecca craved the rush she got from yielding to Kurt. When he loomed above her, skillfully manipulating her senses, she wanted to surrender to her heart's desire to submit, to lose herself in his attentions. She was terrified to see what would happen if she let go. Was this predisposition genetic? Is this how her mother had felt? Had she chosen to go with the tide instead of swimming against the current of need?

Was Kurt worthy of her unequivocal trust?

She'd agreed to obey him but she didn't have to relinquish control of her emotions or her soul. When he'd recognized her as his partner, he'd freed the professional part of her but put the woman behind the new doctor at risk. Still, she couldn't stop wanting him.

Licking her lips, she caught the hint of his salty taste and moaned. She considered masturbating to relieve some of her tension but Kurt had threatened to come in after her if she dallied. She couldn't stand to have him find her needy only to push her away again. It would shatter her newfound resolve and have her pleading for all the intimacies he avoided.

She pledged to enjoy the experiences she'd craved for so long. Savoring the warmth of his embraces, she would bank memories to take with her when their time together ended. If she could block off anything more than physical release maybe he would stop running. It would have to be enough.

Finishing her shower with brusque efficiency, she took care of the essentials then steeled herself to tackle the hardest phase of the experiment yet. Braced against his disorienting presence, Rebecca opened the bathroom door. Her stomach dropped. She was alone.

A note on the desk informed her to wait in his office for their first session.

☃

"You're late checking in." Luke sounded annoyed but Kurt knew it was only because he worried. They'd been friends a long time.

"I know, sorry, I didn't have a chance. Things have been going well. Really well."

"So you have the proof we need for initial board approval?"

"Almost. I have the dream sequences on file, now I just need to prove she responds more to them then the baseline. She will."

"Are you sure she's ready for this? Can she handle it?"

"Yes. She can take anything I'd ask of her." The confidence and pride he felt colored his declaration but he didn't care. Kurt shared everything with Luke. They were closer than brothers.

"How are you holding up? You sound...different. Is there something you're not telling me?"

"No. I'm just thinking about the session today. I won't force her to remember, Luke."

"Not even if it means throwing away several years of research?" his friend asked with quiet patience. Luke knew how much was at stake.

"That doesn't matter to me right now." Kurt chuckled. "But I did stack the deck in my favor. I've made sure there are context clues. The place, the clothes, everything I could think of. I want to make it good for her."

"Of course." Luke's smile came through in the tone of his voice. "Well then, what are you doing wasting time talking to me?"

"Good point."

"I'll call the meeting for 10 a.m. day after tomorrow. Be ready."

"We will be."

⌈⌉

The familiar comfort of Dr. Foster's office embraced Rebecca. When she'd first started working at the clinic, the raw masculinity of his space and the sheer heft of the furniture had intimidated her. Now, though, the sanctuary seemed sturdy and safe, not at all overwhelming. She breathed deep for the first time in days, inhaling the calming spice of his cologne along with the musk of leather-bound medical tomes. By his absence, she deduced he intended to keep her waiting.

Disappointed, each cell of her body throbbed. If he'd hurry up and start the day's events, she could steal one damn modicum of relief. The flare of Rebecca's temper startled her. She couldn't contain the mood swings zooming through her anymore. Sexual frustration was driving her insane. No man had ever made her want to do the things she craved now.

Wasn't that the point of volunteering? Her laughter held a bitter edge. Her plan might have worked a little too well. She could definitely identify with the cases she'd worked involving people unable to obtain the fulfillment they craved. The resulting hunger made her irritable.

Pacing around the room, memories bombarded her—Kurt in this office, taking care of patients, working case files, teaching her everything she knew and researching new theories. She smiled when her finger trailed over the spine of the book she'd given him for Christmas last year. It was prominently displayed on his shelf. She lingered for a moment, considering the place of honor among all his other texts before continuing her circuit.

Her gaze snagged on the chaise lounge near the back of the room. She stumbled as she remembered the way he'd touched her there when he'd accepted her for the experiment and changed her life forever. Had it really only been three days ago? Her insides quaked.

Desire erupted again when she heard the door open behind her. She smelled the rich scent of Kurt's soap before she pivoted to take in his damp hair falling in slim clumps over his forehead. He looked magnificent striding toward her in dark slacks and a dove grey pullover sweater. She thought the choice odd for the middle of summer but she recognized it as his favorite. The V-neck dipped, exposing his corded throat, while the supple fabric hugged his defined chest and shoulders. The garment made him look like a powerful animal as he stalked toward her.

The rose silk robe he'd laid out for her, while beautiful, left her decidedly underdressed.

"Lie down on the chaise, Becca," he ordered without preamble as he neared. When she didn't move fast enough to suit him, he pressed his hand on her shoulder until she sank onto the sofa. Situating a slick leather wingback within arm's reach, Dr. Foster settled in beside her.

"Today we need to discuss the dreams you experienced last night." Kurt began the formal process. If he didn't follow the book to the letter to start with, he would never make it through this session. They needed to stick with procedure for the sake of the trial but he would have anyway, to ensure he didn't harm Becca by exposing her to desires her conscious mind wasn't yet ready to admit to.

"The next stage of the study involves comparing your recollections to the images captured by the Dream Machine. By doing so, we can prove the scenes recorded are your actual dreams." He had no doubt of it but the board required verification.

"For the board to be satisfied with the accuracy of the Dream Machine, I need you to independently corroborate any dreams you remember having last night." If she got any tenser, he feared she would shatter. He regretted having been so harsh with her earlier but she had to understand he'd thrust her away because it had been the only way to keep himself from taking her right then and invalidating the study. Didn't she?

"I've reviewed all six of the REM stages you experienced last night but I won't reveal anything you can't recall on your own. As you know, dreams are an outlet for your subconscious. You may not be ready to face all you dreamed of. I won't breech the internal safeguard your mind has put in place. Therefore, I need you to tell me what you remember."

It was now or never.

"What did you dream about last night, Becca?"

Kurt didn't know what he would do if she had no memory of the fantasies he'd witnessed in the recorded files this morning. At the limits of his control, he prayed for the strength to walk away if she required his patience. They desired the same things but he wouldn't force her. The urgency tearing at his guts caused his voice to rasp out harsher than he intended.

"Concentrate."

He braced himself as though he headed into a fight instead

of a session, determined to bring them both through it in one piece.

Rebecca closed her eyes against the stern look on Kurt's face. She drew on all the mental tricks she knew to quiet her psyche. She couldn't bear to disappoint him. Thinking back to the moment she'd awakened this morning, she tried to hone in on the hazy images that had lingered when she first opened her eyes. Flashes of the events just after waking distracted her. The decadent sight of Kurt touching himself had driven all other thoughts from her mind.

"I can't remember any dreams," she confessed. "I'm sorry, Dr. Foster."

"Don't strain so much. Let your mind relax." His fingers tracked over her furrowed brow, smoothing the tension, before he retreated. The profound silence overflowed with his will for her to remember.

His hushed support comforted her. She could almost wrap it around her like a security blanket. Settling into the sofa, she let her consciousness drift. The barest hint of something came to her.

Rebecca's mind turned toward the flicker of remembrance but, like a reflection or a wisp of smoke, it dissipated when she strove to bring it into focus.

"Try again. Don't attempt to remember the whole thing at once. Start small. This will be the hardest step. You've trained yourself to hide your desires and suppress your needs for so long it's become ingrained. It's okay to remember."

The verbal equivalent of holding her hand, his words promised to lead her down a path in the pitch dark. Lost, faltering, all she had to decide was if she trusted him to steer her safely, guaranteeing she didn't get hurt.

"I'm right here. Let go."

She believed his whispered promise.

"Do you remember any colors? Scents? Sounds?"

Sounds? In her mind, she heard a husky, guttural moan. Embarrassed, she angled her head away. Kurt pounced on her slight reaction.

"No, Becca. Don't withhold anything from me. Complete honesty, remember?" He surrounded her hand with his.

"I...I heard a moan." Far away, her face heated.

"Good girl. What else?" The lightest stroke of his hand on hers mesmerized her. His fingertips painted a hypnotic, swirling path over her skin. The sensation made it easier to open her awareness to the brief impressions circling the edges of her consciousness.

"Warmth. It was hot." The burst of Kurt's exhaled breath landed on her cheek.

"Yes. That's good."

Something tickled her memory but she didn't know quite how to voice the emotion.

"Keep going. Don't think, just let it out."

"I felt...protected."

Kurt's hand squeezed hers, bringing the impression she attempted to describe into better clarity. Gaining momentum, her mind recalled more and more details. A faint picture formed in her mind.

"I was inside, a room, someplace I know."

She heard his approval in the satisfied sound he made but he didn't interrupt. On the right track, he left it to her to remember.

"God, you're so close." His barely audible whisper made her wonder if he'd meant her to hear it at all. He sat statue still as though afraid to breathe for fear of breaking her concentration.

And then, abruptly, it was there. Similar to detecting the trick in an optical illusion, once she saw it, there was no going back.

She remembered the place, the scent, the colors, the textures and the sensations though they stayed a bit hazy and ethereal like most dreams. She tensed, wondering if the scene playing in her mind now had inspired Kurt to action this morning.

"You remember."

"Yes." She choked on the weak, thready sound.

"You have to tell me, Becca. Say the words," he commanded

137

her, leaving no room to waffle or escape.

Her eyes opened. The truth made it impossible to glance away from his penetrating stare.

"I dreamt you fucked me on your desk."

With those words, something inside Kurt tore loose. He dropped to his knees and kissed her viciously, need pouring out of him. His hands tangled in her hair. He clasped her to him.

"Yes, you did." Hands trembling, he separated them just far enough to search her emerald eyes. He had to be sure. "Becca, you know what this means?"

She looked dazed by the intensity of the recalled dream. He knew how powerful it had been. Bold enough, clear enough, he hadn't been able to stop himself from jerking off while he watched it. Trying to temper his reactions, not to mention his aggressive kiss, he sat on his heels.

She shook her head in confusion. "It means I want you. You have to know that after the way I've acted the last few days."

A pretty blush tinted her cheeks but he chose to be blunt.

"No. It means I need to take you." He growled against her throat as he licked and bit a trail down the side of her neck. He couldn't help himself.

"W-what?" Kurt heard the disbelief in her question as her brain tried to process what her body already accepted. She leaned forward, closing the gap he'd tried to create but her voice wavered, unsure of his meaning. "Stop. I can't think when you're doing that."

She was right. He drew on a hidden reservoir of restraint, battling the instincts encouraging him to steal the pleasures within his grasp. Damn it, she'd started shivering so hard her teeth clicked together. He had to slow down.

"It's not enough to establish that the Dream Machine records your dreams. For it to be useful, we have to demonstrate how it can aid patients in uncovering their latent desires. I need to test the theory that the subject of your dreams makes you respond more intensely than other stimuli."

The explanation poured out without thought. He'd

considered the feasibility of the process for close to a year before he'd pitched the idea to the review board. Persuading the more conservative members had taken months, and a lot of fast-talking, but he'd finally convinced them to sponsor his research behind the nontraditional invention. In the end, he suspected they'd only agreed because they believed the idea outlandish and impossible.

In fact, once he'd completed the prototype, more than two years from his first conception, he hadn't bothered pitching a human trial to the board. He and Luke had concurred the machine would never become a reality. They'd never have let him test it. Until the break-in. Until that asshole, James Wexford, revealed what a perfect setup they had. They'd grant Becca what she desired most and the role posed no hardship to him.

Now, Luke gathered support for the initial findings even as they created this shred of evidence.

Along the way, the experiment had become secondary to his personal journey but the academic camber of his speech penetrated her shock and denial.

"Take me?" This time disbelief, not confusion, tinged the words.

"Baby, I need to prove fucking me makes you hotter than things you haven't dreamed about." Kurt steeled himself to make her comprehend the ramifications of the situation. If he took this step now, without her complete understanding, she might resent him later. He couldn't stand the thought.

Becca curled up on the sofa, drawing her knees to her chest. She looked him straight in the eye. He hadn't realized the level of confidence he had in her answer until she stunned him.

"No."

Kurt observed her quaking beneath the force of her cravings. Her reluctance baffled him. "Why not? What's wrong?"

"I won't make you fuck me." She cringed but didn't blink. Her eyes had to sting from holding back the unshed tears turning them glassy. Her rigid self-control, stubborn pride and independence wouldn't allow her to cry in front of anyone, never mind taking advantage of any comfort they might offer.

Nothing could have perplexed him more. "*Make* me fuck you?" he asked incredulously.

"I know you don't want me that way. I'm sorry I keep putting you in this position. I won't let you do this for the sake of an experiment. I won't let either of us be cheapened, getting it on just to prove the machine works. There has to be some other way."

A single tear trickled over the side of her face. It hit him in the gut with the impact of a baseball bat. Her delicate hands attempted to shutter her reaction from him. She couldn't contain the tears overflowing her fingers, though. To Kurt, she looked lost and broken like patients he'd seen suffering from the most tragic wounds. Overwhelmed, she sat paralyzed in a ball on his couch in direct contrast to her usual fighting spirit.

Only her pure agony kept him from laughing.

"Becca, I don't know how you got this crazy idea. Would you look at me?" With one hand, he tugged her damp fingers from her high cheekbone while the other grabbed his crotch. His straining cock mashed against the zipper of his pants. The bulge testified to his lust as though he hadn't had an amazing blowjob less than an hour ago.

"You're a healthy man. It's natural for you to get turned on by discussing sexual fantasies. That doesn't mean you want *me*. I've thrown myself at you several times, including this morning, and you've pushed me away on every occasion. You made it clear you aren't interested. I'm sorry. This has to be uncomfortable for you. I'm sorry I dreamt—"

"Stop it!" Wrapping his fingers around her ankles on the sofa, he shook her. "Stop apologizing. Listen to me. I want nothing more than to act out your dream right now." Kurt couldn't reason with the need raging inside him, distracting him.

"I understand. The study is important to you." Her flat eyes focused on his hands clenched around her fine bones.

He refused to let her use the excuse of responsibility or duty to navigate this monumental juncture. She had to take him without pretense or, as much as it pained him, he couldn't have her.

"*You* are important to me, Becca." He snaked his arm around her waist then tugged her closer until they touched. The heat of her abdomen seeped through the seductive silk she'd dreamed of and into his chest as he spread her legs around him.

He thought back to her earlier words, when she'd begun to remember the first dream. *I felt...protected.* She had no idea the gift she'd given him. Better than any lascivious caress, knowing he gave her a sense of security pleased him. It also went a long way toward soothing his conscience for smashing the last of her resistance.

He reached up and cupped her face in his hands. "I want to satisfy you. I *need* to make your dream come true." He swiped a tear from her cheek with the back of his finger.

Kurt studied the drop of moisture as it dangled from his knuckle before licking it off.

Chapter Twelve

Rebecca sat in mute disbelief following Kurt's confession. She'd wanted him for a lifetime though she'd tried to deny it. Her overwhelming infatuation made it easy to pretend he meant the sweet words the way they sounded. But he was generous and kind by nature. He'd never reject her after exposing her girlish crush. Especially since he intended for them to be partners.

Opening her mouth to refuse him again—she couldn't bear being a pity fuck, not even for the sake of their experiment—he surprised her by guiding her mouth to his for a rich, drugging kiss. Her breath caught in her lungs. The simple glide of his lips against hers seemed more intimate than anything else they had done together. Profound and personal, he couldn't fake this kind of emotion.

He convinced her with his touch.

Indignation and pride melted away as her nature took control.

"Mmm." She purred against his mouth as he alternated a long lick with a gentle bite. The contrast captivated her. No one had ever treated her like this before. Rebecca felt cherished and hunted simultaneously. Her body cried out, begging her to stop running and submit.

"That's right, baby. Lean on me." As though he could sense her resistance fading, his hand curled around the nape of her neck. She whimpered when he ended their first, fantastic kiss.

Kurt nestled her tighter against his chest. Then he whispered in her ear, "What did you tell me? While you tried to remember the dream? You said you felt protected. Follow your instincts. You know I'll take care of you. That's the best gift I've been given in a long, long time. Maybe ever. Will you trust me now, Becca? Trust yourself, please."

Every gut intuition confirmed the truth of his declaration. His concern swaddled her, sheltering her. She relaxed. Calm certainty exposed her objections as an excuse.

This situation had nothing in common with her mother and the producer.

Kurt would never hold this experiment against her when it came to their professional relationship. In fact, he'd used the opportunity to help her. Her mind had convinced her heart that he couldn't be attracted to her as a means of protection. Now, she couldn't refuse the barest hint of desperation buried in his plea. It didn't seem possible a man like him would beg for anything. His intensity crashed through all her resistance.

There was only one possible answer. Only one possible outcome.

"Yes." The reply sprung from her lips before she could change her mind. But the truth would never change. "I trust you. I trust us."

"Thank you, sweetheart. Let me make you feel good," he whispered against her ear. "I promise you'll enjoy this."

She whimpered, unsure of what to do. Her mind urged her to back off, to find her self-control but, too far gone, her body refused to listen. There weren't enough cold showers in the world to restore her sanity this time. She couldn't fight both herself and Kurt.

One nod broadcast her surrender. He seized the moment.

He shot to his feet, then collected her into his arms. He crossed the room to his mammoth desk in three strides. When he deposited her on top of the shiny surface, she squealed at the jarring sensation of her backside and thighs landing on the cool desktop.

"Shh, baby." He kept one hand on her, stroking her, steadying her, while he reached into his top drawer to grab something light and flexible.

"What are you doing?" Some of her sense returned while he

checked the object in his hand. She couldn't think when he invaded her space, touching her, igniting riots of overwhelming lust.

"It's a measuring device similar to the probe in the laboratory. Except I designed it for remote use." A wicked grin illuminated his face as he stepped closer once more.

He placed the tool on her outstretched palm so she could study it. The thin-walled cylinder, made out of the stretchy material he'd invented for the probe covering, seemed too insubstantial to be of much use but held up under her exploratory squeezes and tugs. Clear, it provided visibility to the circuits, receptors and transmitters inside but could have fooled her tactile senses if her eyes had been closed. It felt like warm skin. Each end of the tube had an opening.

Suddenly, she realized what he intended.

"You'll wear it, while you..." She couldn't finish the statement. Blood rushed to her face.

"Yes, Becca. It's a sheath. I need to measure your reactions while I fuck you." She hated her telling flinch at his clinical description. Unsure if desire roughened his voice or if he forced himself to the duty, she hesitated to question her judgment. For a moment, when he had kissed her with such honest passion, their connection had seemed like more.

Kurt had never mentioned tenderness or emotion, though. His language revolved around needs. Partnership, desire and mutual satisfaction. All those things, he had pitched to her. She could see that clearly now. Afraid she wasn't wired for such a phlegmatic relationship, Rebecca wished she had more time to erase any lingering doubts but, in all honesty, the answer wouldn't matter.

As she had resolved earlier, she would take what she could get for now and fight to keep her emotions separate. The reminder he also did this to advance the development of the Dream Machine had her body cooling and sanity returning.

"Dr. Foster, I don't know if this is the best way."

"Don't be frightened, Becca." He began to unfasten his pants. "I'll never hurt you."

Maybe not on purpose. When his gaze met hers, the longing

his bottomless grey eyes leveled at her sucked her back into the moment.

"I've waited so long to take you, I'm afraid I can't restrain myself anymore. Tell me now if you can't do this. We can end the experiment right now." As he spoke, he dropped his belt on the carpet then tugged down his zipper.

Rebecca's heart jumped as she caught a flash of tan abs through the gap in his pants. He left the smooth black slacks unbuttoned and open where they rode low on his trim hips. She followed the light sprinkling of hair, visible between the bottom of his bunched-up sweater and the top of his dress pants, to the point it disappeared beneath the opening of his fly.

She didn't say anything at all to discourage him.

She definitely didn't object.

Unmindful of the silk robe gaping open in front, Becca sprawled on the desk, watching him with desperation mirroring his own. Kurt stepped closer, relishing the glimpse of creamy skin between her breasts and the enticing flesh below. Approaching the edge of the desk, he settled her against his chest. Immediately she leaned forward, burying her face against his shoulder, nuzzling into the fuzzy cashmere.

"You like this sweater, don't you?"

She moaned as her hands came up to his chest and fisted in the material. With her cheek pressed against him, she answered. "God, yes. It fits you like a glove. I can see the contours of your chest and the muscles in your arms. I love the way it smells and how it stroked my skin when you accidentally brushed against my arm while handing me case files one day last winter. Ever since then I've dreamed of it. It's so soft, and you're so hard underneath."

When he tucked his hand beneath her chin, forcing her to look at him, a furious blush spread over her skin as though she hadn't meant to say so much.

"I've noticed you watching me when I wear it, Becca. That's why it's my favorite."

"I didn't realize I was so obvious."

"Don't be embarrassed, baby. I loved knowing you looked.

Besides, it made me feel better about lusting after your sexy shoes every day."

Amazed they could laugh at a time like this, warmth spread through him. They suited each other so well. How could he ever detach himself from this experience and go back to the way things had been before?

"I hate that you understand all about me but I never know what you're thinking. You have some walls of your own, Dr. Foster."

The vulnerability in her voice drew Kurt from his thoughts. He considered telling her just what he'd been wondering but it would sound crazy. The realization of all his hard work and the intensity of the moment had made him sentimental. It skewed his perspective.

"Right now, the sweater's got to go. I need to feel you against me."

Reaching behind his head, he grabbed a handful of the cashmere covering his back. He tugged it over his head in one swift movement, mimicking the precise gesture Becca had imagined last night.

The dream had been vivid and detailed. He'd always suspected the depths of her sensual nature but now he'd confirmed a passionate creature dwelled inside her conservative exterior. The intensity of her fantasies had surprised even him.

Turning, he saw her fascination with the simple gesture. He had thought to play into her fantasy, to perform for her, creating this scene exactly the way she had imagined it. But he found the motions came natural to him. Maybe she knew him better than she realized. The things she had envisioned were natural reactions he had in the moment.

In a way, it alarmed him. He remembered her mental image of him—more suave and attractive than he thought of himself—although self-confidence had never been an issue for him. His hair feathered across the collar of the sweater as he yanked it over his head, recalling how the strands had drifted over his forehead sexily in her imagination. He couldn't bear to disappoint her. He wanted to fulfill every desire she'd ever had then inspire a few more.

In reality, she acted more reserved than she had in her dream. She'd had more sexual experience in the past few days than all her life before. It still amazed him she had suppressed those desires for so long. Her absolute trust inspired and awed him. He would settle for nothing less than her complete cooperation, total surrender to the moment.

"Come on, Becca. Touch me. Do what you've dreamed of. I want to be your fantasy."

With a sound of longing, she reached out and buried her hands in his hair. The way her fingers rubbed his scalp spurred him on. He bowed his head to give her better access. She sighed her approval when the strands ran between her fingers. Forgotten now that she touched him, Kurt tossed the sweater on the floor behind him before closing the tiny gap between them.

Bare chest pressed against bare chest.

They gasped in unison.

Reaching around her waist, Kurt slipped the silk robe, heated by her body, from her while raining light kisses on her shoulders and arms. The retreating hem revealed her glowing skin. The garment pooled on the desk below her. He couldn't resist exploring her body before moving on. As soon as he got naked, he wouldn't be able to hold back. Not this first time, after waiting for years. Once he loosed his control and finally allowed himself to take her, there would be no stopping.

Becca braced herself on her palms. Her elbows locked straight, arms behind her. Delighted, Kurt watched as she threw back her head, reveling in the trail of exhilaration left by his meandering mouth. A wave of possession raged through him. He bit her between her breast and collarbone. He appraised the faint mark then traced the slope of supple skin with his mouth, closing in on her tight nipple.

"Please, more." She moaned then tried to wrap one hand around the back of his neck to position him closer.

"There's no rush, Becca. I'll take care of you, I swear." Despite the tidal currents of ecstasy roaring through his veins, cradling her close soothed Kurt. Soon he would take her. Tasting a woman like this had never been so fulfilling. Every tremor of her breast, every ragged breath or sigh affected him as though it were his own.

Some of them might have been.

Teasing, he flicked the tip of his tongue across her nipple while his hand cupped her other breast. The hard center poked his palm. Becca strained against his mouth.

"It feels good, doesn't it, baby?"

"Yes. More."

She wouldn't be able to deny the pressure building between her legs. He wanted to give her what she needed, what he needed too. But, first, he wanted her to beg. Sucking harder now, he caught her rock-hard peak between his teeth while he trailed his other hand lower, rubbing her belly. Quivering beneath his touch, she thrust her hips at him then tried to clasp his waist with her legs. Obliging her, he stepped into the vee of her thighs, grinding his hard-on against her dripping pussy. Her arousal left a glistening trail across the placket of his dark slacks.

"Dr. Foster, I can't wait. Please, fuck me. Please."

Becca seemed beyond caring about the urgency in her voice. The only color in her face now stemmed from the mantle of passion she wore so well.

"You're beautiful." A sense of wonder filled him. He took one moment just to observe. This instant would be branded on his memory forever.

"Please don't torture me, Kurt. Now. I need to feel you inside me. Fill me."

Her begging and the involuntary use of his name obliterated the last of his restraint. His flesh pulsed, straining to be released. He attempted in vain to calm himself and react as the study dictated. Still suckling her, he shoved his pants off his hips. Having perused her medical files, he knew Becca took the pill. He'd double checked to make sure she'd taken them from where he'd stashed them with the rest of her personal items. They were both in perfect health. He couldn't wait for her to surround him. Skin on skin.

He lifted her ass off the desk just enough to slip the robe out from beneath her and fling it to the ground. Setting her back down, he gestured to the sheath tool clenched, forgotten, in her hand.

"Put it on me." Kurt reminded himself of the intent of this session. He had to obtain readings for the board.

Reaching out tentatively, Becca gripped the base of his erection and squeezed. A moan burst from his chest as his cock jerked in reaction.

"I can affect you, too." The discovery seemed to surprise her although he considered it obvious. He didn't act like this with anyone else. Only with Becca was he so out of control, his sexuality so raw and primal. How could it not be when she greedily measured the length of him with her hands and eyes as though the idea of having his dick buried in her turned her on more than anything she'd experienced before.

"Come on, baby, hurry. There will be time to play more later." Kurt's harsh breathing echoed as he noted the marked contrast of her delicate, porcelain-white fingers on his flushed, straining cock.

Becca stretched the bottom ring of the sheath open with a finger on each side then tried to tug it over the bulging head of his cock. "It's too tight, Doctor."

Her innocent flattery did him in.

"It'll fit just fine." The double meaning brought her worried gaze up to his. He couldn't help but kiss the spot on her bottom lip she nibbled in nervous anticipation.

Guiding her hand, he reached between them to scoop up some of the moisture between her legs. Together, they smeared it over his cock, lubricating it. The slick glide of her hand across his aching member sent sparks through his entire body.

He helped her position the sheath over his slippery hard-on. It gripped him snugger than when he'd tested it out earlier. He should have anticipated Becca's participation would have this effect on him. He made a mental note to build a larger version.

The device enclosed the center of his dick, covering about three inches and leaving more than two thirds uncovered. He'd left the maximum amount of skin exposed to enhance his enjoyment of the moist clasp of her inner muscles. The instant the tool shifted into place, Kurt fisted his hands in her hair. He kissed her roughly, thrusting his tongue deep inside her mouth, swallowing her moans of approval and encouragement.

Easing back until his lips dusted hers as he spoke, he growled, "Tell me what you want, Becca."

"Fuck me, Dr. Foster. I can't wait any longer. Please, now."

"If that's the way you want it, baby…" Kurt swept his wrist behind her. He knocked Becca's arms out from under her but caught her secure against his torso. Pressing her back, he laid her flat on the surface of his dark, gleaming desk. Then he climbed on top of her and notched the purple head of his cock at her soaked entrance.

The moment they touched, she cried out. Electricity flew along his spine when the mouth of her pussy gripped the tip of his raging hard-on. The earlier phases of the experiment had prepared him for her petite build but he didn't have the necessary control to work her open with his fingers first. Besides, that's not the way she'd dreamed it.

For the first time in his life, he couldn't hold back a moment longer. Placing his hands on the tops of her shoulders, he anchored her on his shaft as he thrust. His cock lodged a meager fraction of an inch inside her tight channel.

They both froze, staring at the joining of their flesh.

The sight turned Rebecca on so much it amplified her body's demand for him to bury his hard-on to the hilt inside her, even if she worried it would hurt. She craved the excessive length and girth of his shaft though it intimated her. She squirmed closer, attempting to force him deeper, but he held still. When he ignored her pleas, she leaned forward and bit his lip.

Kurt's gritty laugh sounded as he met her eyes. "Feisty little one. Work with me, sweetheart. Don't want to hurt you. Can't fight us both." His labored breathing fragmented his speech. In that instant she knew what she wanted. Without doubt.

"Take me, Kurt. Make me yours." He surged forward again, advancing down her channel. Filling her in gradual increments defined sweet torture. The flare of pain accompanying each thrust morphed into waves of pleasure as she accommodated him.

Rebecca felt stretched wide, full to bursting, and he had barely breached her. He retreated to rest against her sensitized opening for a moment before piercing once more. With each pass, he sank a little deeper. She cried out every time he left only to be rewarded with more of him when he returned.

This time the ridge of the sheath tool entered her. She went wild, convulsing around the throbbing head of his cock. Hearing his guttural moans in the distance spurred her higher.

Afraid she would come before he'd fused them by burying himself to the root in her throbbing body, she tried again to rush him. He halted her attempt with a restraining hand on her hip. Being pinned beneath him boosted her response. A wave of liquid pleasure rushed along her pussy, easing his way. Kurt withdrew until the clenching muscles ringing her opening hooked around the ridge beneath the head of his cock on the verge of exiting her.

He teased her with shallow twitches in and out, rubbing the bulging tip across her sensitive tissue. Then, with a savage groan, he entered her again in one fierce lunge that drove him nearly to the hilt, spreading the moisture from her weeping entrance to the far reaches of her body. Rebecca writhed on the desk beneath him, crammed so full he must occupy every space inside her.

"God, Becca, you're so damn tight. Open up and take me. Almost there. Take all of me." Kurt rammed inside her once more. Their abdomens collided. Her clit bumped against the smooth, flat plane of muscle above his dick. He impaled her completely.

His body curled over her. He laid his head on her shoulder then licked the side of her neck. His whisper came as his lips glanced the shell of her ear. "Damn, that's good. Your cervix is cradling the head of my cock. We're a perfect fit, Becca."

She moaned when his hard shaft throbbed inside her. "No room to spare." She managed to choke out. His eyes blazed as they roamed over her. He stilled, waiting for her muscles to accept his girth, while her inner walls stretched around him.

"Are you okay, baby?"

For once, she needed to reassure him. He couldn't stop now or she'd die.

"Never better. It's amazing."

The rhythmic undulation of her muscles milked his thick shaft. Her orgasm gathered without the added thrill of him shuttling inside her or touching her clit. She was going to come soon. The sensations coursing through her sparkled, vibrant and violent. Afraid to let them take over, to let them free, she fought against the tide of ecstasy. She didn't want this dream come true to end so soon.

"No, Becca. No hiding. Give me everything." He began thrusting with sharp jerks that forced his pubic bone to stroke her clit on every entry. "Yes, baby. I can feel your body tensing."

She straddled the razor edge of desire as he began to fuck her with long, liquid strokes. The intensity frightened her. What if the boundaries protecting her heart shattered along with her body? She struggled to resist the heat burning like a river of lava through her.

With a feral growl, Kurt opened his eyes. Some primitive instinct clued him in to her plight. He wouldn't allow her to play it safe. He encircled the base of her throat with one hand then increased the angle of his penetration. Bearing down on her, his hips ground against her inflamed flesh, sending sparks straight to her core.

"You're going to come around me." The order contained no hint of a question. He bent low over her then alternated rasping delicious suggestions in her ear with sucking on the lobe. "Show me how much you love my cock. Squeeze the sheath tight and come for me. Give me all of you."

The irresistible combination of his sleek body slamming into her, his scent surrounding her and the arousing words he whispered secured her surrender. His trimmed pubic hair feathered over her swollen clit. His sweat-damped chest slid back and forth across hers.

Kurt grasped her wrists then yanked them over her head. He pinned them with one arm while he increased the tempo and pressure of his fucking. Dipping his head, he bit her neck hard enough to sting but not break the skin. Her pussy clenched in response to his domination. His dick swelled impossibly in turn. Each action furthered the cycle of escalation until something had to give.

"Let go, Becca. Now."

His voice compelled her straining body to obey. Unable to fight anymore, her needs crushed the last shred of her resistance. Her legs clung to his waist. Euphoria washed over her. Her inner muscles clamped around his impaling cock as she screamed his name. The shattering terrified her even as it exhilarated her. Through it all, Kurt held her close until—with one last plunge—he buried himself balls deep and began to come with her.

The rush of his hot semen bathed her spasming pussy with his seed. His hands clasped her hips tight enough to leave bruises but it comforted her to be anchored against him through the hurricane of sensation and emotions swirling around them. He groaned her name when the last of his come sprayed inside her before they both collapsed on top of his desk.

Chapter Thirteen

Together they lay, chests heaving, hearts pounding against each other as they regained their composure. Becca still floated, eyes half-closed, when Kurt rose up on his elbow to brush the dewy hair from her face.

"Are you okay, baby?" He kissed her cheekbone then her lips. Her swollen pussy still hugged his semi-erect dick. The aftershocks of her orgasm set off periodic contractions around him. He wished he could make this instant last forever. Arms shaking from the power of their first joining, he dropped down then buried his face against her breast. She sighed, closing her eyes as though savoring his heaviness, which had to be squashing her delicate frame.

Afraid he had used her too harshly this first time, Kurt retreated enough to examine her but not far enough to separate them. She moaned. Thinking of the way he'd pounded into her, he cursed. What had come over him?

"I should have been more careful, sweetheart." Running his fingertips over the marks he'd left on her wrists, neck, chest, thighs and hips, he realized how violent his need had been. He'd never lost control like that before. Not even when he'd taken women who liked things rough. With an innocent like Becca, he couldn't believe how hard he'd pushed her, how badly he'd wanted to leave his signature, make her sure she belonged to him.

Lost in thought, he didn't realize Becca had begun to stir beneath him until she placed her fingers on his cheek. The gentleness of the gesture underscored the savageness of his appetite for her. He tamped down the impulse to turn his head and nip her fingers. For someone who claimed not to know what he thought, she hit the nail on the head.

"I loved it. All of it." She gazed deep into his eyes as she spoke. He couldn't deny she shared the truth. "You didn't hurt me, Dr. Foster."

How was it possible someone could fuck like her then blush?

Kurt didn't like her shyness around him one bit. Neither did he get pleasure from the use of his title. True, this session was part of the study but the usual pride and satisfaction he enjoyed when a woman deferred to him during sex dissipated.

With Becca, it would take more than a respectful address to satisfy his yearning for her sexual submission. He craved her complete trust, hungered for her to admit more hung in the balance than the damn study.

For them both.

But at the moment, a devilish combination of lassitude and contentment reduced his capacity for argument. Becca's long lashes fluttered when her eyes closed. Her body steeped in the aftershocks of pleasure coursing through it. He loved the way her pussy trembled and twitched around his dick with the remembered force of her orgasm. She looked fragile beneath him, though he knew a wealth of stubborn determination lurked beneath her deceptive appearance.

Hell, his forearm was almost as wide as her neck. He could compare since they rested next to each other on the chilly desktop, which didn't make the most comfortable place to linger now that his adrenaline had receded and awareness of his surroundings had returned.

Kurt separated from her inviting body with a reluctant sigh. Even flaccid, his flesh didn't escape her grasp without effort. Her whimper matched his groan when his cock dislodged. He leaned against the desk, praying his knees would hold. It would be damn embarrassing to fall on his face now.

While he stood collecting himself, a stream of their come dribbled from her pussy in an erotic strand before beading on the glass protecting the antique furniture. Lost in contentedness, Becca didn't appear to notice but Kurt's cock defied the laws of nature to swell once more.

"I think my desk might be ruined forever." He chuckled as the image of Becca lying sated, replete and spread snapped into his memory. Already he had quite a few mental pictures saved. Each one more potent than the last.

"Oh, God, I'm so sorry." With the refinement of a newborn foal, she attempted to coordinate her uncooperative limbs and scoot off. Before she moved an inch, Kurt plastered one hand across her waist, stilling her.

"You misunderstood. I'm talking about the fact that I'll never be able to concentrate when I try to work in my office." He laughed but he couldn't have been more serious. "Every time I sit here, I'll think about this."

The experience had rocked him. True, he'd waited years to have her but the reality had transcended physical rapture. He didn't want to scrutinize the resulting bond they'd developed or the strength of the emotional response sneaking past his guard. He knew better than to let chemical reactions override his logic.

The smirk lifting the corners of Becca's mouth gave him hope. He wanted nothing more than to keep her happy, always. Finally, he'd taken the first steps toward demonstrating the viability of their total life partnership. Kurt lifted her, rocking her limp form in his arms. As he walked through the corridor, he pecked her succulent lips.

"Thank you, Doctor," she murmured then snuggled closer to his pounding heart.

Kurt feared she would once again retreat from him on a personal level in the wake of their release. He refused to lose ground, so he devised a plan to appeal to the academic in her. He had all the components required to prove she needed him. Some unknown combination of genetic traits made them ultimately compatible.

A scientist at heart, she wouldn't be able to refute the cold, hard facts when he illustrated how she responded more intensely to his touch than anything else.

A foreign sense of unease brewed within him. He hadn't seen the data yet. What if they hadn't proved his hypothesis?

What if the universe hadn't just shifted for her the way it had for him?

Never before had he cared if a lover grew tired of their games. He'd watch them walk away with no hard feelings if they wished, though he almost always left first. A typical tryst had a brief lifespan for him. Once or twice with a woman assuaged his appetite. By then he could rule out the possibility of her holding his interest for the long term. However, with Becca, he'd barely scratched the surface. He refused to let her go until he'd had his fill, if ever. He didn't question his burning impulse for her to admit she needed him just as bad.

It was the only way he could bear this overwhelming obsession.

Rebecca drifted along, absorbed in the aftereffects of her encounter with Kurt and the surreal sensation of flying as he carried her toward his quarters. There'd never been a man in her life to sweep her off her feet before him. Not a father and certainly not a lover. Complete reliance on anyone was a novel experience. One she could get addicted to. Expecting him to set her down on his luxurious bed, or in the shower, the laboratory's comfortable but firm examination table caught her off guard.

"Doctor?" Her breathy voice sounded distant to her own ears. The reality of the situation hadn't set in yet. It seemed so much like her dream she kept forgetting it had happened outside her imagination this time.

"Shh. Rest for a minute. I'm going to upload the data from our session." He stroked her shoulder with absent caresses while he adjusted the table beneath her. He angled her until the instrument panels came into clear view then secured her once more, ensuring she couldn't avoid the truth.

Still recovering from the most intense sexual experience of her life, a diminutive whimper escaped Becca as the embrace of the restraints tucked her against the platform. She marveled at the sense of security enveloping her when bound this way. It thrilled her when Kurt restrained her. Her muscles relaxed further, if possible, counting on the straps to catch her. She could let her body rest without worry of falling.

For someone always on the lookout, independent, accustomed to staying alert for possible danger—taking care of herself and others around her—the bonds provided a surfeit of freedom. They forced her to depend on Kurt to protect her and use her well. The wide, plush bands enveloping her arms, legs, torso and even—carefully—her neck soothed and comforted her.

Instead of panic, absolute assurance in Kurt permeated her spirit. Welcoming the chance to lie back for once, to let someone else worry about the details, she yielded to his wishes with faith he would provide for her needs. At peace with this new facet of herself, Rebecca accepted her proclivity for bondage.

He must have sensed her serenity making her boneless beneath his hand because he turned to face her. "I half expected you to have fallen asleep."

The message behind her repose hadn't been lost on him. A smile spread across his face, lighting up his expression. Distracted from his preparations, he began to play with her hair.

"Thank you, Becca," he murmured against her ear. Dipping lower, he imparted a moist caress on her open lips. "Do you have any idea how appealing you are? Naked, bound and exposed to me. Your faith and submission are staggering gifts. I'll do everything I can to deserve them."

Tenderness poured from him, engulfing her in a bright glow of hope and satisfaction. Right now, his approval was the only thing that mattered. He'd given her so much in their short time together, opened the doors of her soul to delights she'd never imagined she'd enjoy or thirst to repeat.

"I want to please you," she whispered.

"You do, sweetheart." Smiling against the curve of her neck, he trailed light kisses next to the thin band encircling her throat.

Emboldened by his show of affection, she persisted. "Not the experiment, Doctor. You've already given me so much insight into my desires. Let me repay you."

As though stung, Kurt jerked away from her.

"Damn it, Becca. For all your pliancy, you still don't understand, do you? There's no debt between us. I wanted this as much as you." His clipped tone bounced around the bright lab. The rapid fluctuation of his moods threw her off balance.

"I know the experiment is important to you." Surprised by his sudden withdrawal, she considered keeping quiet but she wanted him to appreciate her perspective. She goaded him, true, but the new Becca refused to demur. He'd seared away the careful distance that would have stopped her before. This is what he'd get.

Tired of half-truths and innuendo, she had to understand once and for all if his fondness extended beyond their professional relationship. Passion had muddied the water earlier making her perception murky. She refused to live with uncertainty any longer.

"That's not what I meant, though. I want to do something for *you*. The man, not the doctor. What do you want from me, Kurt?"

"Becca, stop." He covered her mouth with his palm as though to prevent her from tripping him over the edge of reason. "You don't understand what you're asking."

She thought he was the one who didn't understand. Frustrated, she cursed her lack of experience. She knew what she felt for him but she couldn't decode the mixed signals he broadcast. He got angry when she implied he fucked her for the sake of the experiment but stopped her from expressing her budding attachment. What other options were there?

Her determination wavered. What if she made a fool of herself?

The scent of his skin made her weak so she obeyed his order for silence. However, she continued her relentless assault on his control. Going with instinct, she bestowed a soft kiss on his palm as if she were a subject paying allegiance to a king. The gesture mitigated some of the unintentional damage she'd done to their easy mood. He withdrew his hand to trace her lips with his finger, eyes softening again.

Regaining some of her composure, she whispered, "Then show me. Make me understand."

As she waited for him to proceed, she couldn't help but taste him. She closed her lips around his finger then sucked on it, moaning when his pupils dilated. The grey depths of his eyes looked like a sky reflecting a coming storm. Her pussy responded to his show of desire. Longing blossomed inside her.

How could she possibly want him again so soon?

"You need a demonstration of how we affect each other." The pensive statement made it seem he spoke to himself. "First, the easy part. I'll confirm your body responds more to my touch than to other stimuli."

Rebecca groaned. She didn't need Kurt to validate his skills as a lover. She'd already admitted he brought her more pleasure than she'd ever dreamed possible. She wondered about the effect she had on his mind and heart but the evident determination in his stance made it clear he wouldn't be swayed from whatever course he'd set for them.

After tugging his lab coat over his bare muscles, he displayed the readings from their session the day before on the monitor in front of her.

"Look, Becca." He pointed to the line on the top half of the screen then assumed his lecture tone as though he had to stay detached in order to make it through this lesson undistracted. That he relied on the crutch gave her hope. "This is the baseline average of your response from initial touch to orgasm during our trials yesterday."

Even her newfound boldness couldn't prevent her face from heating as she recalled coming again and again while he observed her. Rebecca whimpered.

In a dangerous mood, Kurt narrowed his eyes, almost daring her to object. Unsure of what had displeased him, she concentrated on staying still and relaxed in the grip of the restraints although her earlier sense of security had dissipated somewhat. Unqualified surrender would be so much easier if his feelings were clear to her.

"Now, the results from today's session are being added to the graph." His grin turned sinful as the readings spread out in a line trending blatantly above the baseline.

"Compare the level of your arousal from beginning to end. Today's sample is higher at every single data point." A groan reached her ears as he performed a quick review of the results.

They must have confirmed his experience because Kurt nodded to himself. Then he pointed out a marked difference. "Here, just before and during orgasm in this afternoon's session, the line spikes off the charts. The subject's vaginal muscles squeezed the sheath tool with enough pressure to compress it to the absolute minimum thickness."

She gulped, squashing a plea for a repeat performance of his thick cock tunneling through the muscles that had clenched around it. Instead, Rebecca waited for him to continue, to see where he took this line of reasoning.

How could he keep it physical and ignore any hint of emotion?

"You've completed many successful experiments as my assistant. You're an outstanding researcher. Although there aren't enough records for a complete scientific study, this is enough to form a theory." He paused, and then asked in his most patient voice, the one he reserved for slow students, "What does this tell you, Becca?"

She resisted putting herself in a one-down position by admitting her desire for more if he wouldn't do the same. Reluctant to divulge her imprudent infatuation with the doctor—though it was plain as day to her, Dr. Foster and, soon, the rest of their colleagues on the review board—she drew on her professionalism and reserve. She avoided the obvious answer to his question with tact.

"There are a number of theories one could generate based on the given data set."

Afraid Kurt would recognize her cool logic for a convenient mask to cower behind, she maintained a straight face. Either he believed her or he couldn't resist playing along simply to make her admit the truth. Why would he do this? Why make their relationship more awkward if he didn't return her affection?

"True. Tell me a few," he commanded. Crossing the room to the whiteboard, he uncapped a dry erase marker and prepared to take notes. This familiar routine called to mind many previous brainstorming sessions despite the fact she'd never been naked and tied open for his perusal during one before.

Rebecca dissected the question as she would in any other

case, hoping to gain some distance from the intensity of the situation. "The baseline involved manual stimulation by the subject whereas, during the trial, an outside source aroused the subject."

"What else?" he pushed.

"The object inserted in the subject's vagina was larger during the trial than in the baseline creation phase, which could have been the cause of the subject's enhanced response."

Her mind screamed for her to stop talking. She made the situation worse with every syllable she uttered but the researcher in her couldn't help but uncover the flaws inherent in his comparison. Besides, she didn't want to admit either to herself or Dr. Foster that she would never obtain sexual fulfillment this complete in all her life once the experiment finished and Kurt reverted to being her boss...no, partner. Not her lover.

"Any other discrepancies, Becca?" Kurt's arched eyebrow dared her to come up with more reasons to deny their connection. After all, he intended to prove her wrong.

"You're so hot." The thought slipped out before she could translate it into scientific language.

At least he didn't laugh in her face. Although, judging by his lips clamped together and his shaking shoulders, it required monumental effort on his part not to. She scrambled to recover.

"W-What I mean is, the inserted device during the baseline creation had a much cooler average temperature than the one used during the trial this afternoon." The memory of his heated flesh scalding her chest, between her thighs and inside her pussy made Rebecca shiver as though she might freeze without his searing touch. The band across her abdomen seemed to constrict when her hips shifted at the memory of Dr. Foster fucking her.

Kurt jotted down the last of her ridiculous assertions with hasty strokes before adding his own theory in bold, printed letters.

"The subject responded more intensely due to her underlying attraction to her partner."

Snapping the lid on the marker, he deposited it in the tray

before spinning to face her. In the small space, he crossed to her side in two steps.

"And I'll prove it to you."

Chapter Fourteen

When Rebecca opened her mouth to ask how Kurt intended to confirm his theory, he silenced her with a brutal kiss. This time she thrust inside the inviting warmth of his mouth, parrying jabs of his tongue with her own. Dazed by the rush of pleasure, she didn't realize he'd started to retreat until their lips separated with a smack.

As though he could read her mind, he said, "You'll see."

He rummaged through the cabinet behind her, hunting for God knew what. She drummed her fingers on the table. Not a very patient person, curiosity got the better of her. "What are you looking for?"

"One of my more recent inventions. I hadn't intended to use it yet but this is a perfect opportunity for a test run."

She strained against the bonds to lift her head but couldn't see what contraption he'd retrieved no matter how she squirmed and struggled against the straps. After removing another component from the closet, he crossed to the sink then tinkered with something on the countertop. As he worked, he spoke in his seductive, midnight tone.

"So, we have as possible alternate theories that the inserted device in today's session was bigger, hotter and remotely operated as compared with the method used in the baseline creation session, correct?"

When she didn't respond, Kurt pivoted. His dark eyes bored into her, daring her to defy him.

"Yes, Doctor."

"Then this should help disprove your suggestions." He

offered a deflated sphere, constructed of his flesh-colored material with a slender tube protruding from the back, for her inspection.

"What...what is it?" Her stomach did summersaults at the thought of yet another of his devious implements.

"I don't have a name for it yet. Maybe you can suggest one after you try it out." His dimples reappeared. The straps sank into her flesh as she squirmed beneath them. Judging by the sight of his cock rising higher with every heartbeat, Rebecca deduced he'd relish debunking her hypotheses.

"God, baby. Look at you." Kurt's eyes raked down her body, kindling an inferno of need.

Her nipples hardened beneath his appraising stare, her mouth fell open and she began to rock against the clasp of the restraints. She surrendered to the passion flooding her.

"You enjoy being my subject, don't you?"

Her eyelids fluttered closed as she tried to bring herself to refute his claim. It was no use. "Yes, Doctor."

"Good girl." Kurt patted her hip as he circled the table to stand between her legs. "I bet if I push my finger into your pussy right now you'll be soaking wet. Should we test out that idea, too?" Without waiting for an answer, he slid one digit inside her. "You're still so snug. Even after taking my dick less than an hour ago."

Her moan reverberated off the white linoleum floor and the stainless steel cabinets, which amplified the animalistic sound. Kurt removed his finger from her grip. As she watched, he tasted the remnants of their desire. Slipping his finger in his sexy mouth, he ingested the mix without glancing away from her, not even to blink. What would the mingled flavors be like?

"I love the way you taste, Becca," he murmured as she strained beneath him on the table, desperate to get closer. "Soon I'll have you again but, for now, we have work to do."

Rebecca had lost track of their intent. Struggling to focus, she grasped for a shred of self-control. He returned her to the task at hand with a light slap on the inside of her thigh. The resulting sting didn't really hurt but it got her attention. Instead of shrieking or protesting, another moan escaped her when the spark of arousal ran up her leg.

Kurt began a narrative documenting his actions. He dictated each step of his procedure as he had on the more mundane experiments she'd assisted him with over the years. The familiarity of the situation contrasted with the building tension she braced herself to contain.

"First, I've rolled the device into a thin cylinder of material. I'll take the moisture seeping from your slit to lubricate it." Hearing him speak such blatant, unprofessional and arousing words aimed at her was surreal. His dirty-talk inflamed her already rioting senses but his speech couldn't compare to the initial brush of his fingers against her moist, swollen flesh.

"Mmmmm."

Kurt doused the end of the device in the copious secretions coating her pussy. The rolled up material would be smaller than his erect staff but the anticipation, while it hovered a hairsbreadth from entering her, drove her wild. As though he understood, and couldn't resist toying with her, he paused.

"I've prepared the device and will now begin the insertion." Kurt aligned the blunt tip of his creation with her channel. He embedded it in her pussy with a single long stroke.

"Yes, Becca?"

Unaware she'd cried out for him, she couldn't say if she'd begged him to stop or do it again. Every nerve ending stood at attention. Tender from their earlier session but craving the dark pleasures he could subject her to, she teetered with indecision.

Before she had recovered from the intrusion, Kurt continued. "As you can see, this tube connects to the portion of the device buried in you. I'm about to hook it to temperature regulation module I've already connected to the sink faucet. It's accurate to a one-hundredth of a degree."

What did he have planned? Nerves made her jittery but only because she intended to control her reactions this time.

She would demonstrate she could disconnect her emotions if he could. His impromptu exhibition turned her on enough she had a shot at corroborating one of her theories. This could make her hotter than fucking him had.

Liar! She suspected the set up only made her this horny

because he ran the show but she didn't have to admit that to him.

Already, her inner muscles clamped around the device lodged in her pussy as it began to unfurl. Frustrated, she wished Kurt's long, veined cock replaced it instead, throbbing deep inside as it stretched her.

He finished calibrating the device while Rebecca studied the thermometer unit with her three remaining brain cells. All the others already clamored for release. She hadn't seen him lay the component beside her trapped arm on the examination table.

Unparalleled pleasure dulled her keen observation skills. Kurt scrambled her logical and controlled mind. Always keeping herself distanced from possible distractions on the path to achieving her goal, she had pushed aside everything else to concentrate on the most important thing in her life. Sometimes, that had been studying for a test, working at the practice or protecting her family. Now, what she wanted most was for him to fuck her again.

He returned to her side then raised the section of the table beneath her hips until she reclined at a shallow angle. Shaken from her meandering thoughts, the slight tilt encouraged blood flow to her head. The resulting tingle added to the arousal building within her.

"I have a valve system rigged into the tubing. I realize it's too close to your body for you to see—tied as you are—but trust me, it's there."

Comprehension dawned. Her eyes winded in shock at his nefarious scheme. He wouldn't. One glimpse at the smug expression on his face assured her that he would. She could say no right now and he'd allow her to leave. She could end it, but she didn't want to. If she stayed, she granted her permission to proceed with all his arousing tests.

Nodding in acceptance when she refused to object, Kurt forged ahead. "In a moment, I'm going to open the valve." His impressive erection strained against his abdomen. "The temperature gauge is set to five degrees above the average body heat reading the sheath tool recorded when I fucked you on my desk earlier."

The mention of their erotic interlude forced more cream past her tensing muscles. The cool breeze of the laboratory's air-conditioning highlighted the wet trail leading toward her ass.

"When I open the valve, warm water will begin to fill the device inside you. Are you ready, Becca?"

"Yes, Doctor." God, if he didn't do something soon she would beg again. She needed him to ease the ache inside her. The glint in his eye aroused her suspicion. He wouldn't make her wait before he allowed her release, would he?

Kurt rested against the side of the table then reached between her legs. His solid, straining cock branded the outside of her thigh as he opened the valve. She wished she could extend her hand and touch his engorged flesh, stroke it, but no matter how she tugged, the strap held her wrist immobile. Before she thought to ask him to free her arm, the slide of warmth running up the channel of her sex ripped her attention away.

It reminded her of the way his hot come had coated the walls of her pussy. She bucked within the limits of the bonds, her muscles reacting with wild flexes. Her body strained, eyes squeezed shut, as the heavy liquid and heat rushed inside her. "Oh, yes. Kurt, more. More."

He didn't grant her wish. Instead, he gave her a moment to adjust to the initial sensation. Once her gasping reverted to slower, deeper breaths, she realized that what felt like Niagara Falls pouring inside her was more of a slow, steady stream. She opened her eyes to find him scrutinizing her reactions.

"Damn, baby, maybe I'm wrong after all." His voice resounded with disappointment. "Maybe you're amazingly responsive and it didn't matter who fucked you earlier."

As if on cue, the machines behind him beeped. The initial readings had activated the sensors. He spun around to inspect the monitor receiving input from the inserted device. Although her apparent arousal soared above the readings measured in the baseline session, the new line tracking across the screen fell far short of the one from their reenactment in his office.

"Then again...maybe not." Placated, Kurt grinned while

noting the output on his clipboard. Then he increased the flow into the device.

The moment of uncertainty that had clouded his features brightened something at the core of her soul. If she imagined his reactions to her, why would he care if she wanted him specifically? Before she could reason any closer to the answer, he drew her attention to the pleasure saturating her.

"Do you know what's going to happen, Becca?" He spoke in an intimate growl against her ear. His hard-on throbbed against her hip as he leaned over her. In subtle arcs, he thrust himself into the side of her leg, stroking his arousal over her skin between the restraints.

Clearing the haze threatening to cut off her judgment, she realized the pressure inside her continued to amplify as the stretchy material of the device unrolled and bulged with water.

"It's going to fill me." She groaned in realization.

"Yes, baby. It's going to expand to take up as much room as you can give it. The flexible material will conform to your shape. You're going to be stretched and packed until you can't stand anymore. It's going to be warmer and bigger than my cock." He nipped her earlobe before retreating with a groan. "I don't want to influence the readings by touching you."

Rebecca whimpered. "I'm going to burst." The water trickled incessantly, increasing the size of the object bit by bit. She squirmed, flexing and relaxing her vaginal muscles to accommodate the expanding ball.

Kurt's strained laugh cut through her protest. "We've just begun. You'll see, you can take a lot more than you think."

As the volume increased, the weight and force inside her ballooned. His palm slid over her abdomen, testing the size. She couldn't help but moan.

"I bet that feels good, doesn't it? Shit, I can't keep my hands off you." He checked the monitor to ensure levels of her recorded pleasure remained lower than during her dream reenactment before he continued to goad her. "Do you want to come for me, sweetheart?"

She wheezed now as her muscles rippled against the bulge inside her, causing it to shiver and quake. The resulting waves bounced around, enhancing the powerful pleasure forcing her closer to release.

Kurt wouldn't need the monitor to alert him to her impending orgasm. In another second, she'd start screaming her need. She trembled on the razor's edge of completion when he dialed down the flow of water entering her.

"No! Please, I'm so close."

"You're so petite, I don't want to stretch you too far." He leaned in for a closer look. His finger nudged around the opening of her pussy, between it and the device, testing the fit. The motion triggered a sensual sloshing against her sensitized nerve endings. She groaned as the rhythmic squeezing of her own internal muscles reflected and amplified the ripples.

"Did that hurt?" His head raised as he peered at her in alarm.

"No, feels so good. Please. A little more."

"You've had enough, Becca. This is a new invention. I don't want to push you anymore. In fact, I can see a slight protuberance in your abdomen." His cock jerked when he relayed his observations. She could tell he loved the sight. She watched the drop of pre-come oozing from the slit in the head. It beaded, doubling in size before dripping down the crown. His hand hovered near his engorged dick for a moment as if he resisted the urge to take the tight flesh in hand.

"Do it, please. Keep going." The evidence had to be valid. They had to finish what he'd started. Amazing as this felt, hovering on the edge of bliss, it couldn't compare to their previous experience.

Even if Kurt wasn't interested in her, the results needed to be irrefutable. This might be the single chance she had to corroborate her deepest longing without having to lay her heart on the line.

"Becca, look at me." He commanded. "Are you sure?"

Heavy lidded, brimming with pleasure, her eyes met his. She nodded once.

"The object inside you now is stretching you completely. It's far bigger than my cock and warmer." He paused in concern when a violent shudder ran through her body.

"Hurry," she whispered. "Finish it."

"The evidence is clear, baby. You want me more than this. Look at the proof." Dr. Foster pointed at the glowing lines streaking across the display. "Say it, Becca. Tell me you want me."

She thought she might explode. "Please just let me come. Touch me."

If she could think of anything except the pleasure driving her mindless she might have been mortified for begging.

"No."

Rebecca whimpered, her hands clenching into fists at her sides. He couldn't be pushing her away again. None of it made sense. Why did he keep doing this?

"I will not let you come until you say it. Now." Kurt wouldn't relent.

"What?" Her desire-fogged mind hadn't grasped his request.

"Tell me you need me." His fierce command forced her to speak her deepest desire. No matter how badly she yearned for him to stroke her clit, to push her over the edge, he wouldn't release her from this trap until she admitted she wanted him more than he wanted her. Though it hurt, and embarrassed her, she couldn't hide the truth.

But in a terrifying moment of clarity, her stubborn pride decided to rebel. She hated that she'd pleaded for release and still he'd denied her. Again.

Didn't he know how hard it was for her to ask? She would claim at least a little victory by feigning indifference as much as possible in her current state. "Could be...the lack of remote stimulation...I proposed in...theory three."

She fought to choke out the words as her body trembled. Her breath sawed in and out of her lungs. So close, she teetered on the brink of a powerful climax, poised to fall into the oblivion of ecstasy.

Kurt growled. "Fine."

With a savage yank, he reached in the drawer built into the table and removed a gadget. Still, the water flooded her until Rebecca feared she might spring a leak. If her hands had been free, she'd have reached down to circle her clit with the one caress it would take to fly. No matter the repercussions.

"I'll put this on you, Becca. It's a clitoral vibrator designed to attach to the base of many of my inventions. You'll come for me. Then, I'll make you admit it. I won't stop until you scream out your desire for me. You'll shatter in a million pieces and still it won't be as good for you as when I fucked you. We both know it."

When she met his troubled stare, Rebecca wondered if she'd injured more than his ego. Suddenly, she wished she'd capitulated. She'd only wanted to horde a sliver of her pride for later. Of course, it was true.

Kurt aroused her more than anything else she could imagine. The fear crowding out her will to submit stemmed from the knowledge he didn't reciprocate her emotional investment. To give up control—succumb to her wild desires—when he didn't, distressed her.

While she struggled with her emotions, Kurt waited with his legendary patience. When she focused on him once more, he held the tool a fraction of an inch beyond her reach. He switched it on. A loud buzzing joined their labored breathing and Rebecca's occasional whimpers. Yet she wouldn't give him what he wanted.

Each pounding heartbeat that passed carried her a step further from the ledge she'd toed as her desire ebbed a tiny bit. A minute more and her reactions would be back under control.

"Why do you fight it, baby?" he whispered. "I'm sorry. I won't let you lie to yourself."

With a grimace that could have been disgust or desire, he clipped the vibrator to the base of the invention. As soon as it touched her ripe clit, she exploded. The walls of her pussy stretched and contracted at the same time. The vibrator jiggled the contents of the device. The motion drove her over the edge. She writhed in ecstasy.

After what might have been several minutes, the pulsing attachment chafed her sensitive nerve endings.

Bound, she couldn't escape the intense sensations.

Her eyes snapped open and found Kurt staring at her, his gaze boring into her. His purple cock overshadowed his balls, drawn tight against his body, as he witnessed her plight.

"T-turn it off." Her sharp entreaty bordered on hysteria as the vibrations began to turn from satisfying to unbearable. "PLEASE!"

"No."

"Oh God, please Kurt. Please turn it off." She begged shamelessly as her stretched pussy quivered and shuddered around the still swelling intrusion and the buzzing on her clit.

"Say it."

She couldn't understand what he meant. The intensity of the vibrations shut down her brain.

When she hesitated, he reached over and resituated the attachment against her clit. The overstimulation morphed into impossible pleasure at his hands. Rebecca's traitorous body tensed again. It hurt, but the wonder underlying the discomfort would soon overtake any lingering sting.

Her head thrashed within the confines of the restraint.

"Tell me how much you want me, baby. Not this damn piece of plastic. You want my cock, don't you?" As he spoke, he realigned the vibrator with her pussy to provide a modicum of relief from the direct contact while driving her arousal higher.

Juices streaming from her saturated the invention. She was going to come again but no machine could satisfy her craving for the doctor. He rotated the base of the invention, transforming the liquid into a whirlpool of pleasure.

"Now, Becca."

"Kurt! I need you. Loved it. Fuck me." She screamed his name as she came apart.

A low groan rumbled from his chest as he flicked the valve, allowing the water to rush out through a second, much larger, drain tube. In an instant, the liquid abandoned her, leaving her empty, hollow.

Kurt restrained himself until the device deflated enough to slide out of Becca's pussy with a torrid slurp before he mounted her bound form. Staring into her eyes, forcing her to acknowledge the truth in his own, he annunciated his words.

He couldn't afford for her to misunderstand.

"The second part of my demonstration is harder. Believe this. I want your body every bit as much as you want mine. I've never possessed so little control with a woman. I have to fuck you right now."

Kurt slammed into her. Her pussy wrapped around him like a moist electric blanket after soaking up the heat of the fluid he'd pumped inside it. His entire being shuddered with the memory.

His invention would have seemed gigantic in contrast to the meager toy she had in her nightstand drawer. Her resilient muscles conformed around his cock even after they'd been stretched but he plunged balls-deep into her with a bit less resistance now.

The freedom of motion and the compulsion to squelch her defiance drove him to pummel her greedy pussy, goading him with rhythmic contractions. Compared to this, the fucking in his office had been gentle. Watching her come had pushed him to his limits.

Standing between her legs, he gripped the black straps crisscrossing her porcelain skin for leverage. He thrust his rock-hard cock inside her with driving strokes as his lab coat flapped around him.

"God, baby, I can't wait. You destroy me." Leaning forward, he ground his face into her neck, taking her flesh between his teeth. His sac drew flush with his body, preparing to release his load into her throbbing channel.

Kurt tensed between her legs, groaned and bucked one last time. His cock flared, the ridge of the tip growing more pronounced before jets of his come threw Becca into another shattering orgasm beneath him.

She never once complained or questioned his intentions, a fact that delighted him. Her natural submissive traits, open and expressive, brought him joy the likes of which he'd never been blessed to experience before. He treasured every minute of their journey. And he'd never come so hard in his life.

What the hell was he going to do when they completed the experiment?

Chapter Fifteen

Rebecca registered Kurt unbinding her in the dim recesses of her mind. Her thoughts whirled. Once again, the honest passion she'd glimpsed in his fierce expression when he filled her had shattered her preconceptions. No matter how he steered her from entangling emotions in their tryst, he desired her for more than the experiment. She'd received her training in psychology from the best. Patterns had begun to emerge in his behavior. She wouldn't doubt her instincts any longer.

Regardless of the mind-blowing pleasure of her previous multiple orgasms, the difference had been obvious the moment he'd penetrated her. Having him inside her—on top of her—when she came catapulted the experience beyond euphoric.

He was right. Nothing could compare to the ecstasy their union imparted. Not only for her but also, she suspected, for him. The lightness invading her soul, giving her hope for what they could build together, might not be prudent but she couldn't resist it. He stood next to her, holding out his hand.

"Come on, baby. Let's move somewhere more comfortable." His sated tone hitched around a yawn he couldn't quite stifle.

For once in her life, her inhibitions relaxed enough to make demands, to ask for what she wanted but didn't need. She lifted her arms toward him and smiled.

"Carry me."

If her request startled him, he hid it well.

He laughed. "You make me weak, I hope I don't drop you."

They both knew there was no chance of that. Grinning, he bent to enfold her in his strong arms. She loved the way his lean muscles cupped her back and knees. Safe in his embrace, it seemed he'd never let her down.

He carried her to his room with such care she felt cherished and fragile. Unbidden optimism for their future suffused her. Could she have it all? A career, hot sex and the man she'd adored for years?

Following her onto the bed, he tucked her against his brawny chest. It still rose and fell with elevated respiration. Enchanted by the sound of his racing heart, Rebecca nuzzled closer.

After their breathing had returned to normal and her skin chilled, Kurt shifted to tug the blankets around them. He stared at the ceiling instead of meeting her gaze when he asked, "So, are you convinced of my theory?"

His unusual hesitancy made it sound as though he dreaded the answer but had to ask anyway. His sheer bullheadedness wouldn't allow him to recede without her total surrender but her will to fight had vanished anyway. She wavered in deciding how much to reveal about her newfound convictions until she'd had the chance to mull over the repercussions then devise a strategy for convincing him.

"I admit I want you. The evidence is conclusive on that point." Her response trickled out as she selected each word but she couldn't see any way around the truth. It was plain for anyone to see.

"That's a start, Becca." Kurt rolled, forcing her to her back while he levered himself up on one elbow to peer at her. "But what about the second part of my demonstration? I want you, too. Don't ever doubt it." As he spoke, he maintained constant contact with her skin. He brushed wisps of hair from her face, traced her lips and eyebrow with a fingertip.

She struggled to decide whether his actions or words soothed her most while marveling at their closeness, which left her speechless.

"How could I not want you? I wish you could see yourself as I do. You're beautiful as well as smart."

The sweetness he'd never before revealed stunned her silent. Mistaking her lack of response for disbelief, intense determination invaded his speech.

"Do you think I'm so poor a lover I can't hold myself back? I've never lost control like that before."

Confusion clouded her rationality. He thought he'd disappointed her? If his performance had been him rushing to the finish, what would it have been like if he'd been calm? Somehow, she was glad he hadn't been. Her ability to affect the stolid doctor exposed his latent desire. Signs any rational observer couldn't deny tipped the scales.

"I believe you." She laughed as weight lifted from her soul. "I'm not sure I understand but, I think, I actually believe you."

Dropping his head until their brows met, he smiled slow and huge as his hands came up to frame her face. "You have no idea how long I've waited to show you. I've craved you from the beginning but you weren't ready."

Startled, she scanned his face for any sign of deception and found none. All this time, she'd admired him from a distance but her focus on goals acted as a convenient blinder. The epiphany liberated her. She understood what Kurt had meant about freeing her desires. He'd told her she needed to learn to trust, accused her of lying even to herself.

"You were right, Kurt. I wouldn't admit how much I missed in my life. I was too scared." Her eyes filled as she ached for all the things she might have experienced by now. She buried her face in the light sprinkling of his chest hair as she wrapped her arms tight around his solid back. Allowing herself the luxury of a few tears of joy, she leaned on his shoulder. She refused to veil her emotions a moment longer.

"Thank you for giving me the confidence to accept this part of myself. And the push to explore." Everything came together at last. She had all the tools necessary to reach her aspirations. She had earned her partnership in the firm. Soon she would start a career, hoping to help even one person suffer less. Kurt's invention would be successful and her sister would attend Elembreth. She might even have a chance at forging a lasting relationship with the man of her dreams.

"I'll never forget all you've done for me. Never." Burying her face against his neck, she absorbed his warmth and surrendered to complete relaxation.

In a rush, guilt swamped Kurt. He'd pressed Becca into admitting her weakness and confronting it under the guise of benevolence. Sickness cramped his gut as he appraised his true intentions.

He wanted to have her for his own.

God, he'd stood back and allowed the board to persuade her that this whole escapade had been her idea in the first place. He might as well have flat-out lied for the damage his passive omission could do now.

Disgust clawed at him, tainting what should have been one of the best moments of his life. She'd praised him for his altruism in making her face the truth when he'd been the one lying to himself all along. He couldn't hide from the facts now.

He'd succeeded in convincing Becca he desired her but she would never continue to believe it if she discovered how he'd played on her inexperience and deceived her. Having her in his bed for the duration of the experiment no longer qualified as a satisfactory result. He craved all of her—companion, partner and lifetime lover—and the knowledge she accepted him wholly in return. Never before had he met someone with such compatible desires. Now he stood to lose his perfect woman because of his dishonesty.

For a moment, he considered blurting out his revelation. Fuck the board. He'd confess his foolishness then offer his pitiful excuse. He'd only done it because he couldn't think of another way to break through the barriers she'd erected to constrain her nature.

But her bravery outstripped his by a mile. He couldn't chance her rejection.

Meeting her seeking lips, he kissed her with aching delicacy. He couldn't risk losing her now. Instead, he'd ensure she never found out. For close to an hour, he cradled her pliant form while she dozed on his chest.

She could enter the first stage of REM sleep any minute. The knowledge finally prodded him from his sleepy paradise. With quick and efficient movements, he attached her to the

Dream Machine for a second night of data gathering.

The reminder of his deception seasoned the moment with a bitter flavor. Trust forged the strongest partnerships but he didn't deserve hers.

Collapsing beside her, the consequences of his earlier admission slapped him in the face. She *did* make him weak. He couldn't help but gather her to him again, to savor her lissome body draped across him though her gratitude had made him feel like a cheater in a championship race.

The purgatory of his conflicted mind refused to calm long enough for him to join in her angelic slumber, so he contented himself with the silkiness of her hair against his cheek for several hours while he wondered what she dreamed of tonight.

CB

"Wake up, baby." Kurt mumbled as he nudged her shoulder. Groaning, she tucked her face against his chest and snuggled closer, as though unwilling to give up the comfort soaking deep into her bones to face the reality of the day.

If he didn't escape in the next ten seconds, neither one of them would be getting up anytime soon. Though Becca tempted him to linger and revel in her surrender, he had a ton of work to do. He had to scramble to assemble a plan. She protested when he rolled to the edge of the bed, but remained half-asleep as he removed the diodes.

"You recorded my dreams again." Her drowsy statement held no alarm. The lack of concern at his intrusion marked a change so drastic Kurt realized just how much the events of the past few days had affected her. Hell, the experience had changed him irrevocably as well.

The indelible marks she made on him would continue to darken now. No longer worried about his reaction to her fantasies, he postulated the more intense yearnings lurking in her subconscious would emerge. Bits and pieces of her dreams from the night before flashed through his memory and he shivered in anticipation.

His lust didn't prevent his conscience from berating him,

though. Torn, he reached down to release the receptor from her pussy, hissing out a breath when the heat of her arousal scorched his knuckles. God, she was so wet already.

The sound of surprise drew her attention. She roused enough to peer at him as he hovered over her, naked and sleep rumpled. Sure his hair stood on end, a self-conscious twinge encouraged him to rake his fingers through his hair. Ridiculous for a man of his age and experience to act like a teenager with his first girl.

Becca brought her hand to his, rumpling what he hadn't smoothed anyway. "Only a man could make this sexy."

When she laughed, he thought of a million corny song lyrics. What the fuck was wrong with him!

As he watched her come alive, Kurt's dick hardened. She stretched, exposing her neck and thrusting her full breasts up in invitation. He stumbled back a few steps to ensure he didn't grab her and make love to her right then. First, he had to review her dreams, plot a course for their research and create a presentation for the board meeting.

The day sparkled with promise. If everything went well, they'd have irrefutable evidence to petition the board to move to stage two of the experiment at tomorrow's meeting. They already had a strong case, but one more example would clinch the deal.

Kurt found himself devising reasons to delay the proceedings, extending this opportunity to explore with Becca. Maybe he could forge a bond strong enough to transcend their involvement in the project as well as their practice if he had more time.

Things hadn't worked out according to his initial plan. First, he'd been sure a few days with Becca would wipe this crazy obsession out of his system. Then, when he realized how well-suited they were, he'd taken for granted she would recognize it too. His lust had warped his judgment for the first time in his life. He was meticulous, a planner, a man of logic but, when it came to Becca, even his strengths unraveled.

Luke had tried to warn him. Why hadn't he listened?

"I need some time to get everything ready for today." If he

didn't separate them he might do something unwise, like explain all the sordid details of the situation and pray to every god he didn't believe in she would forgive him.

It was an impossible risk to take. He had to pursue the only viable option—continue with the agenda and hope their passion could overcome his deception.

Off balance, he glanced away from the insightful gaze Becca leveled on him. He jerked in surprise when she breached the gap between them to kiss his cheek. "I'll go take a shower, then I need to check in with my sister. Can I borrow your phone?"

"Of course." He retracted his arm before it could return her embrace. He had to think. Instead, he deflected the motion into a vague gesture aimed at the pile of clothes in the corner. "It's in the pocket of my pants."

As soon as he heard the spray of water, he plugged in the headphones and began to observe the sequences. As much as he'd like to postpone the board meeting, they had more reason than ever to proceed. They already had the evidence necessary to prove the validity of the machine's recordings. Now, he had some time to survey the depth of Becca's sensuality.

Their time was limited. The board could deny the continuation of the experiment if they weren't convinced the benefits outweighed the risks or ethical concerns surrounding the study. Desperation compelled him to make the most of the experience despite his fear of digging himself a hole by abusing Becca's trust. Sure, she was willing, but the guilt over his dishonest intentions festered beneath his lust.

His fascination overpowered reason. He'd set the course and they'd see it through.

In order to take her to the next level, he'd have to bank on every bit of progress they'd achieved to date while making her as comfortable as possible. Not give her cause to throw hurdles between them. Therefore, he resolved to postpone any discussion of his plans for their personal partnership until the study concluded.

They would conduct the initial phase of today's session from this private room where she could relax. The detail and inventiveness of her fantasies playing before his eyes inspired him to drive her higher and push her boundaries further.

The need to fetch her from the shower and plow his aching cock into her drenched pussy caused him to grit his teeth until his head ached. He distracted himself by preparing his notebook then finishing the documentation of her REM stages. He hoped the normalcy in analyzing work-related information would bring him back to his senses.

It didn't.

When Rebecca emerged from the steamy bathroom, the fierce concentration etched on Kurt's face discouraged her. How could he be so involved in the trial when her entire body screamed at her to forget the experiment and crawl into his lap?

Then again, for all his declarations of wanting her last night, he hadn't fucked her outside of the experience in the laboratory.

Although the lack of action wasn't very surprising considering the intensity of the orgasms they'd shared, his obvious arousal had throbbed against her belly as she'd drifted off in his arms. She'd been eager to ease his hunger but he'd pressed her hands away. He'd captured her wrists in his unyielding grip before encouraging her to sleep while he brooded, drilling holes in the ceiling with his troubled stare.

Did he regret the things he'd said to her?

Desire coursed through her entire body, making her brazen. Dropping the towel as she approached, she waited for him to direct her as he would. He didn't spare a single glance for her bared figure.

"Sit, Becca." Gesturing to the bed, Kurt twisted his desk chair to face her. He'd piled several plush cushions to act as a sort of lounging area on the bed. It reminded her of a sheik's harem. Scooting against them, she folded her legs beneath her then settled in for another session with Dr. Foster.

"I know you're familiar with the basic theories behind dream analysis. Therefore, you realize a normal person has five to seven REM stages per night. Over the last two nights, you've undergone six periods of dream activity each evening. Typically, a person experiences their most intense dreams closest to waking. Those encapsulate a person's most profound desires."

Locked into lecture mode, Kurt played the professor this morning. The man she had fallen asleep with had disappeared without a trace.

Rebecca nodded her understanding of the facts then waited for him to continue while she contemplated the implications of his disassociation. It was time for her to start acting like the trained equal he claimed she was.

Her revelations of the night before hadn't vanished into the sultry night air as his appeared to have. Luckily, she could affect him, too. The knowledge empowered her.

"In fact, both nights you dreamt very similar things in all six stages. Again, I won't reveal anything you aren't ready to admit to yourself so I need you to tell me what you remember. Then, we can compare your fantasy to reality and gather additional evidence to support the Dream Machine's capabilities. One occurrence won't be enough to convince the board that yesterday's results were more than a fluke."

Closing her eyes, she settled into the luscious embrace of the cushions. "I remember dreaming about you having sex with me in your office again." Without thought, her hands drifted across her torso, rubbing her achy breasts as she recalled the sensations. Kurt remained silent, letting her work through the first stage.

She decided to torture him with the details she envisioned.

"This time I think it was a little different." She paused to gather her recollections and then said, "Yes, I dreamt about the real thing instead of my previous fantasy. Similar, nearly exact, but the awareness of the experiment worked into the dream. I even included the device you wore to take measurements when you slid inside me. The ridge of the sheath tool enhanced the glide of your thick cock stroking the inside of my pussy."

A strangled noise from Kurt's direction brought her feigned innocent gaze up to his, quizzical.

"Sorry, I didn't mean to distract you." A tremulous smile crossed his face. She noted his white-knuckled grip on the armrest of his chair with amusement. "I like this new side of you, frank and confident. Jesus. It was hard enough to resist you when you hid from the truth."

She stroked herself with deliberate motions designed to advertise how much she would welcome his touch.

Instead of reaching out, he shifted in his chair then cleared his throat before continuing his line of questioning. The nervous gesture revealed a side of him she'd never glimpsed before. He paused in his routine long enough she wondered if he might be debating whether to continue or not before pressing on.

Did he think he'd pushed her too hard already?

He'd mentioned he wouldn't reveal anything she couldn't remember. Determined to surpass his expectations, she focused on remembering the contents of her next dream without his guidance.

As though he couldn't stop himself, Kurt blurted, "How did it make you feel to know you were part of an experiment?"

The personal question triggered a whimper. Rebecca didn't object to the betraying sound, which would have horrified her yesterday.

"It made me twice as horny," she admitted.

Although she'd disclosed her attraction to him, a tiny part of her craved his reassurance in light of his withdrawal. Of course, she'd never ask for it but, if some sign of his acceptance manifested in his features, she would gladly snatch it. She didn't have to search past the gleam in his eyes at her confession.

"Good girl, Becca," he soothed. "Now, what else do you remember from last night?"

She relaxed under his careful scrutiny and let her mind wander, fitting together the flashing images like pieces of a puzzle.

"It's difficult to sift through the bursts of action. They're not very coherent. It's like someone keeps flipping the channels in my mind." Concentrating, she spoke aloud, not directing the comment at him but explaining as she attempted to filter the glimpses of memory.

Kurt beamed at her with something like pride. "You're remembering more than one stage at a time. Pick a vision and follow it through. You can do this."

As he continued to study her, Rebecca's eyes flickered behind her now closed lids. Her fingers twitched as she clenched then relaxed them. A vision, stronger than the others, pushed to the surface of her consciousness. She grabbed hold and watched as libidinous images flooded her memory.

After what could have been moments—or minutes—filled with desire, she whispered, "I sort of remember most of it but... It's a little weird."

"Tell me, baby."

His supportive tone compelled her to share. It washed away the last of her lingering doubts. After all, he'd already seen her dreams and he hadn't run away screaming or treated her with disgust. No man could fuck her with such raging passion if her darker desires affronted him.

"I floated in the middle of a room...weightless and rocking, almost like a kid on a swing set. But I also remember being tied up, I think. No, that's not quite right..."

Kurt waited with his infamous patience as she fought to bring the details into focus. His handsome face caught her attention and her mind wandered, thinking about how it seemed normal to refer to him by his first name now.

Somehow, he'd fallen from the pedestal of idolatry she'd placed him on before. Instead, an amazing but real—sometimes flawed—man had replaced the caricature she'd adored. This man held the potential to satisfy her desires in a way the doctor never could.

In the wake of her realization, a picture blazed to life. It wasn't herself she saw but her mind had borrowed the image when it created the related nocturnal adventure.

She tried to speak but her dry throat made it obvious all dampness in her body had migrated to her pussy. Moisture seeped from between her legs. Attempting to deny the lurid vision would be futile at this point.

"It's okay, Becca. Trust me. Just say it. Start with the small things if the whole scene is too hard." Instinctively, he leaned forward enough to wrap her hand in his.

When he twined their fingers, she smiled. Staring straight into his stormy eyes, she explained, "Do you remember the

Johnson case from March?"

In response, Kurt's straining dick throbbed against his abdomen. The flimsy cotton shorts he wore couldn't obscure the jerk of his flesh. Of course he'd remember. And he'd understand which REM stage she had recalled.

"Yes." His gravelly response confirmed her suspicions. It turned him on, too.

She eyed the bulge stretching full to his hip as he shifted in his chair again. The deliberate way he laid his palm on his thigh made her aware of his struggle to restrain himself from taking his erection in hand. She rooted for his lust to win out over his control, deciding to add fuel to the fire with her confession.

"While I filed the finished cases in the archive one night, the photographs included in the package Mrs. Johnson provided fell onto my desk." She had to clarify this point before moving on. She would never violate a patient's privacy. Her discovery hadn't been intentional but once the first had landed on her calendar blotter, she couldn't tear her eyes away.

"I'm sorry, Doctor, but I couldn't help it. I saw the pictures when I picked them up and put them back." Her eyes opened as she evaluated his expression. Would he be angry at her intrusion? The rapture on the woman's face had sparked her curiosity, compelling her to inspect the remaining scenes.

"Becca, we're partners now. You have the right to review any case file in the office. You were doing work at the time, I understand. What did you see?"

"After their sessions in the office, Mr. Johnson admitted to his wife he'd always wondered about suspension. Following their successful therapy sessions, where you encouraged them to indulge each other's fantasies, he sent you some photos. Since his wife is an exhibitionist, I assumed they had agreed to trade desires." Her breath came harder now. She had to clear her throat to continue.

"How does this relate to your dream, Becca?" Kurt asked though he must've already understood. He still needed her to demonstrate the Dream Machine's accuracy.

"I dreamt it was me." She gasped at the wicked idea brewing between them. "Dreamt I hung cocooned in the black leather sling. I dangled helpless from the ceiling, rocking back and forth while you...fucked me." She barely stopped herself from divulging he'd made love to her in her reverie.

Kurt groaned. She glanced at the pen wobbling in his trembling hand. The moment of uncertainty must have shown on her face because he stamped out her imagined doubts.

"Visualizing it makes me so damn hard. Watching your dreams forced me to jack off yesterday. But...shit. Hearing you say it is more than I can bear."

The raw need reflected in the husky timbre of his speech drew an answering response from her body. Her nipples pebbled beneath his intense gaze and her belly rippled with the involuntary clench of her muscles.

"You're ready for this," he assured almost under his breath. Rebecca wondered if he talked to her, or to himself. After witnessing her dreams, he must realize she had more to give if he could convince her to continue her testimony.

"Go on, Becca." His order carried an edge of harshness as though he couldn't wait for her to finish at her own pace. "What else do you remember?"

The first had been hard enough to admit even with her newfound resolve. Telling him the rest surprised her, frightened her a little. Is this really what she wanted?

"Trust me, Becca. Nothing you tell me will change how much I want you. I swear it."

Yes. Taking a deep breath, she decided to get straight to the point. "I'm curious about anal sex."

"Fuck it, I lied. I want you even more now."

Chapter Sixteen

The desire flaring in Kurt's overcast eyes at her admission stunned Rebecca. The focus of his attention stole her breath. He jolted from his seat like a compressed spring bouncing free. When he hustled her toward the laboratory with a firm grip on her upper arm, she wondered if she was prepared to live this particular dream. She'd struggled to take all of his beefy cock in her pussy. Plus, being tied down seemed tame in comparison to being trussed up and left hanging at his mercy.

The pressure of his unyielding grasp increased, supplemented by his hand in the small of her back, which kept her in motion when she faltered. The intensity of his silence unnerved her.

Could she make this monumental leap of faith? She'd opened herself to utter vulnerability. Despite her earlier conviction, panic invaded the fringes of her arousal.

"Stop thinking, baby. Just feel." His voice, a bare whisper of sound, came from right next to her ear as his lips dusted her face.

Relying on Kurt seemed instinctive now. She capitulated, allowing him to guide her over the threshold to his lair. The thrum of anticipation jumped inside her as the motion sensitive halogens of the laboratory blazed to life. Off to one side, a white yoga mat covered the linoleum flooring. When she reached it, he ushered her to her knees with pertinacious pressure on her shoulders.

He grabbed the remote touchpad, which controlled the examination room facilities, then tinkered with the settings. The whir of motors hummed through the room as a panel in the ceiling opened to reveal a complex system of wires and pulleys. An extended frame of black bars with embedded eyehooks descended from the contraption.

Kurt shaped her malleable frame into a submissive pose—head bowed and arms clasped, wrists to elbows behind her back—before continuing his arrangements. From the periphery of her limited view, Rebecca caught a glimpse of the rigging. What she saw caused her trepidation to transform into a tidal surge of lust. The further they explored her fantasies the more powerful her response became.

When he seemed satisfied with the downward progress of the mechanism, he reached into the cabinet beside her to withdraw a wad of leather and metal. Buckles jangled as he straightened the device until she could discern the intent of the tangle. It was a harness, similar to the one she'd seen in the case file, consisting of padded leather straps looped into various sized openings.

"Spread your legs wider, Becca."

She complied with his command. The cool material bumped against her thigh, causing her muscles to tense in response. He crouched on the floor beside her to thread the straps over, around and between her legs in a mysterious web. Next, he encircled her hips, torso and arms. Every clash of his fingers against her hypersensitive skin sent sparks of arousal shooting through her core. The taut encasement of her flesh competed with the soothing stroke of the downy fur, resulting in sensory overload.

"Mmm." She couldn't stop the moan from escaping.

When she tipped her head back to rest against his thigh, Kurt's hand bracketed her jaw. His fingers stroked the side of her neck. She swallowed against his palm, which cupped her throat, when he loomed over her, forcing her to meet his gaze.

"This time will be different. Your explicit dreams require me to be rough with you. I can't hold back or it won't be a true test."

Pensive, she considered his words, construing them as the serious warning he intended. Did she have what it took to follow this through? Before she solidified her answer, Kurt continued.

"Listen, baby. The truth is, I don't think I could go easy even if the experiment didn't exist. I don't know what the hell is wrong with me. I'm fighting to keep myself in check. You need to know that when you decide. This isn't for show. All the months—craving you, planning, and hoping you could be what I need—have tested my control."

She was speechless. He'd thought about this? With her as his subject? For months? Her attempt to process the rush of elation prevented her from answering. Mistaking her silence for indecision, he demonstrated his gallant underpinnings by offering her an escape route.

"It's okay if you decide it's too much. Do you understand me?" Kurt growled. "I won't think less of you if you're not ready for this."

The determination in his eyes along with his clamped jaw underscored the depth of restraint he possessed no matter how he cautioned her otherwise. If she changed her mind right now, he'd let her walk away. That knowledge gave her the confidence to fling herself off the edge of the cliff and surrender to his mastery.

"I'm ready, Doctor."

"Are you frightened?" For a moment, his features softened.

"A little." Fear and arousal fused into one heady tumble of emotion but nerves played a starring role.

"It's hard for me to remember you're new to this kind of play. Your passion is so pure. Everything will be fine. You're going to love this. If you don't, we'll stop. Just say the word and it'll be over."

"But what about *your* desires?" Her novel sense of freedom liberated her to speak her mind without embarrassment. "Do you need this, too?"

He stroked her cheek with his stubbled jaw before kissing her. Lingering caresses communicated his longing without speaking. The gentle gesture made his words even sweeter.

"It's not about what I need, Becca. It's about what you want."

Something inside her shifted. The artificial boundaries

she'd drawn around her physical response dissolved. Affection seeped into every nuance of their interaction. The circular current of their intimacy fed each other's desire, spiraling them both higher with every turn. Together, they became so much more than individuals.

"Whatever you need is what I want most."

With a feral, inhuman sound of longing, Kurt snagged the first carabiner dangling from a wire attached to one of the myriad leather loops encasing her body. He clipped it to a corresponding eyebolt, which had been welded onto the metal structure hanging above her head. Meticulously, he rechecked the security of the harness as he strung each cable until she imagined herself as a risqué marionette.

When satisfied, he turned to her and asked, "Do you trust me?"

She nodded once.

A series of commands entered on the control panel initiated the rig's ascent. Slack disappeared from the wires. Spools gobbled the excess yardage until taut lines increased the pressure on her body as she struggled to maintain balance in her kneeling position.

"Relax. Let it take you."

Her legs unfolded beneath her when her upper body levitated from the ground. The motion of the shifting metal frame stretched her arms wide into Kurt's pre-programmed position. The pulleys retracted select cables until she resembled a T with her toes dangling inches off the cool, polished tile of the laboratory. Gravity sucked her against the padded restraints on her arms, around her rib cage and between her legs. The delicious pressure caused her to squirm, which triggered a lulling sway.

Though her bindings provided ample support, the air swirled across her exposed skin as she swung in shallow arcs. The instinctive fear skittering up her spine should have disconcerted her but it couldn't come close to overpowering the exhilaration saturating her. Her spirit soared like a crane cresting the Himalayas.

She squeezed her eyes shut against the overwhelming

pleasure.

"Are you okay?" His immediate concern followed the gesture. "I won't let you fall."

"Oh, God. Yes." When she shuddered in the harness, it set off a tinkling of metal fasteners, transforming her into an erotic wind chime.

Lost in arousal, she basked in the glow of pleasure without a care for the outcome of the scenario. Nothing she did would alter what was about to happen because she couldn't change her nature. Or Kurt's.

The mechanism hummed as it elevated her. Her gradual ascent provided an opportunity to study every inch of his tensed body as it passed before her eyes. The doctor observed the process, vigilant to test various wires and straps ensuring her comfortable safety. The motor paused. He stalked around her. His fingertips trailed across her skin, raising goose bumps in their wake.

"Very nice." His hand dipped to pet the juncture of her thighs, tucked tight together. "But I want to see more of you."

He pressed another series of buttons. Her wrists inclined as her legs separated until she hung in a flying X. He stepped behind her.

"Turn your head to the right." She did as instructed but spun back after catching a glimpse of herself in the mirrored surface of the one-way glass on the opposite wall. The picture they made—her fair skin striped with dark leather, suspended in front of his imposing figure—blinded her with lust. Kurt slapped her ass hard enough to leave it stinging.

She wished he'd do it again.

"Focus. I want you to see what I see. Admire the play of light enhancing the lines and curves of your silhouette. You're spectacular." She peeked at the mirror but, instead of what he visualized, she only had eyes for him.

Rebecca's rapid, shallow breathing perpetuated the sway of her body in the harness. The motion drew his attention like a cat locked on a dangling string. His consumed stare inflated her confidence.

With one fingertip, he traced the furrow of her spine

between the straps until it culminated in the cleft between her ass cheeks. Her gasp reverberated through the examination room. Their eyes locked in the mirror—hers imploring, his possessive. Kurt rasped from behind her, "You've never had a man touch you here, have you, Becca?"

"Only you, Doctor." Her shy reply conflicted with her raging desire to experience his forbidden caress.

"We'll go as slow as I can manage, baby. We will do this, and you will like it. I promise." The smug assurance held no boast. A virtuoso of the flesh, Kurt could strum her body until it sang.

She squirmed in a desperate attempt to apply friction to her aching core but, no matter how she thrashed, she couldn't squeeze her legs together or rub against the bonds hugging her inner thighs. The doctor chuckled at her futile effort as he circled her.

Once again situated before her, Kurt grasped her hips then tugged her closer until he could drag her nipple into the moist heat of his mouth. Instantly, it beaded beneath his ministrations. He flicked the sensitive tip with his tongue then nibbled it before releasing his hold on her waist.

The pressure on her breast increased tenfold. Only his teeth and lips fixed her at the shallow angle before her nipple slipped free from his light grip and she rocked away.

On the return arc, he seized her hips as he played with her other breast. She moaned when she watched his midnight hair brushing her chest and his tongue glazing her pebbled nipple as he raised her. Then he sucked hard and let go. His teeth raked the plump flesh of her breast as she escaped once more.

He repeated the pattern, building a rhythm her body learned to anticipate. The swinging motion mesmerized her. It gave her a moment to cool off before he boosted her higher again, each trip expanding his caresses to another exposed part of her body. Each touch was more intricate and inflammatory than the last.

When she expected his next wicked embrace, Kurt shifted. Reaching into his pocket, he selected a button on the remote. The motor reengaged with a buzz. The wire attached to each leg cuff zipped through a pulley on the side of the suspension bar, drawing her appendages wider apart. Before she could adapt to the new position, she rose until her pelvis aligned with his.

"Enough playing, Becca. Time to get serious." Though he directed the words at her, she understood he'd scolded himself to stay on track. After all, she was helpless.

She heard the whiz of a cable unraveling a moment before she pitched forward. She shrieked, fearing she'd splatter on the floor in the next instant. Instead, Kurt steadied her with a broad hand on her shoulder, murmuring reassurances.

Heart racing, she watched as the ground pivoted in front of her in a controlled descent. The cables connected to her upper arms and torso bands went slack while the lines attached to her thighs and knees contracted. As a result, she rotated forward. She stopped parallel to the yoga mat she'd kneeled on earlier as though she lounged on her stomach in bed, or flew like Superman. But spread-eagled.

Hip high, the position provided an excellent, up-close view of Kurt's impressive equipment. The flex and bob of his shaft in time to his pounding heartbeat fascinated her. She hardly noticed him placing a supporting headband rest around her forehead, taking the weight off her neck, because she couldn't focus on anything but his throbbing hard-on.

He stepped closer to attach the latest cord to the main support. While he concentrated on the task at hand, she snaked out her tongue then lapped at the bead of pre-come dripping down the head of his cock.

Kurt's rock-hard thigh muscles quivered in front of her eyes. He slapped her ass again, drawing a groan from the inner recesses of her chest. Her pussy flooded with arousal.

"Don't distract me, baby. I won't jeopardize your safety."

Though his serious tone attempted to squelch her rebellion, she couldn't help but test him. As soon as he rechecked his work, she strained her neck as far as she could to mouth his sac.

"Becca!" The chastisement came out as a rough moan. He couldn't restrain himself from thrusting his groin against her greedy lips for a few seconds before stealing her treat.

"Did you intentionally disobey me?" The rhetorical question highlighted the error of her self-indulgence. But hadn't she expected him to punish her? Hoped for it? She made it easy for him.

"Yes."

He yanked the cables, spinning her ninety degrees until her hip came even with his front and her face pointed to his right. He gave her left cheek five rapid, stinging spanks. The crack of his hand against her ass excited her as much as the tingling heat spreading across it. When he finished, his harsh breathing echoed in the room. She wished she could see his face instead of the corded muscles of his tense calves.

"Baby, if you want my hand on your ass, all you have to do is ask. Do not disobey me again."

"Yes, Doctor." She grinned at the tremor in his voice, knowing he couldn't see. "Please, may I have more?"

His muffled curse accompanied another shift in her world as he spun her in the other direction then repeated the sharp slaps on her right cheek. She panted, recovering as he rubbed her ass to ease the sting. The throbbing ache between her thighs prevented her from requesting additional punishment. He had to fuck her.

At her silence, he rearranged her to suit his purpose. His hands guided her legs into position, accompanied by the whir of motors. Her knees bent until her heels rested on the back of her thighs where Kurt banded them with yet another tie. He brought her arms together, folded so that her wrists rested at the base of her spine. The weight of her breasts swaying beneath her fanned the fire in her core.

Then, his touch vanished. He couldn't have gone far but, from this position, she couldn't find him. Her whimper became the only sound in the room. A moment of panic snuck in through the desire.

"Doctor?" Her question sounded like a distressed cry.

"Yes, baby?"

"Don't leave me. Please, touch me."

"I'm right here, sweetheart." His hand stroked her flank, reassuring her. "Just stepped back to look at you for a minute. I can't believe you're real." He kept up a constant stream of insignificant ramblings as he retrieved the rolling tray with supplies he'd stashed out of Rebecca's line of sight.

Had he done that on purpose? What did he have on there?

She writhed in the bonds, attempting to steal a glimpse at the contents but couldn't manage it. Kurt dropped a restraining hand on the inside of her thigh mere inches below her pussy.

"You're soaked." Reverence saturated his tone. He must have bent closer because his breath teased her slick flesh. "You smell so hot, it makes me crazy. I have to taste you..."

The last of his words were muffled as he sipped from her pussy.

"Oh, Kurt. Please." Pleasure arced across every nerve ending in her body.

"No, Becca. You can't come. Not until I give you permission. You're not hooked to any machines yet." Pulling herself back from the razor edge of intense arousal, she panted, trying to squelch the electrifying sensations. Even as she registered the warmth and velvety glide of the doctor's tongue lapping the juices from her slit, she heard a latex glove snapping into place.

His gloved finger spread a cool glob of lubricant over her anus. Shocked at the disparity in temperature, as well as the imminent possibility of penetration, she cried out.

"Tensing your body will make this hurt, baby. Relax." The lazy, seductive cadence inspired confidence. Rebecca's muscles loosened up one by one.

Before she could frighten herself again, Kurt began to massage her pucker with his gloved and lubricated finger as he bent forward to lick a path from the bottom of her swollen, dripping lips to her clit. She bucked against the ecstasy. His finger nudged against her tight hole until the tip began to infiltrate a fraction of an inch at a time.

It felt forbidden, uncharted and so right to succumb to his penetration. In that moment, she realized she would surrender anything to Kurt. Not for the sake of the experiment, not for the resolution of her family crisis, not for the enrichment of her professional empathy but because she genuinely wanted to please him.

A strangled groan wrested from her constricted chest but she concentrated on the delight Kurt's tongue imparted as it rubbed a track down the edges of her slit before piercing inside then swirling around her clit. On every pass, he withdrew his finger, spread additional lube across her back passage, and then delved further inside as he distracted her from the burning discomfort by caressing her bud of nerves with his talented tongue.

When, at last, his knuckle passed the final ring of muscle then plunged deep inside her, they both groaned. Though she tried to relax, she was so turned on all her muscles clenched rhythmically. She gripped his finger.

"Please."

"No," he growled then bit the globe of her ass. "Damn, baby. Your pussy is snug, but this is even tighter. We need to do some more work here or I'm afraid I'll tear you when I fuck your virgin ass."

Withdrawing the digit once more, he selected a tool from the tray. He showed it to her before going back to work. The flat leather base would fit the standard attachment he'd built into many of his inventions. For now, he clipped on a remote probe tool embedded in a thick dildo then pressed it inside the mouth of Rebecca's pussy with one hard stroke.

A wave of sparks radiated from the intrusion. She had to bite her lip to keep from coming right then. He'd instructed her to wait. But the bands wrapped around her body, the gentle swaying, and Kurt's touches pushed her closer and closer to orgasm with every passing second.

"Doctor, hurry. I can't wait much longer."

Kurt hooked the straps on the inserted device to clips in the bands encircling her waist. Now secured, the tool would measure her response without being ejected from her convulsing channel while he concentrated on preparing her ass for his penetration.

Rebecca cried out when her inner muscles clenched around the implement but that alone couldn't satisfy her. The taboo pleasure zinging from his probing advances might push her over the edge when coupled with the instrument.

"I want you to wait, Becca. The probe is engaged now so I'll capture the data if you slip. But I want you to wait for my permission." She would do it. A large component of her satisfaction came from pleasing him.

"I'm going to stretch you now, baby. Open you up for my cock." Kurt removed another apparatus from the tray. She watched him spread a generous coat of lube on the constricted ring. The device formed a ball with a dent running around the center like inverted rings around a planet. Beyond reasoning, she didn't venture to guess how he'd use it. "This is the smallest Stretcher I've made, but I think it's still going to be uncomfortable for you."

"Do it," she begged. "Please."

Instead, he knelt in front of her. Rebecca sensed the intensity of the doctor's attention through her closed eyelids. When she peeked from beneath heavy lids, Kurt captured her mouth in a blazing kiss. She matched his vigor and then some.

While engaged in the kiss, Kurt slid the Stretcher inside her ass. The leading slope of the round gadget filled her, spreading her wider until the indentation ringing the sphere cradled her anus. The bulges on either side trapped it in place.

He was right. The instrument felt huge, although she'd seen the modest size of the object when he'd cupped it in his palm. Her eyes rolled. She grunted at the burn in her ass. She struggled against the bonds and the invasion.

God, if this is what the small intruder did to her, how would she ever take his cock? She couldn't do it. The thought of disappointing him upset her, causing her to tense further.

Kurt grabbed a fistful of her hair, redirecting her focus back to him.

"Relax, baby." As waves of pain and pleasure collided in a cacophony of sensation, he nuzzled her neck, pushing her over the edge from discomfort to arousal. The gentle vibrations of the objects embedded in her registered in her mind then began to enhance her stimulation. Stuffed, both her pussy and ass clamped around his amazing inventions.

After a few moments, he smiled against her throat then raked her exposed pulse with the sharp edges of his teeth. He rubbed his cock with the palm of one hand as though it hurt as much as she did.

"Good girl, Becca. How do you feel now?"

Words refused to coalesce in her usually articulate brain. All that would pass her lips was, "Mmm."

His contented laugh vibrated through her chest. Satisfaction layered on top of desire when she realized how much she pleased him.

"It's almost time, baby." Kurt clasped her shoulders then shoved. She spun around like the blades of a helicopter until she faced the opposite direction. Without hesitation, he clamped his mouth to her dripping folds, sucking her, licking her around the base of the probe. Her cries built in rapid succession as she neared the peak of her ardor.

She struggled to ignore the way her complete submission to his desires, as well as the devices embedded inside her, goaded her to come at once. A few more strokes of the doctor's tongue would make her fly over the edge.

As her weightless body strained toward release, Kurt tapped the device in her anus to make an adjustment. It flared, coaxing the ring of muscle further open.

Rebecca spiraled out of control. She twisted beneath his touch. Her heavy breasts rocked beneath her. Her overflowing pussy and ass spasmed around the devious invasions. The ring in her anus bulged further. The gradual expansion awarded her the chance to accommodate it and enjoy the sensation of being stretched.

She couldn't wait any longer.

"Kurt. Please. Now."

Instead of granting his permission for her release, he retreated, abandoning her on the cusp of a brilliant orgasm.

"No!"

She watched him lunge to his feet in the mirror now in front of her. While she absorbed the shock of the loss, he pried the Stretcher from her then replaced it with the engorged, blunt head of his straining cock. It seemed even bigger than before but she was so close to coming she reflexively squirmed closer. Or tried to.

"Take a deep breath," he commanded. Coating himself in her arousal and the abundant lubrication, Kurt notched his hard-on against her back passage. He gripped the cables then used them to tug her onto his impaling flesh. The head of his dick stretched her entrance. "When I tell you to, exhale and push out around me. We're going to do this. In one stroke. Just like you dreamed it. Fuck, I don't think I'll last more than that in your tight, hot hole."

Reaching beneath her waist, he flicked his fingertip across her clit in the deft swirl guaranteed to bring her off. When she squirmed against him he yelled, "Now, Becca."

His smooth pump buried his cock in her to the hilt.

She felt unbelievably full.

Held immobile, at his mercy as his thick staff stretched her beyond comprehension, a sense of complete submission overpowered Rebecca. It blazed inside her, lighting her soul with a rightness she never could have predicted. Simultaneously, Kurt roared out his possession, making it clear he was the first and only person who would ever take her this way.

Her heart heard and understood.

They shattered together.

Chapter Seventeen

Morning returned Rebecca to reality. The sensual haze that had surrounded her and Kurt for the past few days dissipated. She mourned the loss of the intimacy they had shared although it had been selfish to assume it could last.

Yesterday, following the life changing session with him, she'd passed out cold. When she awoke, it was to an empty bed. The man who'd barged into her heart had made himself scarce all afternoon.

He'd popped his head out of the laboratory once—still wearing the lab coat she'd never look at the same way again—to check on her. After she'd assured him she felt fine, he'd disappeared into the workspace with a muttered excuse about preparing their case to present to the board. Her stomach had lurched when the bolt slid into the lock with an audible click from the other side.

She'd idled the time away first by indulging in a nap, exhaustion still plaguing her. When she couldn't stand it a moment longer, she'd amused herself by flipping through the channels without much interest, reading some of the scientific journals stacked on Kurt's desk, calling to check on her family and pacing around the three square feet of floor space in the private quarters about a million times. But nothing had distracted her from imagining Kurt hiding on the other side of his fortified door.

She'd wished she could assist him or even lounge at his side while he worked. Yet, he still hadn't returned by the time she ate leftover pizza for dinner. She'd accepted his avoidance when he hadn't shown up to tuck her in or attach her to the Dream Machine. Lonely, she'd given up then snuggled close to his pillow, inhaling his scent while she surrendered to sleep.

This morning had been more of the same. He'd busied himself with last-minute additions to his case notes. When she'd crossed the room to his private desk to massage the bunched muscles of his tense back, he'd yielded for a moment before shrugging off her touch once his breathing grew erratic.

The presentation to the board marked a major milestone. Today, the council would either approve continued study into the applicability of the Dream Machine for commercial use or it would terminate the experiment. Rebecca couldn't bear the thought of what would happen then. Although Kurt had convinced her he'd enjoyed their carnal interactions as much as she had, he'd distanced himself from the explosion of emotions their extreme coupling had induced. He now epitomized the aloofness she'd associated with her mentor before this adventure.

The doctor had laid out a new, skirted suit for her. When she tried it on, his eye for fashion impressed her. The professional yet provocative ensemble highlighted her figure in a way her old attire never had. Of course, the well-cut silk outfit probably cost as much as her entire wardrobe combined. It flattered her curves while allowing her to maintain the air of the distinguished psychologist she longed to be.

He'd also provided lingerie rivaling the wild garments she preferred with their inventive lack of material and lacy panels, which obscured most of her tender parts in shadow but displayed a lot for temptation. The shoes, however, captured her rapt attention. After going barefoot for days, the designer heels made her drool. Simple, black leather stilettos wrought with such artistry and flair should be illegal. The additional four inches added to her stature polished off her makeover.

The individual changes were subtle but the cumulative effect was drastic. The sensual component of her nature emerged from the cage she'd locked it in, transforming Rebecca into the complete woman she'd never again abandon. Her time with Kurt had taught her she didn't have to bottle her desires in order to succeed. In fact, trusting her heart, placing faith in her fellow human beings and staying open—even when it made her vulnerable to hurt—enhanced her effectiveness as a psychologist.

No matter what happened at this morning's meeting, the Dream Machine had worked for her. She prayed her testimony would convince the board of the effectiveness of Kurt's invention and the benefits it could bring to others.

Maybe then, he'd be happy.

CB

Silence shrouded them during the ride to their appointment, both Kurt and Becca lost in their private musings. He ran through every possible objection the board might raise and formulated a counterargument to nullify it. They couldn't shut him down now. He wasn't finished with his subject. She fascinated him. He burned to learn more about her but he wouldn't blame her if she no longer wanted him after the way he'd severed their intimacy.

Guilt had corroded the elation rocking his world after the earth-shattering release he'd achieved in her supplicant body. Once the storm of pleasure had blown over, his first thought had centered on preventing her from discovering his deception in today's board meeting.

What an asshole. Self-loathing had driven him to sequester himself in the laboratory as punishment. He'd wanted nothing more than her company while he compiled evidence for the board but he'd denied himself the satisfaction. Besides, the time in isolation had allowed him to refocus by ridding his mind of the fanciful ideas perfect chemistry had implanted in his brain.

As he led Becca through the polished chrome and glass doors of the board's office building, the heartbeat racing in her veins skittered beneath his fingers, which braceleted her wrist. Even though it made her nervous to face her colleagues when they all had knowledge of the experiment requirements, she exuded confidence and a freedom Kurt found highly attractive. The clothing he'd had tailor made suited the enhanced woman well.

Knowing this strong, intelligent creature would submit to him acted as a more powerful aphrodisiac than the intoxicating thought of coaxing her to embrace her sensual nature had.

"You'll do fine, baby." He reassured her as he stroked the inside of her delicate wrist. "The board granted unanimous approval of your position in the firm. These are people who respect you."

"I know, Kurt." She slowed as she turned to face him with an expression he couldn't read. "I'm anxious for you. For the experiment. This is a pivotal moment in your career and I believe in your work. I don't want anything I do to jeopardize that."

He stopped short. The trial would have monumental ramifications for their field but all morning he'd focused on how this meeting would affect their relationship, not the success of the Dream Machine. Science he understood. The sound research and evidence left no wiggle room for denouncement. Hell, he'd known the Dream Machine worked before they'd set out to prove it with empirical evidence.

He stroked her cheek. "Thank you, sweetheart. But there's no need to worry."

As they rode to the top floor in the mirrored elevator, the true irony of the situation hit home. He couldn't decipher the unintended results of their procedures. Becca had reacted to the study as he had planned. However, he hadn't anticipated the effect the liaison would have on him. Kurt couldn't condense their changing relationship into a column on a report, couldn't graph the way she made him feel. It disconcerted him.

Debating the likelihood of a hormonal reaction strong enough to trigger these complications, he considered the merits of a follow-up experiment. They reached the meeting room before his wandering mind realized they had arrived. The atypical distraction concerned him. He fortified his resolve and swept his attention back to the challenge at hand.

They took seats near the head of the gigantic conference table. At the opposite end of the gleaming seating area, an unfurled screen hosted the title slide of his briefing, beamed up by a computer projector attached to a laptop. Luke had arranged everything as he'd requested.

The other board members joined them within moments, ratcheting up the background of chatter and greetings from colleagues. Many offered Becca congratulations on her hard-earned partnership.

If anyone noted the gleam in Kurt's eye as people praised her or the possessive way his hand rested on the back of her chair, no one mentioned it. They'd witnessed him fighting off the other firms contending first for stellar interns and then top graduates in order to keep Becca for years.

Before long, the room had filled. Only the seat at the head of the table remained vacant. Doctors swiveled and rocked in the imposing leather chairs. Anticipation mounted while they waited for the council chairman. Kurt's hand never strayed from its perch on Becca's knee. Five minutes later, Dr. Luke Malone strode into the room in his dark suit, commanding the attention of all in attendance.

Their close friendship was no secret. They'd known each other since high school, been tight since college where they'd roomed together, studied together and played hard together, though no sign of their bond showed now. In their professional roles, favoritism had no place as they pushed each other to be better scientists through healthy competition.

"Are we ready to begin?" All business, Dr. Malone directed the question to Dr. Foster—not Luke to Kurt—with raised brows.

At Kurt's nod, Luke initiated the proceedings.

"Due to the sensitive nature of the case we are about to review I'd like to direct your attention to the folders in front of you. Inside you'll find a standard non-disclosure form. Please take a moment to sign them now before we begin."

The rustle of pens whipped from portfolios and purses resounded through the long room. A secretary stood by to collect the formalized bonds of doctor patient confidentiality. What happened in this room would stay in this room.

"Thank you, Lucy." Dr. Malone dismissed the assistant once the last doctor completed his form.

"Begin when you're ready, Dr. Foster," Luke instructed as all eyes focused on Kurt.

Rebecca fidgeted under the scrutiny of the board, although she wasn't as flustered as she'd expected. Kurt sat beside her, his discreet hand lending support. He approved of her performance, which made the entire process bearable.

In prior case debriefs she'd attended, the sanctioning process included an overview of the procedure and a dry, academic discussion of results to date. While the review would invite the speculation of her colleagues, there should be no reason to go into details on the specific fantasies she had experienced.

"As you know," Kurt began, "I've created a machine with the capability to capture and reconstruct dreams from brain wave patterns. This study diverges from most in that the subject is aware of the intent of the experiment. But, the usual double-blind standard doesn't apply to this case because it would be impossible for me to alter the outcome of the experiment."

An older professor with a reputation for his conservative views interrupted. "No one would accuse you of intentional deception, Dr. Foster. However, we all know that a researcher's underlying beliefs about the outcome of the experiment can influence the research."

Before Kurt could respond, Luke intervened on his behalf. "You're right, Dr. Kensington, which is why the board stipulated a third-party witness to all of the experiment proceedings."

The blood drained from her face in a rush. Her heartbeat pounded in her ears. How could she have forgotten? The cameras. Kurt had been clear with her at the beginning of the experiment. In place of a human witness, the board had approved recorded sessions but her focus hadn't been on the silent, omniscient eye after the first day.

Would they evaluate the footage here today to ensure no bias had tainted the outcome of the trial?

The tensing of her thigh against Kurt's knee must have alerted him to her nervousness. He squeezed her leg beneath the cover of the table.

She flinched. The gesture intended to calm her only

reminded her of the wild sexual abandon she'd experienced at his hands. It magnified her awkwardness induced by the possibility of her colleagues spying on her.

At least she tried to convince herself embarrassment, not arousal, caused her sudden flush. Sure her face had turned scarlet, she sucked in a lungful of air to combat her dizziness. She vowed to uphold her commitment to embrace her desires. Her chin lifted, her spine straightened and she refused to drop her gaze from the curious glances her companions shot her way.

Her defiant stare swept around the table until it landed last on Dr. Malone. When she withstood his scrutiny, he nodded his approval.

They had one ally, at least.

After brief moments that seemed like a lifetime, she turned to Kurt, who waited for her consent to continue.

"Go ahead," she murmured. "Show them what you need to."

The relieved smile tilting the corners of his sexy mouth rewarded her enough to outweigh any possible professional repercussions.

"To assuage your concerns, Dr. Kensington, I've included video clips from each stage which will run following my discussion. Feel free to scrutinize them for procedural violations. I assure you, there are none." He flipped to the summary slide. "In addition to establishing a baseline, we have so far conducted two Dream Machine sessions."

When the presentation progressed to a graph plotting her biofeedback, Kurt continued. "You can see by the data presented here, the baseline arousal readings are significantly lower than those collected while reenacting scenes recovered from the Dream Machine."

A woman across the table raised her hand. "Yes, Dr. Faulkner?"

"What does the red line between the baseline and the reenactment data sets represent?"

"Ah, I'm glad you asked. Those are results from a second control experiment we conducted to eliminate other hypotheses for the subject's elevated reactions."

Rebecca's mind flashed back to the warm liquid that had rushed inside her as Kurt forced her to admit her desire for him. She squirmed in the seat as arousal dampened her thighs.

"Today we're requesting the board's permission to continue the success we've already achieved in perfecting the use of the Dream Machine. This tool has the potential to aid those who have repressed their passions." His booming voice filled the meeting room with his commanding authority but still they wouldn't let him off the hook.

"Dr. Foster, you realize we can't permit you to continue without reviewing all the evidence as impartial observers?"

Rebecca didn't miss the wicked grin on Dr. Malone's face. In fact, several other attendees shuffled in their chairs either out of excitement or as an attempt to conceal their amusement.

"I do. Therefore, I've prepared a sample of the trials as compared to the dreams recorded. You'll see the REM stages captured on the left side of the screen, the actual trials on the right and the associated biometric data across the bottom of the videos. Please keep in mind, we've only had the opportunity to delve into the first three scenarios thus far. I refuse to discuss the contents of the remaining cycles in Becca's presence due to the possible risk of uncovering desires my subject is not yet prepared to handle."

Luke nodded in agreement before dimming the lights via his master controls. She wheezed, finding it impossible to draw a full breath. She recalled the scope of her abandon, about to be exposed to a committee of near strangers.

Kurt maintained his steady narration but she barely registered his words. She clung to the sound of his voice as a lifeline she'd depend on to help her through the next few minutes. He started at the very beginning, with the baseline session. As the visions and sounds of her—naked, vulnerable, submitting to the doctor—came alive in the room, he slid his hand beneath the hem of her skirt.

He fumbled inside the material until she wondered if he'd lost focus while speaking. Then his fingers found a spot in the seam of the skirt and tugged. The material rode up her thighs as it gathered on either side of her hips like obscene mini-blinds. He'd planned this! Never breaking his monotonous lecture, as though something other than her most personal desires were on display, he distracted her by manipulating her moist flesh through the lacy thong panties he'd given her to wear beneath the sexy suit.

Embarrassment hovered on the edge of her arousal but her attention shifted to his manipulations while she viewed the close-up shots of them having sex. She couldn't look away from his thick cock as it had first pressed inside her on his desk, then the rhythmic clench and release of his muscles as he pumped into her.

In the dark room, she indulged herself in reliving the memories while Kurt's hand grew bolder in the caresses it bestowed. By the time the video had progressed to the suspension sequence, his fingers had delved under the elastic in the crease of her thigh. He tapped his fingers against her clit.

She fought against the need to come right there in the boardroom while more than a dozen people watched the influential doctor fuck her in wicked ways. When she slipped near the edge, his hand retracted, leaving her disappointed. In her peripheral vision, she watched him reach into his pocket before returning his fist to her lap.

But she never expected what came next.

Shock raced through her system when he tucked something thin and short into her pussy. She clenched her teeth against a scream when he flicked the base and it puffed up, locking inside her.

While Luke observed both the amazing drama unfolding on the screen, as well as the reactions of those around the room, his erection chafed against the rough zipper of his trousers. Many of the scientists' hands had ventured out of sight. He could hardly blame them. Who wouldn't be moved by the perfect balance of his friend's domination and his young protégé's submission?

Today he loved his job.

His eagle eye picked up the signs of Kurt distracting Becca

by arousing her beneath the table. Luke only noticed his friend's skillful multitasking because he would've done the same thing in Kurt's position.

Plus, the lucky bastard had filled him in on all of her REM stages. In addition to those the council had witnessed when Dr. Wexford had barged into their last meeting with accusations of scandal then revealed some of her most private longings before they had halted him.

When would she realize this was her fantasy?

On the personal monitor embedded in the tabletop in front of him, which allowed him to view presentations given on the screen behind him, he selected a different input. One moment, the picture flickering on-screen depicted Becca's glorious display in the suspension harness while Kurt prepared her for the ultimate surrender. The next, it switched to the view from the camera currently mounted on the underside of the table a few feet in front of her lap.

While the other doctors scrutinized the first three REM stage reenactments, Luke had a private viewing of the fourth. Her thighs glistened with arousal, proving she responded not only to fantasies she could recall but also to those she'd not yet admitted to herself. She couldn't hide from Kurt's invention.

His friend had been right about her blazing sensual nature.

How had he not seen it himself?

Rebecca bit her lip to keep from crying out as ecstasy suffocated her inhibitions. She came against Kurt's hand. As a disassociated observer, she watched the woman on-screen bend to his will, the look of rapture on his face as he thrust inside her clenching ass and the entranced expressions of her colleagues. The sights wrung pleasure from her in wave after wave.

Recovering, she squeezed Kurt's hand—which dried her with his handkerchief under the table—thanking him for the relief and an outlet for her nerves. He popped the instrument from her pulsing slit, wrapped it in the damp cloth then returned it to his pocket. No sign of acknowledgement crossed his face while he finished his clinical explanations to the board.

Seeing things from a new angle, she devoured the blissful expressions on Kurt's face that had been inaccessible to her during the experiment. She never expected she could move him on a higher plane than physical satisfaction. Finally, she understood he needed her gift as much as she desired to give it.

As the clip ended and the lights returned to their normal brightness, she blinked to clear the cobwebs before raising her eyes—afraid to see if today's events had destroyed the professional reputation she'd worked so hard for. Instead, as the faces ringing the table became illuminated, they contained a mixture of responses ranging from appreciation to reverence to hunger.

After all, these were sexual therapy experts. The exclusive leaders of their field understood the healthiness of expressed desires. Relieved, in more way than one, Rebecca sagged against the tall chair-back.

Dr. Foster cleared the pregnant silence, "As you saw, the experiment procedures met all applicable standards. The results are legitimate. We request your sanction to finish our research. Then, I'll ask you to grant your approval to manufacture the Dream Machine for use by licensed doctors."

Dr. Malone scanned the room as the board members spoke amongst themselves in huddles of two or three. "The board needs to make this decision in private. Becca, please wait outside until we come to agreement."

She rose then made her way to the door on shaky legs. Each doctor she passed nodded at her or reached out to shake her hand. Their overwhelming support and admiration touched her. By the time she collapsed onto a modern sofa in the waiting room, tears stung her eyes.

Thank God, she'd done Kurt proud.

After she'd recovered somewhat from the shock, she realized how beneficial this experience was for her career. A few, short days ago she would have focused on her goals to the exclusion of everything else except, maybe, the resolution of her sister's financial worries.

Lost in thought, it seemed like no time had passed before the doors reopened. Kurt escorted her back inside. He seated her at the table looking somewhat fierce. She began to worry things hadn't gone as well as she'd thought.

Dr. Malone assumed his official role for the pronouncement of their decision. "Becca, first we'd like to express our gratitude to you for undertaking this experiment. While the whole process is somewhat unorthodox, this board believes the potential benefits are worth the deviation from standard practices. Please be assured the raw beauty we witnessed today increased our esteem for you and your future as a brilliant addition to our community. Unfortunately, there are still some lingering concerns regarding the authenticity of the experiment. Therefore, it has been decided to allow you to proceed to the final stages with a physical witness as a safeguard."

As the implication of their ruling sank in, Rebecca spun in her chair to examine Kurt's face for his reaction. He patted her hand then nodded. She could barely force out the words accepting their terms but she managed. Then it was over. Colleagues rose, shaking Kurt's hand, congratulating them both before exiting, until the only person left besides her and Kurt was Luke.

He slapped Kurt on the back then bussed her cheek while shaking her hand. A smile spread across his handsome face as he said, "Good job, both of you. I'll see you tomorrow for stage two."

With a wink, he sauntered from the room.

Chapter Eighteen

"Are you sure you know what you're doing here, Kurt?" The familiar drawl travelled across his desk from the wingback Luke now occupied.

Anyone else would have overlooked the underlying tension in his friend's relaxed pose. He'd arrived early this morning and sequestered himself in Kurt's office to discuss their strategy for the day's research.

Before he could answer, Luke continued, "I admit it's been a while since I've had time in my schedule to get some real work done at my practice instead of dealing with the board's administrative bullshit popping up everyday..."

"You excel at bullshit."

"Thanks, asshole. Maybe I'm rusty, but I think you're getting in too deep. Are you sure Rebecca can handle this?"

At the mention of her name, Kurt sighed. She'd slept peacefully when he extricated himself from her tantalizing embrace to confer with Luke. Even after he rose, he'd stood transfixed by the sight of her bundled in his bed, getting some rest, until the door buzzer had sounded again, jarring him from his trance. It was no wonder her body soaked up this time to relax. She had worked so hard for so long, it took time to catch up once she gave in to exhaustion.

Already she looked better. The shadowed circles under her eyes had faded and her skin glowed with a rose-hued vibrancy. Then again, Kurt's ego suggested, all the phenomenal sex with him may have had something to do with the improvements. She thrived on their carnal adventures.

"Yes. She's ready."

"And you? Are you taking this all in stride, too?" Luke's penetrating stare made lying futile.

"Hell, no. What if I've fucked everything up? I don't have a choice now. I've set the course and I need to see it to the finish but..." Frustration rose inside him. He shoved back from his desk harder than he intended.

He couldn't sit here without remembering the first time he'd taken Becca.

"Shit!" He smacked a palm against the bookcase behind him, rattling the contents. His head hung low for the span of several ragged breaths before he righted the hardback reference of Freudian studies Becca had given him last Christmas. He aligned it with careful precision, allowing his fingers to stroke the binding before he stepped away.

"I don't understand, Luke. Everything is going well. The experiment is a raging success, Becca's agreed to be my partner and I guarantee the board will approve the final product. But it seems like I'm hanging on to everything by the skin of my teeth. Maybe it's too good to be true." Dragging his fingers through his hair only caused it to stand more on end.

Luke didn't respond. Instead, he rocked the heavy chair back on two legs, grinning like a Cheshire cat until Kurt snapped at him. "Quit that would you? This is serious."

"I'm sorry. But after all the times I've made a fool of myself over a woman, it's nice to see your icy guts in a knot for once." Luke's apology didn't conceal the lingering ghost of his smile. "Damn, though, I give you credit for picking her out of the crowd. You always swore she'd be hot."

"She is, isn't she?" Kurt groaned. "I knew she'd make an excellent partner for the firm from the moment she approached me after our first class to question a flaw no one else caught, not even you, in my latest journal article. Not like one of those smartass punks who argues to prove how smart they are, but because her mind is designed to solve problems. Because she wanted to improve the research. Right then, I wanted her."

"Why the hell didn't you tell her before James..."

"Tell her what? That I was dying to fuck her? That I've had

a perpetual hard-on for her for the past six years?" Kurt cursed, "Probably not the best way to entice your gun-shy intern to team up with you in a professional venture. She would have discounted her talents and assumed all I cared about was getting in her pants."

He clenched his fists but gritted his teeth against the need to pound something. It wouldn't eradicate his shame. "When you told me about the board's decision, part of me cheered. The experiment provided the perfect outlet to expend my lust before it could ruin our work. Hell, then I even started hoping she might want to keep up the smoking hot sex after we finished here. We're perfect partners, in and out of bed. And she did need to learn to trust herself before she could reach her full potential. You saw her yesterday, she's ready now."

"Then what's the problem?" Luke wondered. "You got what you wanted. She's your partner and she's burning up your sheets."

"You're right. I don't know what the hell's wrong with me. I just can't stand the idea she might find out I haven't been completely honest with her."

"Because she'd leave your sorry ass?"

He winced at the thought. "Not just that. I'd hate to see her revert back to the way she was before."

Luke stared him straight in the eye. "Are you in love with her?"

"What! No. Of course not. You know I don't believe in sentimental bullshit." He laughed but the strained sound held no humor. The concept was preposterous. Science didn't permit him to be swayed by the idea of love.

"Sometimes you have to take things on faith."

"Faith is what people rely on when they want to believe something evidence doesn't support."

"We don't have to do this, Kurt." His friend employed the understanding, cautious tone characteristic of his attempts to coax a patient down from the ledge. Literal or proverbial. "The board would have approved the final stages of the Dream Machine study without my involvement. Without the striking videos. It was only your request that swayed them to let me

215

witness the proceedings. Your woman has busted through more than one mental blockade in the past few days. What if she remembers everything? I can call this off right now before we make things worse."

He was torn. He knew what Becca's final two REM stages contained. Damn it, she lounged in his bed dreaming them right now during the hour before she woke. The idea simultaneously fired his blood and chilled it. Selfish urges begged him to end this nonsense. But she craved the fantasy.

"No, Luke, we continue as planned. I'm going to be the one to give her what she needs. I have to take her to her limits. I can't help myself. Even if she hates me for it later."

"I can only argue so much, Kurt, when I'm hungry, too. As your friend, this is the final out I can offer."

He smiled when the taut lines and anticipation in his best friend's expression reflected the primal need consuming him. "Let's go."

ଔ

Rebecca hesitated outside Kurt's office to gather her courage. Sucking in another futile gulp of air, she shivered with anticipation. After last night's relaxing sleep, she'd awakened to an epiphany. She knew what waited for her behind this door.

Although she'd opened and passed through it many times before, doing so today would mean the acceptance of yet another irrevocable change in her life.

She raised her hand toward the knob, not surprised to see her fingers trembling. She couldn't say if fear, desire or both caused the reaction but she refused to run away. Kurt had taught her to go after what she wanted even if it lay outside her primary goals in life. She was willing to change direction if it meant reaching for something better.

God, she thought, please let me be doing the right thing. Before she could second-guess her decision, she twisted the handle then strode inside without knocking.

Two sets of eyes tracked her march to the couch. Similar in

their eager intensity, they varied in appearance. Kurt's steel grey reflected the complete control of his stony, masked expression. Dr. Malone's rich, jewel green shone in welcome, deceptive in their gentleness.

No one who'd watched him twist his opposition into compliance in tough negotiations with the board—or the raw power of his physical competitions with Kurt on the tennis courts near the psych building—would mistake his charm for weakness. Both men inspired her imagination, though she'd always favored the hard edge of Kurt's enigmatic brilliance.

She disguised a shiver as she assumed a stoic pose on the sofa before them. At least she thought she had, but the dilation of Kurt's pupils in response shattered her illusion.

His formality for the sake of the cameras fractured the concentrated silence. "Today we'll begin stage two of the Dream Machine study. Dr. Luke Malone is present to act as a witness for the board."

"I understand, Doctors. Let's get right down to business. I remember all the dirty details." Not wanting to drag out the suspense, Rebecca decided to put it all on the line but her joke fell flat.

Kurt's face paled. Had she embarrassed him by being so forward in front of his friend? Maybe her assumption of control affronted him. She paused, waiting for him to direct her next move.

"All the details of what, Becca?" His tentative inquiry puzzled her.

"My dreams from last night. What else?"

He answered her with another question. "What exactly do you remember?"

"I recall all three stages we uncovered in previous sessions. In addition, I dreamt of a sexual encounter in a public setting where oblivious people sat just feet away. The way it happened at yesterday's board meeting." She snuck a glance at Luke to gauge his reaction but instead of anger or surprise, she detected acknowledgment and desire. "In fact, my fantasy mirrored the experience down to the tiniest insignificant minutiae. I must have incorporated reality into my desires.

Last, I remember...such vivid details..."

Despite the best of her intentions, her voice cracked. She licked her lips to wet the parched surface.

"Go ahead, baby." Kurt nudged her.

"I dreamt two men fucked me at the same time."

Her gaze locked with Kurt's. "You."

Then Luke's. "And you."

Though no longer afraid to embrace her unconventional tastes, her inexperience cranked up the flush racing to her cheeks. What if her dreams had changed since the last time Kurt documented them with the Dream Machine? He hadn't had time to review last night's feed since he'd left before she rose and she'd searched him out instead of waiting for his return.

What if he hadn't seen this? What if her confession shocked him?

The meeting the day before had influenced her fourth REM stage to morph into the wicked game they'd played below the table in yesterday's meeting. Only a psychic could have dreamed of something that hadn't happened yet. Therefore, the depraved indiscretion must have replaced whatever had filled that slot on previous nights. Maybe the knowledge Luke intended to witness their session today had spawned this fifth dream.

When Kurt's hand uncurled from the dents he had clenched in his pants leg, a predatory grin spread across his face. Rebecca assumed neither her lusts nor her bold speech displeased him. From her seat a few feet away, she discerned the outline of his erection beginning to swell along the length of his thigh. No, he didn't hate the idea.

She bit her cheek, imagining the possibilities. Would they go through with this?

Less sure of Luke's reaction, she peeked over to discover his open admiration of the cleavage showcased in the vee of her jacket. The bulge tenting the front of his trousers expanded as she watched.

Kurt and Luke exchanged glances. With the ease of men who have been friends long enough to be as close as brothers, they swapped silent communication in an instant. Both moved at the same time, converging on her where she sat. Their bulk and strength crowded her, encasing her in their scalding heat. Kurt took her mouth in a fierce, possessive kiss while Luke stripped off her shoes then began to knead the flesh beneath.

Before she could recover from the intensity of their initial touch, broad hands guided her down onto the plush area rug covering the industrial carpet. Fingers flew everywhere at once, over her neck and face, tracing the lines of her suit jacket and teasing the hem of her skirt. Working together, the doctors removed her jacket, shirt and skirt in less than ten seconds.

Rebecca's head spun as they bombarded her with sensations. They were both so attentive it was as though they knew just where to touch her to drive her wild. Kurt gathered her close to his side while he skimmed the lacy edge of her bra with his tongue. Luke mimicked the gesture across the tops of her thigh-high stockings. The feathered touches of their moist tongues drove her higher. She realized the animalistic sounds filling the room came from the back of her throat as she struggled to get closer.

"God, you're beautiful." Luke groaned against her sensitive inner thigh.

"So smart and brave," Kurt crooned in between licks and nips on the upper slopes of her breasts. "You're...perfect."

She reached out to brush the silky strands of Luke's hair between her fingers while her other hand gripped Kurt's biceps. He peeled the dainty bra away from her breasts as Luke tugged her panties off. Kurt assisted Luke by raising her hips. Their tag team approach triggered a flood, which washed her clenching channel with desire.

"Tell us, Becca. What do you want?" Kurt's rough voice and the lines of strain bracketing his mouth conveyed his superior restraint. What she wanted most was to be ravished. To become the center of their pleasure, knowing every touch would burn her alive.

"Use me." She trusted them to shape her into the ideal receptacle. "Please. Take me. However you like. Make it good."

At her desperate plea, Luke bit the tender spot between her

thigh and pussy with enough force to assure he'd received her submissive message. When he groaned against her, the shockwave traveled through her electrified nerves, causing her to gasp and arch.

"You're right, Kurt. She *is* perfect."

Kurt rocked his massive erection against her hip while he worked on her breasts. Her fingers wrapped around the pulsing shaft then squeezed, loving the heft of his satin flesh and the musky scent of his arousal. His hands roamed across her torso and abdomen causing her eyes to flutter closed.

"No, Becca. Watch." He snagged a cushion from the couch to prop her up.

"Taste her, Luke." His friend complied with famished laps. Kurt cradled her as Dr. Malone drove his tongue inside her soaked slit. She nearly came on the spot.

He rumbled his appreciation as more of her slickness coated his face.

Kurt's tight laugh followed. "I know. She's delicious. Feast on her. Make her come for you, Luke."

She shrieked when Luke sucked her clit into his mouth. Her hips bucked against his glistening chin. Kurt's fingers cupped her jaw, drawing her attention to him. "You like this, baby? You like being taken by two of us?"

When she hesitated, his grip strengthened.

"Tell me now. Or I'll make him stop, I swear it."

"No! Please don't. I love it. Let me touch you, taste you." She begged for mercy as the first hints of her imminent orgasm spiraled inside her. If they abandoned her now she'd die.

Kurt freed his hard-on then knelt beside her head, his cock bobbing in time to his pounding heart. "Is this what you want?"

She lunged for his proffered erection, devouring him in one slurp. The engorged tip bumped the back of her throat. After willing the muscles to relax, they parted to let him pass. His head dropped back. The cords on his neck stood out in stark relief as he moaned. Luke drove his long fingers to the extent of his reach inside her pussy. Her spasming muscles hugged the intrusions, rippling around them.

Kurt's dick absorbed her scream as she came and came.

Luke's fingers wrung every drop of pleasure from her pussy, making wet slurping sounds with every thrust. He lifted his head then said to Kurt, "Damn, she's so hot. Let me fuck her."

Lost in the afterglow of her first orgasm, Rebecca followed their distant conversation as if having an out-of-body experience. She watched Kurt nod. Then he retreated from her mouth. His salty flavor acted like a drug on her body. She whimpered, craving more of his taste.

Luke shucked his clothes even faster than he'd stripped hers off then rose like an ancient god above her. Golden skin gleamed with a thin sheen of sweat on muscles that stood out, defined and tense.

He covered her, bracing himself on his forearms, framing her head as he captured her mouth in a flirtatious kiss. He touched her so differently from Kurt. Tender and a little playful. The disparity fascinated her. Though she enjoyed the exchange, she missed the harder core of Kurt's passion.

She tasted her own juices as he aligned his thick cock with her welcoming pussy. As he kissed her, he slid his shaft along her furrow, spreading her excess secretions over his length and nudging her clit with every stroke.

Her post-climactic glow flared into a blaze of renewed passion when Kurt guided her hand to his cock, showing her how their wanton display affected him. Then, with two fingers, Luke applied downward force to his shaft. The fat head notched in the mouth of her sex.

The rings of her muscles grasped at it, greedily attempting to suck him in as Kurt reached between them to fondle her breasts. Luke sat on his haunches to give Kurt room to maneuver.

Kurt lounged beside them so he could look her in the eye. He dipped his head for a sweet kiss then asked, "Do you like the way he feels, baby?"

"Mmm," she purred.

Kurt laughed while the quivering muscles of Luke's abdomen advertised his obvious strain. Rebecca realized he waited for Kurt's permission to penetrate her. "Please, Doctor.

Let him fuck me."

"Good girl, Becca." Kurt pinched her nipple between his teeth then nodded at Luke. "Do it."

With a series of short strokes, Luke buried himself in her clinging sheath. She groaned as he stretched her. His cock was longer than Kurt's but not as wide. The deep invasion forced a gasp from her chest as the head stroked the sensitive tissue lining the back wall of her pussy.

He hit his stride, fucking her with graceful, liquid strokes. All the while, Kurt ate—biting, licking, tasting—at her chest, neck and mouth. Pleasure overtook her. Her second orgasm stole over her without warning. She clamped down hard on Luke as her pelvis rocked against him, grinding her clit into his lower abdomen.

With a growl, Luke strangled the base of his cock to prevent himself from spurting inside her. "Damn, that was close," he panted. "Honey, you're so snug when you come. I love the way you suck at me."

"Enough," Kurt barked. "Roll her over."

Luke obeyed. Still embedded in her, he wrapped his arms around her waist. Then he rotated until she draped on top of his sculpted chest, trying to catch her breath while the last of the spasms wracked her.

Glancing over her shoulder in search of Kurt, she found him grinning at her with savage lust. "You want us both, don't you?"

The unintelligible sound she made conveyed her total approval. Inside her pussy, Luke's cock jerked.

Kurt reached into the drawer on the end table. She heard the snick of a cap then flinched when he spread cool gel along with the thick cream from her previous orgasms up from the juncture of her and Luke to the tight rosebud of her ass. The thought of his fingers so close to his best friend's dick caused her pussy to spasm again.

Luke groaned. His head banged against the floor as his cock twitched inside her again. "Hurry, Kurt."

Kurt slicked his hand along his lubricated shaft one last time before he straddled them both then notched his cock at the entrance to her back passage. His teeth marked her shoulder as he began to work his dick inside her.

Rebecca had never imagined being packed so full would induce this extreme ecstasy. Kurt pushed in another fraction of an inch before retreating to the very cusp of her ass. She moaned and squeezed her muscles around the head of his cock to prevent him from leaving her.

As Kurt invaded her from behind, Luke began to thrust inside her in short strokes that renewed the stimulation on her clit as they fucked her together. They were far too accomplished at tandem loving for this to be the first time they'd shared a woman.

The strong arms banded around her, the muscular wall of Luke's chest, his searing kisses and the primal possession of Kurt behind her combined to set her on the edge of oblivion in minutes.

"Please Kurt, now," she begged. "Please."

He surged into her, filling her with all he had. He moaned against her neck before he sucked her earlobe into his mouth. So close, he whispered, "You're mine, Becca. Mine."

He rammed into her again and again. Luke rocked beneath her as she thrust her ass against Kurt. Pressure built in her like water on a dam.

"I can't hold back. Feels too good." Luke called mercy below her. His muscles tensed impossibly. Then his guttural cry sent a shockwave up her spine as he emptied himself inside her pussy. The heat of his come blasting inside her in jets of pleasure made her shudder around him. But the shout from above had satisfaction exploding through her as Kurt spilled his semen in her ass. It set her off like the grand finale of a Fourth of July fireworks display.

"*Mine!*" he growled in her ear as they both spent themselves in her willing body.

"Kurt," she screamed as she came.

First, she saw stars as she clenched her eyes shut.

Then, the whole world went black.

Rebecca either slept or hovered in a disembodied state of

euphoria. Groggy and sated, she bobbed there. Sentient awareness of her body didn't translate to control of her muscles, leaving her unable to escape the horror stalking her.

A dream lurked on the fringes of her awareness.

Sex with two amazing men had doused her in rapture—opening her mind to infinite carnal possibilities—but something ominous chased her in the quiet after the storm, permeating her ecstasy with a sense of doom. Utter mental relaxation allowed the scene to play in her mind though she wished she could block it out.

Not a dream. A nightmare.

Everything had been a lie.

She moaned low in her throat as the pain of Kurt's deception smacked her. Yet, the perturbing vision continued to play as if she had a front row seat to the latest horror blockbuster. A corrupted daydream about an experiment flashed in her imagination. Her ultimate fantasy—the sixth REM cycle—featured her as the subject of a fiendish experiment.

In an instant, it all made sense. Kurt must have tested the Dream Machine on her before this week's adventure. She couldn't understand how or when but the whole study had been a ploy.

Not only had he used potentially harmful emerging technology on her without her consent, but he'd also previewed her desires then played right to them. He'd manipulated her into believing he needed the same things she did—that chemistry, or magic, had led her to the one man who could fulfill all her fantasies without effort.

Instead, she'd been nothing more than a temporary fuck toy. The entire experience had been a sham. This couldn't be happening. She thrashed to the surface through the sinister remnants of her dream but gentle hands sheltered her shoulders, preventing her from moving or injuring herself.

"You're all right, Becca. Lie still, catch your breath and everything will be okay. You just passed out for a second." Luke attempted to calm her. She collapsed on his chest, which still rose and fell in rapid succession, confirming little time had passed. She'd really been unconscious just a few enlightening moments. Everything required proof as she began to doubt all her presumed truths. The trust she'd built with Kurt over the past week crumbled to dust.

Nothing would ever be okay again.

"No." She tried to shove away from him with wet-noodle arms but, still disoriented, she slipped.

Luke wrapped his hand around her upper arm to steady her but his kindness only compounded her confinement. She had to flee from their betrayal.

"No! Let me go."

Kurt struggled to gain his footing behind her. His questioning gaze seared her back. She couldn't stand the tearing agony anymore. Before she could suppress it, a sob broke from her splintering chest.

"Calm down, baby. Everything's fine." Kurt reached out to stroke her hair but she wrenched from his putrid touch. Luke's flaccid flesh slipped free from the clasp of her traitorous, still clenching, sex as she flung herself off his torso. She banged her hip into the corner of the couch but the bruising impact couldn't compete with the rending of her soul.

"Stay away from me," she shrieked.

"Baby, what's wrong?" Kurt crooned.

Luke caught sight of her wild eyes then cursed under his breath. "Oh shit, Kurt. She knows."

She whipped around. Panic emanated in searing rays from Kurt's tense shoulders and slack jaw. Their gazes collided.

It was true.

"You lied to me." The simple accusation hung between them. She couldn't utter another word before the bile in her stomach threatened to choke her. Then, in a whisper she didn't mean to articulate, "I trusted you."

While she scrutinized Kurt's expression, desiring with the last shred of hope to see some flicker of denial but finding none, Luke inched closer. "Give him a chance to explain, Becca."

Trapped like a caged animal between two tamers, she crab-walked backward. She stamped out the throbbing twinges of pleasure still zinging through her as she scrambled from between their sleek bodies.

How could she have been so stupid? Her mother's experience had warned her. Men always lied to get what they wanted. But Kurt had seemed so sincere about his intent to make her his partner.

She should have known all he cared about was the Dream Machine.

Dazed, still trying to filter fantasy from reality, Rebecca blinked at the two men in front of her. She couldn't bear to look Kurt in the face so she missed out on any clues to his thoughts. Yet, he hadn't denied her accusations.

He took one halting step closer. Self-perseverance kicked in. She bolted as her mind raced to puzzle everything out. Streaking up from the sitting area, she dove for the coat rack beside the door. She tore one of his long overcoats from the hanger as she fumbled for the knob with her other shaking hand.

"Becca! Wait!" He tried to catch her but she heard Luke intervene on her behalf.

"Let her go, Kurt. She needs to sort this out on her own."

Wrapping the slicker around herself haphazardly, she dashed out of the office barefoot then sprinted toward her apartment as tears streamed down her face.

Chapter Nineteen

Rebecca shed Kurt's coat and the lingering scent of his cologne on the way to a hot shower, realizing she'd jogged all the way home as naked as a flasher under the jacket. For some reason the image struck her as funny. Hysteria tinged her cackle.

"Am I losing it?" she asked herself in a voice raw from sobbing as she stepped under the steaming water. She doubted she could scrub away the disgust clawing at her but she had to give it a shot.

She almost never allowed herself the luxury of tears but the betrayal slicing her heart overwhelmed what inhibitions she had remaining. In the wake of such agony, she couldn't deny the magnitude of what she'd surrendered to Kurt.

Dear God, she loved him.

Nothing could have obliterated a lifetime of denial, her personal coat of armor, and altered her so thoroughly unless it was that. Her outstretched arms locked to brace against the shower wall as she bowed her head under the weight of the revelation. Though she suspected she'd loved him for years—or at least the seeds of affection had lain dormant, waiting for the slightest encouragement to grow—she'd admitted it to herself too late.

Cruel fate had bestowed her wildest dreams then yanked them from her before she understood what lie within her grasp. But every sparkling promise her interlude with Kurt had implied had turned out to be a tarnished lie.

From the start, he'd shown her infinite kindnesses. He'd

mentored her, supported her through school, let her experience life on her own, and chosen her out of a field of talented candidates to develop. He'd seemed like a sexy, benevolent genius to her naïve mind.

Everyone had flaws, but how could she have misjudged him so completely?

Traversing the tracks of sweat, tears and desperation dripping from her face, her fingers walked their way down her body. The slippery mixture of all three of their secretions lingered between her thighs. Touching the evidence drove home the evolution she'd undergone in the past brief days. From a young, inexperienced student to a world-weary doctor, the transition hadn't quite gone according to plan.

Yet, beneath the confusion, grief and outrage, a flicker of arousal stirred in her gut at the memory of two well-muscled bodies sandwiching her. The permanent alterations the experiment had wrought in her sexuality would not die along with her childish notions of love and honor.

Maybe someday she could find solace in that.

C3

Rebecca slouched on the floor of her living room, staring straight ahead with unfocused vision interrupted by an occasional blink. The ticking of the clock echoed in the lonely space, marking the passing time just as it had all through the long night and longer morning. Every instant carried her further from the bliss she'd thought she'd discovered at the hands of a traitor.

How could she have been so blind?

Is this what her mother had experienced so many years ago? Was she doomed to repeat her torrid family history?

Before she consciously accepted her intentions, her hand snaked onto the coffee table in front of her then retrieved her cell phone. A single touch on the first speed dial setting connected her to her mother's house before she thought better of the action.

"Hello?" Her mother's question sounded lucid. Rebecca speculated at what had possessed the woman to answer the phone. A rare occurrence. Her sleep deprived and pain-fuzzed mind prevented her from responding while she debated hanging up.

"Becca, is that you? I see your number on the caller ID."

"Um... Y-yes, Mom. It's me. Sorry." Forcing her ragged vocal chords to produce sound irritated her throat.

"Are you sick? You don't sound well."

"No. Not sick. I'm..." She couldn't utter the largest lie of her life and claim to be fine.

Horrified, a sob bubbled from behind her clamped lips.

"Becca?"

The terrified note in her mother's inquiry prompted her to reassure the woman but, for once, she couldn't. For once, she needed someone to comfort her.

"What's wrong? Is it Elsa?"

"Elsa? No, Mom." The soul searching Rebecca had done during the sleepless night nagged her. Some of the strain in her relationship with her mother stemmed from her need for control. Growing up, her mother had been willing to hand over the family reins but Rebecca had snatched them up to avoid being vulnerable.

Maybe it was time to start opening up. It couldn't hurt any worse than it already did.

Her mother waited with patient silence for Rebecca to divulge the reason for her call. Pressuring her had never worked in the past. Little did her mother know, today differed from all the others in her life.

"I need to ask you something." She dragged a breath through the razor wire of her constricted chest. "I hope it doesn't upset you."

"Go ahead." Did she imagine the spark of encouragement and anticipation in her mother's tone?

How much had Rebecca driven the solitary existence she'd led by calling her independence necessary for survival? Her whole world had warped in a matter of hours. She saw everything through a new lens.

"How could you love my father even after he betrayed you?" The question escaped before she could censor it.

A harsh inhalation, painful to hear, rushed through the speaker of her phone. After several calming breaths, her mother's voice wavered across the line.

"You've never understood, Becca. How could you? You're so much like him. So caught up in thinking you forget to feel. You've always seen me as weak."

Shame layered over the agony of loss rending her soul in two.

"I'm sorry, I didn't mean that as the accusation it sounded like." She suppressed another sob but tears ran hot down her cheek. "I-I need to know. Why can you love someone when they've hurt you so much? It's not fair, damn it!"

Her mother sniffled on the other end of the line as Rebecca's contagious misery spread.

"Someone's broken your heart." Resentment spiked her mother's statement. The protective instincts she rarely displayed broke through the underlying tension of their conversation. "I wished you girls would never experience heartache. I thought you were safe, Becca. I didn't think you'd let anyone in."

The admission stung. Had she really become so cold? She wouldn't make that mistake again. She could reveal this much at least. "I'm afraid, Mom. What if I never get over him?"

"I can't promise you will, sweetheart. We both know it's not true. If he's really the one for you, no one will be able to replace him. I'm so sorry. I wish I could say otherwise."

"Is that why Joe left you? Did Elsa's dad know you didn't love him as much as you loved my dad?"

"What made you think he left me, Becca?" Her mother's soft question alerted her to the dangerous grounds she trod.

"I...I guess I just assumed. You were so depressed, then he stopped coming around." Rebecca's breathing hitched as she now understood the stinging impact such a separation could inflict.

"Maybe it's time I told you this story from the beginning. I was younger than you, just eighteen." Her mother's pause before her trembling exhalation broadcast the effort it cost her to share her experience with her suffering daughter.

She was stronger than Rebecca had given her credit for.

"You don't have to do this." By now, Rebecca's words slurred with her unabashed crying.

"I do. I want to. You know I was a dancer. Your father was an amazing producer. He had a natural eye for what would work, the kind of thing you can't teach. As struggling artists, we shared the same circle of friends. I knew him and bumped into him from time to time. He would flirt with me and suggest we go out but I never accepted. I couldn't. Ever since I was a child, I often experienced periods where I felt lost, helpless and suffocated by despair for no reason. I didn't think anyone would want me."

Rebecca had to interject. "You suffer from depression, Mom. Lots of people do."

"I know, now. Then it seemed so confusing. Everything was going well but I still felt like my life could go to hell at any minute. I worried constantly. I had trouble eating, and my dancing suffered. Your father saw me struggling and offered to help. He was so kind, so understanding. I had a crush on him from the first moment I met him but, during those dark times, I fell in love with him. I just didn't know how to show him. How to take the next step. He was so worldly, already on his way to the top, and he wouldn't pursue me after I'd turned him down so many times before. He acted like such a gentleman."

When her mother paused to gather her thoughts, Rebecca held her breath. She understood exactly how it felt to long for someone but believe they were unreachable.

"Then he got word the funding had come through for his production. The critics billed it a sure success on his credit alone. I was shocked when he came to me. Told me he wanted me for the show. And for himself. I was so wrapped up in myself, I hadn't realized how desperate he was. Until he suggested how wonderful it would be to work together and be lovers. How the show would benefit from our intimacy. He..."

"He conned you into sleeping with him!" Fury erupted from

her, refusing to be contained.

"No, Becca. I would have slept with him regardless. Do you think me so naive?"

Again, the parallel stunned her silent.

"When I got pregnant, hormones amplified the depression until it became unbearable. Nothing he did could cheer me up. He grew frustrated, convinced my morose moods centered on the pregnancy and the interruption to my career. Nothing I said would dissuade him. I think he suffered from massive guilt, thinking he'd pushed me into something that made me miserable. But it wasn't true..."

The story tapered off as her mother gathered the courage to finish the tale.

"We fell into a vicious cycle. His guilt, my depression and the terror swamping me as I watched him slip away. I'm not proud of this, Becca, but it got so bad I had to be hospitalized. He was horrified. Terrified he'd driven me to the edge. The two things I concentrated on to drive away the darkness were the life growing inside me and what it would be like when I could return to him. But, when I finally was released, all that remained in his apartment was a letter."

They cried together.

"He abandoned me when I needed him most because of his own doubts, and for that I've never forgiven him."

"B-but you still love him?"

"Love is a funny creature, Becca. Your father loved me. I know that to the bottom of my heart. And when you love someone, sometimes you do crazy things. Things you'd never consider otherwise. Things you think are for the best. This is how he came to make his silly proposition. I didn't care, because I loved him too. He only offered what I'd always wanted both professionally and personally. He loved me enough to leave his successful show and sacrifice our relationship when he thought he'd hurt me."

She sighed before continuing.

"And that's why I sent Joe away."

"What?" Surprise jolted Becca from her tears.

"Joe was a private investigator. I hired him to find your

father. We worked together for nearly three years but couldn't trace him for long. Bits and pieces would trickle in over time. I developed a friendship with Joe. I was lonely. He's a good man. He loved me but I came to realize I couldn't return his feelings. It wasn't fair to let him sacrifice his happiness. Even after Elsa, he still searched for your father, knowing I'd never be whole without him. And how would I repay Joe if we were to find him? We both knew the answer to that. You see, Becca? Love makes people do irrational things. There is no logic in love."

"How do you know if it's love, not just someone taking advantage of you?"

"Your heart already understands or you wouldn't have called me. Can you live without this man of yours? If not, you had better go find him and make things right. Convince him nothing else matters if you have each other. By whatever means necessary. If he owes you an apology, get one. Then make sure he knows what's in your soul. Show him so he never wants to leave the one place he'll always be cherished—no matter what stupid things he does—because he'll offer you the same shelter from your mistakes."

Her pulse pounded in her temples as she tried to digest the wisdom her mother imparted.

"Thank you." She meant it from the bottom of her heart. "I'm so sorry I didn't understand. I hope we can talk more...if you want, I mean."

"I'd like that very much. I'm sorry, too, Becca. I should have been stronger for you. I let you take on too much."

"We can't change the past. Let's look to the future."

Her mother's watery laugh lifted a weight off her conscience. "This guy has changed you. For the better. I'm so damn proud of you. Now give him hell. And call me later."

"I will. I love you."

"I love you too, Becca."

She disconnected the phone with a sense of wonder. Her tears evaporated, leaving behind crystals of determination and a tiny helping of optimism. She blew her nose then ran through the surreal conversation she'd just had, trying to digest the implications of her mother's story.

Her cell phone, set on vibrate, rattled on the hardwood floor beside her. Was it her mother calling back? Would she instruct Rebecca to ignore the dangerous hope she'd given her? Admit the total insanity of her advice?

She flipped it open, exposing the display. The buzz hadn't indicated a call but an incoming text message. From Kurt. Her finger hovered over the delete key but her heart refused to allow it to drop. Instead, she displayed the simple communication.

Are you okay?

In a rush, she released the breath she hadn't realized she'd trapped in her chest. Why would he care if she hurt? He'd gotten what he wanted from her. Unless...what if her mother was right?

Her analytical mind engaged as she dissected the possible motivations for, and outcomes of, the experience she'd shared with Kurt. She pondered the quandary until her ass went as numb as her heart had been from sitting on the plank flooring.

In the end, only one hypothesis was plausible.

Kurt loved her, too.

Now she had to prove it to him.

Suddenly, she had a new goal. Once she decided she wanted something, she would stop at nothing to have it. That much hadn't changed.

Chapter Twenty

Luke sat at his sleek, modern desk in the high-rise building housing the board member's workspace. His sharp secretary alerted him via a frantic intercom squawk to the young woman on a rampage headed toward his office, undeterred by instructions to wait in the lobby. He'd been expecting something like this for the last two days.

Putting aside the case review he'd been working on, he kicked back in the oversized desk chair, forcing himself to appear relaxed when his office door flew open. Becca turned then shut the door with a crisp shove, giving him a moment to admire her lush ass in the form-fitting suit. Even more attractive when pissed off and determined, she induced a rare twinge of jealousy.

Kurt was one lucky bastard.

Although they'd discussed his best friend's plans for Becca, Luke had never recognized the full potential Kurt insisted lie beneath her composed exterior. He had to give it to Kurt on this one. He'd been right and then some. The woman who planted her feet before him now bore little resemblance to the intelligent but mousy apprentice Kurt had worked with the past few years.

Every time Luke had come to the office, Becca had acted polite, efficient and aloof. Now, the vibrant woman engaged in her surroundings. Emotion poured off her in waves as she stood—arms akimbo, legs spread—less than an inch in front of his glass and steel desk.

As he watched, wondering what kind of shoes she wore today, Becca slapped her palms onto the gleaming surface with a resounding crack. She leaned in closer, putting her cleavage right at eye level. He chalked up her dismissal of his blatant perusal of her lace-covered breasts as another sign of her renewed self-confidence. Luke couldn't help but grin at the ferocity of her intent. His already immense respect for her grew a little more.

"You knew."

"Knew what?"

"Don't play stupid, Luke. Kurt tested the Dream Machine on me before the start of the official study. He would have told you."

"No, he didn't." Luke called her bluff.

"So maybe you were innocent in the beginning but he must have confided in you at some point and you still let it happen."

"I meant, he didn't test the Dream Machine on you until the start of the trial. Not that he hadn't told me." He'd faced some intimidating opponents as head of the board but her spectacular fury, and the veiled pain feeding the bonfire, knocked the wind out of him.

"Yeah, right. Then how did he set up the whole fiasco to mimic my fantasy? Is he psychic? I can assure you it was exact. I see the sordid details each time I close my eyes for more than a moment."

Her lids fluttered closed then she shifted, for the first time revealing a hint of weakness.

"Sit, Becca. There are some things we need to discuss since you're torturing Kurt by refusing to answer his calls. Do you know how many other times in our friendship I've had to stop by his house every few hours to make sure he hadn't drowned himself in Jack Daniels? None. And thank God, because he's a bear to deal with when he's pissed off, devastated and drunk. I'm about to kick his ass."

Regret washed across her features. A good sign. "I needed some time to think."

"I understand. We hurt you. For my part in it, I'm truly sorry, Becca. Please, sit."

She melted into his guest chair. He couldn't stand to witness her agony from his formal distance. Before he considered why, he rounded his desk then took the seat next to her, angling it until he faced her suffering head on.

Luke reached out to cradle her frozen hands in his. She didn't shy away from the gesture as he'd have expected. Instead, she raised her shimmering gaze to his, letting him drink in the liquid pain pooled there.

"Kurt did *not* test the Dream Machine on you without your knowledge." He reiterated. "Dr. James Wexford, recently fired from the cognitive psych division, did. The night you fell asleep at your desk before final exams."

"Oh my God." She flinched, her eyes squeezed shut for a moment before she shook her head as though to clear it.

"Do you remember?" Luke embraced his practiced calm to cover the rage. She'd gotten to him. The idea of someone violating the tiny spitfire infuriated him.

"A little. I thought I'd been having trouble telling dreams from reality because I was stressing out and skipping some sleep here and there. That night I had a nightmare about something attacking my neck. It-it startled me awake. But I was alone. I had a mark there for a day or so but I assumed a spider bite had jarred me from sleep."

He grimaced at her recollection. It was time to give her the truth. All of it. He hoped she didn't hate them afterward, no matter how much they deserved it. He longed to continue their budding friendship and he'd never seen Kurt so ravaged.

The other man had ruined his perfect attendance record by cancelling his appointments for the entire week.

"Kurt got called out to an emergency at the hospital. He tried to contact me but I...had my phone off. He passed James in the campus parking garage and asked him to keep an eye on you since he didn't have the heart to wake you. Instead, James snooped around the laboratory. He'd always been jealous of Kurt. No one expected he was capable of something like this, though."

Her fingers trembled in his grasp but she urged him on. "Tell me. What happened?"

"James found the Dream Machine. He realized Kurt never intended to pursue a human trial. He thought he'd earn a little fame by going rogue, taking that first step without the sanction of the board. The bastard was in a hurry. He had to know Kurt would destroy him if he got caught. He used a roll of packing tape from the office supply cabinet to attach the diode to your neck then took a sample from your REM stages while Kurt was gone."

He had to hesitate to clear his throat. As the head of the board, the rest fell on him.

"Just say it."

"The next day, James brought the session recording to the board. Though we immediately reported him to the state, fired him from the university and pressed criminal charges, we couldn't deny the potential of Kurt's invention. Not to mention the perfect setup we had to test it. A one in a million opportunity. For the record, once Kurt found out about what James did, he decked the asshole before I could pull him off to keep his ass out of jail."

Luke's gaze shifted to the tips of his shoes. He wasn't proud of what they'd done.

Becca's pregnant silence urged him to continue.

"The board... I...threatened to do the same to Kurt for leaving the door unlocked with such hazardous equipment around. Unless he performed the Dream Machine experiment with you. You-uh, you should know he declined at first. I think he only said yes because I told him the board had agreed to approve his request for your partnership if you could learn to embrace your emotions through use of the Dream Machine."

"You lied."

Her steely tone gave no clue to how she took the news. Luke glanced into her piercing green eyes but he didn't see judgment or condemnation. Instead, the reflection of his guilt-torn expression captured his attention, forcing him to admit it.

"Yeah. They'd already signed the paperwork."

"So the ad for a subject..."

"I had my secretary put it on your desk. Kurt didn't know about it." He sighed. "I found out later she'd called your family and told them your sister's aid had been rescinded after listing the large fee in the phony ad. I told her to make it irresistible. I should have been more specific. Shit, I'm sorry, Becca. I hope you know Kurt would never have yanked his sponsorship. No matter what happened."

"Kurt's sponsorship?"

"Um, yeah. Son of a bitch. He funds the grant you, and now your sister, receive. I thought you knew."

Shock, anger, disbelief, fear, violation and relief cycled through her expression. He squeezed her hand tighter, letting her ride out the storm of emotions.

"It seems I keep fucking things up more but I'm trying to do the right thing here, Becca. I never meant for you, or Kurt, to get hurt. I'm so sorry. I've done despicable things..."

"I forgive you, Luke."

"You do?"

"Yes. You fucked up. The board, Kurt and you, Luke. Big time. But I forgive you."

He nodded in awe. "I'm not sure I deserve it..."

She cut him off once more. "I'm sure you don't. But sometimes our decisions are driven by more than logic. And now you owe me. You *will* help me get what I want."

His tentative smile transformed into an irrepressible grin at her audacity. She could have threatened to report him for improper behavior or challenged his professionalism but she hadn't. This debacle struck Becca on a personal level. The determination to claim Kurt for life flared in her emerald eyes. Her passion scorched him from this distance, proclaiming her a woman on a mission.

His best friend didn't stand a chance.

"Of course," he agreed. "Kurt needs some convincing. You have to understand, Becca. He's never been in love before."

For a moment, her composure cracked. The gap allowed him to glimpse the vulnerability behind her courageous intent. Her eyes flitted from his. Luke was glad he'd said the words. She needed reassurance to stay the course and prove it to Kurt. It wouldn't be easy.

"Did he tell you that?" she whispered, some of the ferociousness leeched from her bearing.

"No, but it's obvious to me." His placed a chaste kiss on the back of her hand. "How do you want to do this?"

She blinked then cleared her throat. "I need you to bring him to the lab. I'll need some assistance to get him on the table."

A chuckle of approval rumbled from his chest. "I like the way you think, Dr. Williams. You'll have to give him tonight to dry out. I wasn't joking about the binge. I'll have him there first thing tomorrow morning. Deal?"

She nodded. "Deal."

Chapter Twenty-One

Rebecca paced the limited open space of the laboratory floor. The fine tremors of her legs complicated the difficult process of staying upright on her five-inch heels as she considered the drastic step she was about to take. If she'd had to endure much longer in isolation with her conflicted thoughts she might have changed her mind but, just then, the door opened.

When Luke entered the room, her heart froze in her chest. He bore Kurt's limp, unconscious body over his shoulder in a fireman's hold. Yesterday, he'd convinced her to leave this part of the plan to him but she never imagined he'd go to such extremes.

She rushed to his side. "Is he all right? What did you do to him?"

"He's fine. I put a mild sedative in his drink at dinner last night then let him crash at my place. I think he's starting to come out of it. Let's hurry." Together they arranged Kurt on his back across the table.

When finished, Luke stretched his arms over his head to work out the kinks then turned to face her. The way he stopped short, eyes widened, pupils darkening, Rebecca assumed her outfit had the desired impact. She'd selected the thigh-high, leather lace-up boots, crotchless fishnet stockings and black satin bustier to enhance her confidence as well as her womanly assets.

"Damn, honey, that's one killer getup." Luke whistled as he circled her. "Don't worry, he doesn't stand a chance."

"Thanks, Luke, for everything. I think I can handle it from here."

"Just in case, I'll be across the street at the diner. If you run into trouble, call my cell." He bent to place a sweet kiss on her lips before walking out, shaking his head.

With quick and methodical motions, Rebecca began to remove Kurt's clothes. She attempted to lever his torso up from the table but his deadweight made the task impossible. He moaned in his unnatural slumber when she jostled him. Desperate, she grabbed a pair of scissors from a drawer in the table base then slit the garment along the seams.

She tugged away the dangling scraps while trying to ignore the way the light played over the definition of his muscled chest.

His slacks were easier to dispose of. A sharp inhalation cut the silence when the heat of his abdomen singed the fingers she slipped inside his waistband. She coaxed the stubborn fastener with shaking hands. Finally undone, she discovered his bare flesh beneath. Her pussy clenched in response.

She rushed, stripping his pants past thick thighs and elegant calves until he lounged naked before her. He mumbled again in his sleep. Did he call her name or did her imagination play tricks with her hope?

When she paused to admire his form on display, she observed his cock responding, hardening. Whether due to her presence, a dream or no reason in particular, she couldn't say, but her mouth watered at the sight of him.

Rebecca began to strap Kurt to the table.

First, she cinched the belt straps around his chest and waist. She had to loosen them significantly to accommodate his powerful build compared to the settings he'd used on her. Then she progressed down his legs to his ankles. By the time she secured his left arm, the only part of him not already restrained, his hand twitched and he groaned. Hurrying to finish before he awoke, Rebecca fastened the last buckles around his firm biceps.

"Becca?" His groggy question rasped through the room.

Standing beside his shoulder, she reached out to smooth

his hair back from his face. "I'm here, Kurt."

"What the hell is going on?" After a few blinks, he started to regain awareness. He tried to sit up. His muscles jerked when he reached the limit of the bonds encircling him. The leather creaked but held without budging.

She continued to stroke his shoulders, calming him as his eyelids popped open and stayed this time. His raptor gaze locked onto hers.

"That bastard drugged my fucking pasta?" Kurt's breath came in rapid pants as he worked himself up from confused to furious.

"I made him help me." Her gentle murmur held an edge of steel.

"Why? What's this all about? Release me now, Becca." He yanked on the ties, testing their strength but, she knew from experience, his attempts were futile. He couldn't escape.

"No, Kurt. I'm not letting you go."

"What!" His incredulous tone lost its tinge of wonder when her seriousness dawned on him.

"I'm not letting you go," she repeated more sternly. Focusing on the fight for their future, she braced herself then plunged ahead. "I'm not letting you loose from this table until you admit you're in love with me."

Kurt sucked in a lungful of air then peered at her, all of her, for the first time. As his stare wandered from her face, scanning the rest of her body, she stepped back to ensure he got the picture. She'd primed for battle.

His rage seemed to ebb as he resigned himself to playing by her rules. He gave her his full attention. Though he acted the part of her captive, he pinned her under his perusal.

"That's not going to happen, Becca. You've misunderstood." His hollow words ached with regret.

Prepared for such a claim, she annealed her resolve. "No Kurt, things are just starting to make sense. Thanks to you and the Dream Machine." She circled the table. Her fingers trailed across his exposed flesh as she paced with the crisp snap of her stilettos on tile. His muscles bunched and tensed in anticipation of her glancing touches.

"Becca, stop this. Let me up so I can apologize properly."

She shook her head.

"There are things I need to tell you. Things that might shock you and I don't want to be stuck here, unable to help you if you need me."

"Things like how Dr. Wexford tested the Dream Machine on me when I fell asleep at my desk? Things like the shenanigans the board pulled on you to twist your arm into participating in the experiment with me? Things like the fact you planned to make me your partner all along, before the situation provided you with the perfect opportunity to exercise your lust?"

"Fuck! I wanted to tell you. They threatened to fire me but it shouldn't have mattered." His head clunked against the table as his hands fisted. If the restraints hadn't immobilized him, she could picture him kicking something.

Then his bloodshot eyes bored into her until she couldn't dismiss his apology. "I'm sorry for deceiving you. It was wrong. I should have told you how much I wanted you. I should have told you about the break-in. Only a total asshole would hurt you like that."

His sincere apology squeezed her heart. He'd made mistakes—true—but in her soul, she'd already forgiven him. The admission gave her the confidence to pursue more than the formal partnership he'd envisioned.

"Don't you see, Kurt? Hiding the truth from me is a compelling piece of evidence. Everything you've done goes against your nature. Hell, look at what I've done to get you here this morning." Standing between his spread legs now, she skimmed one fingernail down the center of his chest and abdomen. His cock jerked in response. It grew with each heartbeat.

"Becca, what are you talking about?" His bewildered gaze flicked between her face and hand. She suppressed a grin when his arousal distracted him. Like her, Kurt needed to stop thinking and start feeling. Until they made a breakthrough, she would start with the basics.

"You love me, Kurt. And I'll prove it to you." With a sigh, she turned from his swelling erection. She ripped off the sheet covering the whiteboard in the corner, revealing a list of premises required to support her theory.

"Don't do this to us. It's not what you think. Don't ruin what we have." He strained against the bonds, ignoring her proof.

"This time I won't let you hide, Kurt."

"Don't make me argue against you."

"Don't make *me* use the ball gag I found in the closet."

His stare whipped to hers, incredulous.

"All I'm asking is that you evaluate the evidence without passing judgment. In fact, I think I'll add to the list."

She uncapped a dry-erase marker then squeezed in one more bit of logic at the top of the chart.

Subject cannot separate emotion from decisions relating to his assistant although he typically excels at maintaining rational objectivity.

She dropped the marker in the tray then returned to his side. "For each point you consider with an open mind, I'll reward you. Fair enough?"

"Shit, Becca..." He gaped at her.

"Dr. Williams."

His jaw hung slack for a second or two. Then a new fire blazed in his eyes when he nodded his understanding. "Yes, Doctor. I admit you distort my judgment. It's harder for me to think rationally when you're around. Now, get your pretty ass over here and touch me."

"Your begging needs some work." But she longed for skin to skin contact. Bravado hid her nerves, but didn't erase them. Only the passion he inspired would ground her.

She began with a kiss.

They both contributed emotion to the simple act until the glide of their lips evolved into a complex expression of desperation, relief and turmoil.

She sank into the seductive caress of his tongue on hers until she realized he had her on the verge of relinquishing control. With a sigh, she separated them. Kurt growled, attempting to pursue her until he reached the limit of his confinement. His muscles flexed, restless, beneath the leather straps.

"Next point." She indicated the list on the whiteboard.

It took a few breaths for him to gather his composure, but then he turned his face to read her argument as she paraphrased.

"You could have your pick of women. Ones much thinner, prettier, richer and more desirable than me. Instead, you went to a lot of trouble to have me."

"There's no one more attractive than you, Becca. You're smart, dedicated, loyal..." The points he ticked off dug him deeper as his gaze turned smoky. "...voluptuous, sensual, generally submissive..."

She almost laughed at the rueful look he shot her but she bit her cheek to maintain her game face.

"...and—now—uninhibited. You're all I could want in a lover."

"Thank you," she murmured, humbled by his reverence. Her hands pet his chest, kneading the tense muscles there until he calmed.

"Mmm. Yes, Be—Doctor." She rewarded his learning by following the path of her fingers with her mouth. She nuzzled, sucked and nipped a moist trail along his neck, over his collarbone, to his firm pecs. She placed a tender kiss above his heart then licked his nipple.

When he jerked on the table beneath her, power flooded her veins. The spike of adrenaline helped explain the seductive power of the games they'd played. Like trying on a costume for Halloween, she enjoyed seeing things in a new light but she wished she writhed beneath his commanding touch instead.

"Keep going." His strangled cry contained more demand than plea but she granted his wish. She laved the tan disc then worried it between her teeth before sliding over to do the same to the other. Her fingers lingered with light pinches until his harsh breathing severed the connection with her lips as his chest rose and fell, snapping her attention to her plan.

She turned her back on his imploring stare. Otherwise, she wouldn't be able to resist the urge to climb on top of him then ride until their raging libidos had been satisfied.

"Come here."

She ignored his ragged command. If she didn't, she'd lose control, rendering the whole exercise pointless. She only had one chance to get this right.

She cleared her throat twice, grateful when he asked, "Should I read the next bullet?"

Rebecca nodded though she suspected he rushed her for his prize.

"The subject claimed to conduct the Dream Machine experiment in order to help his repressed assistant. Yet, when he had already succeeded, he petitioned the board to continue the experiment simply to fulfill her fantasies."

He cursed under his breath but she heard the bitterness anyway.

"That's true. But it only shows that I'm a selfish bastard. I wanted to watch you discover your latent desires. It sounds conceited, but I knew I could make your dreams come true."

She smiled. "That's the most amazing gift anyone's ever given me."

Her hand grazed along his tight abdomen until her fingers hovered a hairsbreadth from the glistening head of his cock. Kurt attempted to rock his hips, forcing contact, but he couldn't get enough leverage to maneuver. She raised one eyebrow at him but he refused to beg. As punishment, she continued past his throbbing erection, stroking her hand over his muscular inner thigh, toward his feet instead.

"Becca!" His shout was part outrage, part agony and part plea. She slapped the sensitive skin beneath her palm.

"Doctor," he corrected, "I need you to stroke my dick."

"Not yet." She couldn't withstand such temptation at the moment. He groaned, at first in despair then with renewed hunger when her lips graced his anklebones. She licked the top of his feet until his toes curled. Then she sucked his pinky into her mouth, teasing him with swirls of her tongue.

"Jesus!" His guttural cry spurred her on.

She'd never done this before but his reaction made it clear she'd discovered another implement of persuasion. His skin tasted like his spicy soap. She nibbled her way toward his big toe while her hands worked the soles of his feet with firm pressure to avoid tickling him.

"That feels so good, baby."

She suckled his toes until he called out.

"Shit. I could come just from that."

Straightening, she ignored his frustrated protest but reasoning became harder with every passing minute. Their passion affected her as much as him. In a hurry, she spun toward the whiteboard again.

"In addition to fulfilling the requirements of the experiment, the subject engaged in activities that demonstrated his affection. Examples of this include his use of pet names for his assistant, the gentle care he lavished on her, the way he sheltered her in his arms at night as well as the pride and enthusiasm he displays when developing new ideas with her."

Kurt blinked. "Fuck, I'm not some kind of monster. Of course I care for you."

When she leaned against the table, he tried to grab her fingers with his own but she evaded his touch. His attention divided between her flowing script, which detailed all the times he'd shown her kindness outside the scope of the study, and her black clad form towering over him.

"Becca, I'm not denying I'm fond of you. All those things are true. Hell, I'm not even disputing how much I desire you. It's obvious I want you more than my next breath."

The admission loosened something in her soul. Each step forward they took became more personal. Relief eroded her fear.

She knelt on the platform between his legs then devoured his balls in one long slurp. The tight sac shifted beneath her tongue.

"Oh, hell yes," he roared into the quiet laboratory. She rolled his testicles between her lips with careful pressure until they gathered close to his body. His pants advertised how close he was to succumbing to ecstasy. With a reluctant lick, she abandoned his tempting flesh then laid her head on his taut abdomen to catch her breath.

"You're killing me. End this now."

"Do you love me?" she whispered.

He averted his face, refusing to meet her gaze. The gesture almost squashed the tender shoot of hope she harbored. She refused to settle for less than his ultimate surrender.

"What's the problem, Kurt? I don't understand why you're fighting what's between us. Why don't you want to love me?"

"Son of a bitch. Don't do this to yourself." The oath held no anger toward her, just resolve. "It's not you, Becca. Love doesn't exist. It's just a fantasy people build for themselves."

The cautious hesitancy of his phrasing conveyed her failure to convince him so far.

"It's one big chemical reaction, that's all."

Rebecca's gut twisted at his declaration. It was a perfectly logical thing for him to believe. He was a scientist through and through. She watched him squirm beneath the straps, rejecting his position. Submission just wasn't in his nature. Maybe the ability to love wasn't either.

The knot of pain in her chest took a moment to dissipate. Still, she refused to quit.

"Chemical reactions are always the same." Taking a huge risk, she asked, "Have you ever responded like this to another woman?"

Kurt huffed out a sigh then groaned. "No, Becca. Everything is different with you, I concede that."

She nodded, then proceeded with her next argument in a clear voice. "The subject defied his fundamental makeup when faced with the woman he loves. The obstinate jerk never gives in to the demands of others. However, when the board manipulated him into accepting their terms, he did not rebel as would be expected. Instead, he capitulated with minimal resistance."

She paused to draw a deep breath before tacking on, "In addition, he has never before given a moment's pause for a woman who chose to walk away from a relationship with him until his assistant left. His fundamental characteristics have distorted due to his need for his assistant."

Rebecca prayed Luke's input on this point turned out to be valid. She could attest to the first half—even now, Kurt's stubborn streak influenced his responses—but she had no idea if he'd been unaffected by the early termination of his relationships with other women. She had to trust Luke on that one.

Kurt must have sensed her uncertainty. With more sobriety than his previous outburst, he whispered. "It's true, Becca. I should have told the board to go to hell. I shouldn't give a damn if you tell *me* to go to hell. In fact, I expected it. I definitely deserve it. But I let the board direct me because I wanted what they pressured me to do. I've never felt so miserable in all my life as I have the past two days without you by my side."

She turned to witness the truth flash in his eyes.

"I'm so sorry, baby. I never meant to hurt you."

His regret drew her to him like a magnet, the pull organic and irresistible. As her hand reached for his throbbing erection, he startled her with his objection. "No!"

When she hesitated, he clarified. "Come here. Let me taste you instead. Let me ease your suffering." She couldn't tell if he referred to the sexual rampage whipping through her needy body or the ache in her chest but she didn't argue.

Instead, she cranked the table until he lowered, still parallel to the ground, below her waist. In her massive heels, it didn't take much. She straddled his head without an ounce of embarrassment, then dropped forward until her cheek rested on the flat plane of his ripped abdomen. It felt like coming home.

He moaned encouragement against the dripping folds of her pussy. Her eyes fluttered closed as she soaked in the comfort and satisfaction he imparted. Being so close to him—smelling his unique scent, absorbing the heat of his muscled torso and reveling in his attention—soothed her frazzled nerves.

The wet velvet of his tongue stroked along her slit until his lips surrounded her clit in a light embrace. Everything about his touch communicated his tenderness. His fingers teased the few strands of hair draped over his grasp. A sigh of contentment fell from her mouth, drifting across Kurt's straining erection.

She wanted to reach for him but she still had more work to do first. He must have sensed her indecision. He mumbled against her flesh, "Relax. Let me take care of you."

His talented tongue traced along the rim of her opening. He tasted the dewy secretion of her arousal then groaned. Desire spiked inside her. She ground her pussy against his face, unconcerned about her wanton display. After days of turmoil, she craved release. He used his tongue to fuck her while his chin bumped against her clit.

Rebecca shifted, aligning his touch where she needed it most. Within seconds, she clung to the brink of passion. Her orgasm would be too fast. She wanted to savor the moment but she couldn't force herself to abstain from the delights of his mouth.

"Come, sweetheart, there's more waiting for you." The suggestion tipped her over the edge. He always understood what she needed.

"Yes! Kurt!" She came on his face even as he continued to lap at her with gentle swipes of his tongue. The quasi-relief banked her lust but her greedy body craved more. Pushing up from his chest, she swung her leg—encased in the heavy boot—over his head. She bent until she met his seeking lips in an intimate kiss.

The moment broke only when she left him to kneel between his legs once more. She didn't need to reference the board now. Two points remained. The ones that had finally convinced her broken heart a shred of hope existed.

Kurt's eyes bored into her as her face lingered a fraction of an inch from his cock. He winced but placed her needs above his own again. "Go ahead, baby. Get it out."

"When you fucked me...with Luke. In the final Dream Machine session." She couldn't stitch together whole sentences but he nodded his understanding. "You forgot to record my reactions. You didn't use any measurement tools, the sheath device or your probes. You wanted it so bad, you forgot all about the experiment."

Shock raced over his dumbfounded expression. "Holy shit."

She didn't give him a chance to counter her argument or

devise some ridiculous excuse. Instead, she swallowed his massive erection. The swollen head of his cock throbbed at the back of her throat. She hummed her appreciation around the impressive girth.

"Hell, yes!"

Rebecca took his shouted admission and ran. They were so close to the truth. His musk filled her mouth.

"Suck me." Only he could make it sound like he issued orders while subject to the whims of another.

Her mouth glided along the length of his cock from root to tip as her tongue flickered over the veins lacing the underside. She swirled it around the bulbous head, reveling in his growls of encouragement. Her fingertips tickled his sac while she sipped the bead of pre-come from his slit.

When the corded muscles in his neck, the tightening of his balls and his pulsing cock proclaimed his impending orgasm, she wrenched away from the temptation. Before he could voice his protest, she clambered onto the table. Her knees rested on either side of his trim hips.

His intense gaze stole her breath. She crouched until the ridge of his cock nestled between her labia, teasing her engorged clit with his hard-on. She forced her strained voice to lay out the last piece of proof.

The evidence that had swayed her.

"When you realized I was remembering the REM stages, you knew I'd eventually recall everything. You could have stopped but you pushed on. You granted my greatest wishes, fulfilled my dreams, knowing I might never forgive you. You made a selfless sacrifice of your own happiness for mine. And *that's* the definition of love."

His lips parted as he prepared his rebuttal but she couldn't bear to have the moment shattered. Reaching forward, she covered his mouth with a gentle hand. He licked the center of her palm, inciting a flock of shivers to race down her back.

"Don't argue, Kurt. Just feel, please."

She never once looked away from the depth of longing swimming in his eyes as she guided his straining erection to her pussy. Sinking onto his shaft inch by inch, she welcomed him into her body and her soul.

"Yes, Becca. Yes. Take me."

No other choice existed. She couldn't have stopped herself. She rode him with wild motions designed to throw them both into the abyss of pure emotion. All rational thought disintegrated when instinct kicked in.

"I need you."

"Need, Kurt? Or want?"

"Need! Fuck me, now."

Pleasure zoomed through her entire being. She wasn't going to last much longer. Her muscles clamped around his cock, causing him to yell out her name. With a shift of her hips, she rose off his steel-hard shaft. The loss she suffered was a small price to pay for his hungry stare.

"Tell me, Kurt. This isn't simple attraction or some chemical reaction is it?"

"No," he moaned through his clenched jaw. "Not simple attraction."

With renewed vigor and purpose, she fit him back into her swollen pussy. She indulged in a driving rhythm guaranteed to set them both off. Reaching behind her, she teased his balls with one hand while the other played with her clit.

In seconds, she detected the tensing of his muscles that preceded orgasm.

"You look amazing riding me. Touching yourself."

"I want you to come inside me." Her primal desires commanded them both. "Give yourself to me."

"Damn. Becca." His cock plumped impossibly inside her, stretching her, stroking the center of her ecstasy. "Now! Come with me."

Head thrown back, her spine arched, she ground her clit against his pubic bone. The first scalding jets of his come were the last straw. Her pussy convulsed around him, milking his cock with wave after wave of orgasm until she collapsed on his heaving chest.

"I love you too, Kurt," she whispered against his corded neck as the final lingering pulses of his release invaded her.

When their breathing slowed and Rebecca had made a substantial recovery, she raised her head. She had to hear him say it.

"What did you feel?"

Kurt met her curious look then beamed. She could see the intensity of their shared climax echoed in his grey eyes.

"What I felt was the best orgasm of my life, with the only woman I want as my partner both in the firm and in my bed. Forever."

Rebecca's heart soared.

Her risk had paid off.

Euphoria, unmatched by any physical high, enveloped her soul for a priceless moment. But when she stared dreamily at his face, she glimpsed the obvious regret there then flinched.

Her method of persuasion had failed. He still didn't believe.

Confusion stunned her silent, allowing him to drive the knife further into her unprotected heart.

"You proved we are the epitome of human compatibility, Becca."

The sterile description obliterated her glow of success. She scrambled from her perch on his sweat-slicked hips with so much haste she had to grasp the table edge to keep from toppling. The pain shredding her insides must have been written on her face because Kurt shouted a violent curse.

"Shit! Did you think I meant..." He began to struggle in earnest when he realized what his careless rambling had done— the destruction his revelation had wrought. "Let me go! Right now, Becca! I'm not playing around. We need to talk this out."

But she knew. There was nothing else to say. Because if Kurt felt even a spark of the flame blazing in her soul for him, he could never dismiss it as anything other than love. Her brave façade disintegrated when a battering ram of despair smashed her in the gut.

Survival mechanisms she thought she'd conquered kicked in. A wall fell in place, sparing her from the unbearable pain on the other side. Her whole body went numb. Her brain went numb. She leveled a blank stare at Kurt thrashing beneath the bonds while the rational part of her mind figured out what to do.

She blinked.

Before she had acknowledged the decision, her feet carried her toward the door. She whispered, "Goodbye, Kurt."

Though she heard him bellowing her name, demanding she return to the laboratory, Rebecca continued walking. She didn't run, she didn't cry. Instead, she plucked the long duster she'd used to cover her outfit from the coat rack, then slipped out of the office for what she knew would be the last time.

Chapter Twenty-Two

Luke glanced up when the tinkling of the bell on the diner's glass door announced a new customer. The paleness of Becca's face matched her haunting carriage as she glided into the diner like a ghost. The mask she wore, devoid of any of her recent vitality, made it obvious something had gone terribly wrong. Horrified, he dashed to her side, knocking over a chair in the process.

She didn't say anything.

"Are you okay?" What a stupid question. She didn't bother to respond.

"It didn't go well," he stated.

She shook her head no.

Luke tried to reach for her, to console her, but she stepped back then repeated the pain-laden gesture. He'd never seen so much agony in a woman's eyes. Unsure of what to do with his outstretched hands, he stuffed them in his pockets.

"You left him up there?"

Her throat worked but no sound parted her trembling lips.

"Do I need to go to the lab?"

She managed a terse nod then pivoted before striding out the door, still without uttering a single word. Luke watched as she marched down the street toward her apartment—head high, shoulders back, but so stiff he thought she might shatter.

Kurt had just made the biggest mistake of his life.

Luke stood torn between the needs of his friend and his friend's mate. In the end, he chose to let Becca go. Although his chivalrous instincts screamed at him to pursue her, no one but Kurt could repair the damage.

He sprinted across the street then took the stairs to Kurt's practice two at a time. Halfway up the flight, he began to hear noises. By the time he opened the hall door, furious curses alternated with yells of frustration. Through the open laboratory door, Luke spied Kurt straining against his shackles. Tempted to leave the dumbass to suffer for a while, he slowed before entering the room.

Kurt lashed out in pure rage.

"How could you fucking do this to me? You drugged my food? You set me up!" Without waiting for an answer to his accusations, his voice dropped to an ominous hiss. "Get me the fuck out of here. Becca left. I need to catch her."

"I don't think that's such a good idea." Luke's quiet reply would have warned a sane man.

"What the hell do you have to do with this?" Kurt demanded, still fighting for control despite his prone position.

"You just broke her heart, asshole. I don't like to see my friends hurt. That's why we need to get a few facts straight before I release you." Luke grabbed the discarded sheet, which Becca had used to cover the whiteboard, off the floor. He tossed it across his friend's abdomen, still glistening with the slick remnants of spent arousal. Then he pulled up a chair, straddled the seat, rested his crossed arms on the back and faced the struggling man head on.

"Don't you think I know I hurt her?" Kurt spat. "That's why I need to find her. I need to make sure she's okay."

"Well, hell, now you're acting stupid, too. Of course she's not okay but there's only one thing you can do to fix it."

"You want me to lie to her? Tell her some fairytale about love?" He looked incredulous.

"Kurt, we've known each other a long time now. I've seen you with more women than I can count. Never, and I mean *never*, has one affected you like she does."

"Christ, now you sound like her. You're no naïve girl! It doesn't mean love exists as anything more than a chemical reaction." The fool clung to his ingrained belief.

"Why can't it be true, Kurt? Because your parents sucked at relationships? Your mom married any man who had money, including your father. She pretended to love but it was just a farce. Your dad couldn't handle how easily he'd been fooled. Can't you see past his bitter indoctrination and make your own damned decisions?"

"Shut the fuck up! You don't know what you're talking about."

"Well, you see, I've been pretty intrigued by observing this whole situation, so I decided to do a little experiment of my own." Luke paused for effect, wondering when Kurt would catch on.

"You bastard. You used the Dream Machine on me? When? After you slipped that shit in my food?"

Luke's booming laughter echoed off the stark walls. "I think you're losing your edge. Your IQ's been dropping like a rock lately. Hell, yes, I used the machine on you! You already proved it works. That it's safe."

"You still didn't have my fucking permission!"

The appalled expression on Kurt's face softened Luke's tone. "That's why I'm asking you now. Are you too chickenshit to acknowledge the truth?"

"Son of a bitch." Kurt cursed as his head dropped onto the table and he began to relax. Luke could practically see the gears spinning in his genius mind.

Luke agreed with the sentiment. "Want to know what you dreamed about? Can you remember?"

"The same thing I always dream about?" Kurt calmed the bellowing of his chest into a ragged exhalation then closed his eyes. "Fucking Becca."

Luke grinned, "Well, yeah, there was a hell of a lot of that. On your desk, in the lab, pushing her limits... Your dreams mirrored the ones you documented Becca experiencing during the study. Doesn't that strike you as odd? To share dreams with another person?"

"Not really. The same fantasies turn us on. It's no big deal. I already told you she's my perfect match in bed and out." Kurt's voice didn't sound as certain as he implied.

Sensing a crack in his resolve, Luke debated his options.

The forced realization of a dream Kurt couldn't recall on his own presented a calculated risk. There might be a reason Kurt's mind shielded itself from admitting his deepest desire but Luke didn't think so. The man was just stubborn and didn't take things on faith. His own mental protection had been locked in place so long, he didn't realize the damage it could do.

"Tell me." The strained rasp startled him from his thoughts. "If the machine captured anything more, tell me, you bastard. Otherwise, you've done nothing more than waste your time and ruin our friendship. A bunch of wet dreams doesn't mean a damn thing. It's just sex."

If he didn't act now, Kurt would lose Becca forever. That loss would destroy his friend.

"If it's just sex, then why did a dream of marrying her occupy your final REM stage? A dream of building a life outside this damn charade of an experiment? You dreamt you spent the rest of your lives lost in the bliss of loving each other."

Kurt's eyes clamped shut but Luke could see the zigzag motion of his pupils beneath his eyelids, signaling the recall of the visions. He wouldn't be capable of ignoring this proof. Concerned about the damage the unnatural memory could inflict, Luke began to remove the straps one by one.

When he finished, Kurt lay motionless on the examination table, breathing hard. Luke bent closer then shook his shoulder. "Are you all right?"

Without warning, the angry man hauled his fist around and punched Luke square on the jaw, sending him sprawling. Before he'd finished skidding across the floor, Kurt got right in his face.

"Don't you ever fucking pull that shit on me again! If you weren't my best friend I'd be tempted to kick your ass!"

Struggling to his feet, Luke flexed his throbbing jaw before he clapped Kurt on the shoulder. "Glad to see you're back to your old self but what are you going to do to fix this mess?"

"Nothing."

The word hung in the air, baffling Luke. "What the hell do you mean, nothing?"

"I don't deserve her. I lied to her, I used her and I betrayed her trust. It's obvious, I don't know how to love someone." The desolation behind the sentiment drove Luke to risk another beating.

Besides, it wasn't a half-bad idea...

"Then you don't mind if I pursue her? You were right. Becca is amazing."

Kurt hauled Luke up by his shirt collar before he'd even finished the ridiculous suggestion, pinning him to the wall. "She's mine. Only mine."

From his vantage point—hanging lax in Kurt's rough grip, feet several inches off the floor—Luke broke the tension with a shrug.

"Then don't you think you'd better go convince her?"

Chapter Twenty-Three

Rebecca knelt in the middle of her living room, filling another box with her belongings. As she tucked a few candles into the crate, she bumped the coffee table, toppling the stack of envelopes waiting to be mailed. Though it had been less than two hours since her encounter with Kurt, she'd immediately faxed her resignation to Dr. Foster's practice, printed out the resume's she'd prepared just in case then began to pack.

One step at a time, she erased the future she'd hoped for.

News travelled fast. She'd already had job offers from Dr. Malone's office and several other board affiliated practices in the area, which she declined. She had to escape any reminders of Kurt and all she would never have. He was the only man she could ever love.

As some consolation, she admitted she'd discovered so much about herself over the past week that her confidence in her capabilities as both a psychologist and a woman had solidified. That newfound strength allowed her to ignore Kurt's attempts to contact her. She'd unplugged her home phone and put her cell on silent. She'd never hear the one thing that mattered from him, anything else became noise.

Concentrating on propelling herself forward, Rebecca gathered the resumes from the table then slipped on her sneakers, preparing to take them to the mailbox at the curb. When she opened the door, she spied Kurt's sleek black sports car out front. She slammed the solid oak closed with enough force to rattle the windows. Leaning back against the hardwood surface, she wondered if he'd seen her.

"Shit." Why wouldn't he leave her alone?

She didn't need his pity or his protectiveness. She didn't want him to care enough to check up on her but not enough to give her everything. Yet, she feared if she saw him up close she might not be able to stop herself from succumbing to their attraction and compromising her needs just to stay near him. Therefore, she refused to allow him to corner her.

Sneaking around to the rear of her apartment, Rebecca slid her bedroom window open. She backed out, reaching for the fire escape below with the toe of her left foot.

Warm fingers wrapped around her hips. Broad palms cupped her ass to steady her. The inflaming touch shot her most of the way back through the window.

"Careful, baby." Kurt's seductive whisper came so close to her ear she jumped, banging her head in the process. So much for a graceful exit.

Hauling herself inside, she spun in time to be jealous of his agile tuck through the opening. "What are you doing here?"

"Would you believe I happened to be in the neighborhood?" he asked with a grimace.

"No. Now get out."

"Give me a minute, Becca. Just listen to me for *one* minute. I'm sorry..."

She cut him off before he could go any further. "Nothing you can say matters to me anymore."

Kurt inched forward, trapping her against the wall with his steady advance. "Is that why you're running? There are things I need to say to you." The intensity in his eyes made her shiver in response no matter how hard she tried to ignore his presence.

"You need closure? Fine, get whatever you need to say off your chest then get the hell out."

"No, I need to explain. I understand you're afraid. I hurt you."

"If you won't leave, I will." Rebecca headed for the door. She couldn't resist him for much longer. The ache in her heart, and between her legs, overpowered logic.

Before she got more than three feet away, Kurt tugged her

wrist then pinned her tight against his chest. The heat pumping off him surrounded her. She trembled when the swish of his breath caressed her neck.

"Don't go, Becca. Stay with me." He referred to more than this moment. They both understood what he asked.

"I can't," she whispered, her voice cracking despite her best intentions to keep it steady. Nothing had changed so she stuck to her decision. If she couldn't have everything, she refused to compromise.

"Have I ruined everything you felt for me?"

Rebecca realized she wasn't the only one shaking. Before she remembered she intended to distance herself, she turned in his arms to comfort him.

The pain creasing his brow staggered her. Lifting her palm to the side of his face, she smoothed the lines of tension there. Unsure of how to answer, she gave him the truth.

"I can't live half a dream."

"I know, Becca. I'd never ask you to. I'm so sorry I hurt you, baby. Can you forgive me for lying to you?" His hands cupped her shoulders, fingers stroking the exposed skin around the straps of her tank top.

"*That's* not the problem, Kurt." Although his deception still stung, in a way, she could understand.

"It is to me. I can't believe the way I acted. Things got out of control. I needed to know more about you. God, Becca, when I saw the passion in your dreams, and realized I had been right about you all along, I couldn't resist anymore."

"What do you mean?" Her puzzlement escaped despite her best efforts to conceal it.

"I've wanted you for years. It feels like forever but I didn't think you were ready. So focused on your goals, you had so many other things going on. And you were so young. Damn it, Becca. You have to understand." Kurt hung his head until their foreheads touched then he looked right into her eyes without hiding an ounce of his longing. "I'm explaining this all wrong."

Although determined not to settle, she would hear him out. She didn't want him to regret their time together. She never would, no matter how painful leaving would be. "Go ahead, I'm listening."

His fingers came up to frame her face, teasing her with their gentle caresses. "Everything you said before...it's true. You make it impossible for me to think straight. I adore you. I went along with the board's demands as a convenient excuse."

He sighed before continuing.

"You were right about Luke, too. The board would have approved the Dream Machine without his...personal involvement. I brought him in because I wanted to give you what you desired. I even included the videos at the board meeting to stage your exhibitionist fantasy. Luke watched through a camera under the table."

Stunned, she watched him wince. She condemned the persistent arousal flaring inside her. Anger should have taken its place.

Rebecca reeled from the extent of his efforts, even more elaborate than she had assumed. "You did it all for me? Because you'd seen the experiment was my greatest fantasy?"

Wondering if she should be livid or flattered, she peered into his vulnerable eyes. He was oddly subdued. So used to seeing him in control, sure of himself, this side of him threw her off guard. So this is why he'd chased her? To admit to greater duplicity than she'd suspected?

"Yes. So, I understand if you can't forgive me. But there's something else you should know."

She wasn't sure she could handle another secret. Bracing herself for the worst, she waited for him to continue. He swallowed hard but found his voice after several long seconds.

"My father raised me."

Her eyes widened. He'd never divulged his personal affairs. She'd assumed their stilted conversation stemmed from her unwillingness to reveal her own family issues. After all, who talked about their history when they knew it to be a sore subject for the person they spoke to?

Surprise weakened her knees as he opened himself to her on a whole new level. He guided them to the edge of her bed. Sinking down, he situated her in his lap. She sensed his craving for her closeness as he revealed his secrets.

"My mother was a gold digger." The bitterness in the term made it clear he'd heard it often enough. "She got pregnant with me on purpose to trick my father into marrying her. She insisted on no prenuptial agreement to prove their love for each other. He didn't care about the money, or my mother. I think by then he already knew what she was but he wanted an heir. She stuck around long enough to deliver me then split with half his cash and never looked back."

Rebecca clung to his tense shoulders. Even now, the betrayal had the power to sting him. She raged for the boy he'd been.

"Dad always warned me not to fall for sentimental bullshit. He convinced me emotions were every man's weakness in business and in life. He often said I was worth every dollar he paid, as though I should be glad for the compliment. He's the coldest man I've ever met and I'm afraid I'll die alone just like he will."

Shocked, she flung her arms around his locked shoulders. "God, Kurt. You're anything but cold. Look at you!"

She shook his massive frame then climbed up until she knelt on either side of his wide thighs so she could cup his face in her hands and stroke her thumbs over his chiseled cheekbones.

"And as long as I live, you'll never be alone. I love you." She would never escape him now, even if he couldn't admit what she understood to the bottom of her soul. She kissed him with all the tenderness and devotion she could muster but he broke away.

"Then there's just one more thing I need to tell you."

She couldn't bear another blow.

"I love you, Doctor Rebecca Williams. If you can find it in your heart to forgive me, I swear, I will spend the rest of my life making this up to you. All I can say is, for the first time, I couldn't be rational. I had to have you but I was too afraid to admit it to myself."

The sincerity of his vow radiated from his eyes. She wrapped around him until there wasn't even a millimeter of space between them. Kurt's sweet kiss drugged her, intimate in its gentleness and longing. He surrounded her, cradling her in his arms, never stopping the caress of his lips on hers.

For Rebecca, nothing else mattered.

She retreated a fraction of an inch. Only far enough to whisper, "I forgive you, Kurt. I love you, too. Forever."

Her lips brushed against his.

"Good," he said.

His simple response had laughter bubbling from her at the return of his practical nature.

"Then there's just one more thing to clear up."

"Oh God," she moaned, her heart pitching in her chest. "You said that before! What now?"

"I think I owe you a little punishment for the stunt you pulled this morning."

In a flash, he flipped her in his arms where he sat on the edge of her bed. Before she could react, he had both wrists pinned at the base of her spine in a firm but tender grip. Then he wrestled her sweat shorts off her squirming legs. The first tantalizing spank landed on her ass with a crack.

Rebecca's giggles filled the room. The joy spreading through her overpowered everything else.

"Go ahead and laugh, baby. That won't last long." His primal dominance had returned and it made her wet as ever. More so. Her heart soared on the current of his love.

As the spanking continued, her amusement morphed into moans and whimpers of pleasure. The tingling of her ass increased until she writhed on Kurt's lap.

"You were so naughty this morning. And so beautiful. Do you know what it did to me to lie there and take your torture?" Another light slap spread electric shocks of desire through her body.

The friction of her legs, pressed together, started a liquid simmer in her core that flared into a conflagration of need within seconds.

"Please, Kurt. Take me. Fuck me."

His hand paused in mid-air. He lifted her from her position, draped over his lap, then turned. As his heavy weight settled over her on the bed, bringing his muscular frame into contact along her entire length, she whimpered.

"I want to try something new. A little experiment. I don't want to fuck you, Becca," he whispered, cradling her face in his hands. He buried those long, talented fingers in her hair. "I want to make love to you."

Gently, as though she were made of fragile crystal, he dusted her face with soft kisses. Following the line of her neck, he traced her curves and valleys with his tongue as he removed their clothing. Lost in a cloud of bliss, nothing had ever felt so right in her life.

Kurt's mouth was tender on the swell of her left breast, moving ever closer to her puckered nipple with licks and light nips. His hand cupped the other with a possessive squeeze. When he placed a lingering kiss over her heart, she reached to undo his zipper.

He stopped her.

"Let me take care of you, baby." He nuzzled her abdomen as he sank between her thighs.

He'd tossed her shorts to the floor, leaving her open to his caresses. She gasped when his tongue crept closer to her pussy.

Rebecca couldn't stop her hands from twining in his hair then tugging him closer. The love in his eyes made every sensation twice as vivid. Blossoms of arousal unfurled at each place he touched. Hunger spread from her core until she couldn't stand to be empty any longer.

"Please, Kurt. I need you inside me."

"Soon." He refused to be distracted.

A moan burst from her chest when his fingertip brushed against her dripping folds before sliding deep inside. Her muscles clenched around the digit, drawing it further into her channel. Her orgasm lingered so close, one touch on her clit would send her over the edge.

He must have sensed it because he refrained, denying her release. Rebecca rocked her hips, taking the two fingers now buried inside her to the max while she attempted to rub the bundle of nerves against his palm.

"I want you to come for me, baby." Kurt blew cool air across the top of her slit. So energized, swamped in emotions, the barest of sensations almost triggered her climax.

"Now." He licked a path from the junction of his fingers up and around her clit.

She cried out as her back arched, leaving only her head and hips on the bed. Her orgasm raced through her, accompanied by Kurt's growl of satisfaction. He sucked her clit with wet pulses, prolonging the spasms.

When they began to subside, his fingers retreated from her clinging sheath. She sighed with regret until he replaced them with the head of his cock.

Kurt braced himself over her then dove into a frantic kiss. Their tongues clashed, desperate to proclaim their love. He allowed her a brief taste of their mingled fluids before separating them.

"I love you, Becca." His words guaranteed a lifetime of happiness.

Every ridge of his thick cock enticed her pussy as it pushed steady and sure inside her, joining them. When she cradled all of him in her welcoming grasp, Kurt lay still on top of her.

"You're mine, baby. I want you to tell me you understand." His jaw clenched as he shook from the effort of holding still. The display of controlled power caused Rebecca's blood to reheat. She wanted him to take her but knew he would wait until she accepted his claim.

"I am yours, Kurt. Always."

He groaned in her ear as his head dropped forward and his flesh surged in her clasp. He gathered her in his arms as he made love to her with slow, sweet glides. It took no more than a few minutes before the subtle motion tormented them both.

"I'm yours, Becca. I love you." His proclamation moved her beyond control. She accepted the next rising crest of ecstasy.

Kurt's shaft grew even as her spasming muscles squeezed him tighter. The ridge of his glans pressed against the entrance to her womb as they fit perfectly together. The subtle sensation, along with the reminder of their complete fit, renewed her orgasm.

His possession was all it took to send her flying. He bit her shoulder as he joined her in rapture, his hot come washing over her, triggering several aftershocks of desire.

He rolled to his back, still cradling her in his arms as she draped over his chest. "I want to be the man who makes all your dreams come true," he whispered, as though trying not to dispel the magic of the moment.

"You already are."

About the Author

Jayne Rylon's stories usually begin as a daydream in an endless business meeting. Her writing acts as a creative counterpoint to her straight-laced corporate existence. She lives in Ohio with two cats and her husband who both inspires her fantasies and supports her careers. When she can escape her office, she loves to travel the world, avoid speeding tickets in her beloved Sky and, of course, read.

To learn more about Jayne Rylon, please visit www.jaynerylon.com. She enjoys hearing from readers. You can send an email to Jayne at contact@jaynerylon.com.

Can one man satisfy Alexa's appetites? Or will it take two?

Nice and Naughty
© *2008 Jayne Rylon*

After a disastrous lesson in heartache, Alexa Jones confines her adrenaline rushes to intense boardroom negotiations. Her legendary control cracks and she indulges in a high-octane encounter on the hood of her sports car. She never planned to see the enticing stranger again. When she finds herself across the boardroom table from him, there's suddenly more at stake than just her career.

Justin Winston got more than he bargained for on his summer drive, but he should have known nothing is ever that easy. He's met the woman of his dreams yet he doesn't know who she is. Luckily, he can always count on his practical brother for the things that matter, and this time is no exception. But, when a web of corporate espionage entangles them all, it's clear Justin isn't the only one who's fallen for their mysterious siren.

In Justin and Jason, Alexa finds something as unique and rare as the patent they will risk their lives to secure. The freedom to explore—and satisfy—the full range of her desires. From naughty to nice. Can Alexa accept the love of two men?

Warning: This story contains light bondage, anal play and smoking hot brothers for double the fun and double the trouble.

Available now in ebook and print from Samhain Publishing.

GREAT
CHEAP
FUN

Discover eBooks!

THE FASTEST WAY TO GET THE HOTTEST NAMES

Get your favorite authors on your favorite reader, long before they're
out in print! Ebooks from Samhain go wherever you go, and work with
whatever you carry—Palm, PDF, Mobi, and more.

WWW.SAMHAINPUBLISHING.COM